"Cathleen Armstrong pa[...] of danger lurking on th[...] can-this-really-go-anyw[...] coming like family, and [...] than ideal. With an ecle[...] plot, *Welcome to Last Chance* pulls the reader in from the first blink of the warning light on the dashboard of Lainie's car to the happily-ever-after waiting at the end of her last chance to get her life right."

—**Beth K. Vogt,** author of *Catch a Falling Star*
and *Wish You Were Here*

"An outstanding debut novel! *Welcome to Last Chance* gives us a warm but never sentimental view of small-town life, sprinkled with characters full of quirks and faults—all seen through the eyes of a tough but fragile heroine. Cathleen Armstrong has crafted a story to cherish."

—**Sarah Sundin,** award-winning author
of *With Every Letter*

"With equal parts hope, charm, and tender faith, Cathleen Armstrong spins a tale as warm and welcoming as a roadside café on a dusty highway. Exit from the fast lane and visit Last Chance. It's a place you won't soon forget."

—**Lisa Wingate,** bestselling and award-winning author
of *Firefly Island* and *Blue Moon Bay*

WELCOME *to* LAST CHANCE

A Novel

CATHLEEN ARMSTRONG

Revell

a division of Baker Publishing Group
Grand Rapids, Michigan

Published by Revell
a division of Baker Publishing Group
P.O. Box 6287, Grand Rapids, MI 49516-6287
www.revellbooks.com

Printed in the United States of America

Library of Congress Cataloging-in-Publication Data
Armstrong, Cathleen.
  Welcome to last chance : a novel / Cathleen Armstrong.
      pages cm. — (A Place to Call Home ; #1)
    ISBN 978-0-8007-2246-3 (pbk.)
    1. Self-realization in women—Fiction. I. Title.
  PS3601.R574W45 2013
  813'.6—dc23   2013005610

This is a work of fiction. Names, characters, incidents, and dialogues are products of the author's imagination and are not to be construed as real. Any resemblance to actual events or persons, living or dead, is entirely coincidental.

13 14 15 16 17 18 19   7 6 5 4 3 2 1

For Ed,
who never doubted for a moment

Acknowledgments

Writing, it is said, is a solitary pursuit. If that were the whole truth, you wouldn't be holding this book in your hand, because it never would have been written.

My never-ending thanks to my first critique group, nonfiction writers all, who would settle in to hear my story like kids at bedtime. Loving thanks to dear friend Pat Sikora who applied prayer, encouragement, and outright nagging in equal parts when my feet would drag. The brainstorming with Lauraine Snelling and the reunioners helped me through the hard parts, and the accountability of the BIC coffee shop crowd—Dineen Miller, Shelley Adina, Kristin Billerbeck, and Camy Tang—kept me writing when I wanted to wander. Massive hugs to Katie Vorreiter and Kathi Lipp, who walked with me every step of this journey. I am absolutely indebted to Marcy Wedeymuller, who went over the manuscript with a fine-toothed comb before I ever submitted it, saying, "Drop this," "Beef this up," and "This made me cry." And if it hadn't been for my agent, Karen Solem, who took a chance on me and my manuscript, and the team at Revell who believed in my story, there would be no book. My deepest gratitude to each and all.

1

The warning light, some sort of car part with a circle around it, flashed on sometime after midnight. At least, Lainie Davis guessed it was that late. The clock on the dashboard had read 5:11 since she drove the car off the Long Beach lot three days earlier and headed east. Each mile driven was one mile farther away from Nick and the shadowy world of drugs and dealers that was turning him into a frightening stranger. Now, as she was daring to breathe again, that red light mocked her. "Really thought you were going to make it this time, didn't you? Nice try."

"Nope, you're not doing this." Lainie swallowed fear with a practiced gulp and kept her voice light. "It's just a little electrical short, that's all." She gave the glass a sharp rap with her knuckle. The light flickered and went out.

"That's more like it. I knew you were fine."

Long ago Lainie had learned the value of a little sweet talk, and about the time the air conditioner gave out, forty-five miles east of Palm Springs, she had begun crooning to her ancient Mustang. And until now, less than two hundred miles from her destination, her cajoling had kept things running smoothly.

"Hang on till we get to El Paso, baby, and I promise you'll never have to go anywhere again. But you've got to get me there by morning, no discussion."

She caught her long hair with one hand and twisted it up, letting the hot wind rushing through her open windows blow across her damp neck. "Sheesh, it's got to be nearly a hundred out here. Does it ever cool off?"

The light flickered and came right back on. "C'mon. Off." She slapped the instrument panel with the flat of her hand.

This time it didn't even flicker.

"Don't do this to me." Lainie's voice rose above the roar of the wind. "You can't break down and leave me stranded out here a hundred miles from nowhere."

The light stayed on, but the old car seemed to show no other changes.

"Okay. Deep breath. We're going to be just fine. You're as likely to have something wrong with your light-turner-onner as with your engine, right? We'll just take it easy."

She slowed a bit and patted the dash.

"You know, if anyone could hear me, they'd say I was nuts. And if the radio worked, we could both listen to somebody else's voice." She peered into the darkness rushing past. "Man, it's empty out here."

She glanced at the instrument panel with its glowing red light. The needle was to the hot side of center, but not all that much. Maybe it had always been there? She dropped her speed by another five miles per hour and pulled into the slow lane. Just ahead, on the other side of a barbed wire fence, a small sign read "LAST CHANCE FOR FOOD—22 MILES."

"Well, that's scary." Lainie smiled in spite of herself. "Last chance till when? Doomsday?"

She checked the temperature gauge again and her smile faded. It was definitely showing hotter than it had been. She lowered her speed five more miles per hour and drove another fifteen minutes before looking down. She began to regret tossing her cheap cell phone in a trash can on the way out of town. At the time it made her feel bold and free; she was cutting all ties with her old life. But now she would give anything to have a phone at her fingertips.

The lights of an approaching semi loomed up behind her until her car was filled with their glare. At the last possible moment, the truck swerved around, the long, angry blast of its horn fading into the night with the taillights. Lainie stuck her fist out the window. "Jerk."

To her right, another small sign read "LAST CHANCE FOR GAS—10 MILES."

"Just ten more miles, baby. There'll be someone there who can help us, even if we have to wait till morning to talk to him. Just don't quit on me out here."

The engine had never been quiet, and driving with the windows open made the interior yet noisier, but even with the sound of the wind and the roar of the passing eighteen-wheelers, Lainie heard the knocking when it began under the hood.

She blinked back tears. "Please, please, please."

She didn't know if she was begging the car for a few more miles, imploring the gas station to appear on the horizon, or beseeching whatever god looked after exhausted women driving broken-down cars through the hot desert night, but she repeated the word like a mantra. "Please, please, please."

The small sign said "LAST CHANCE FOR REST—EXIT NOW." Lainie changed her "pleases" to "thank-yous" and pulled off the interstate onto a two-lane road that disappeared into the darkness ahead.

"Now what? Where's the gas station?" Lainie looked around in growing panic, but she could see nothing, not even a way back onto the interstate. She could only drive forward, and the needle in the temperature gauge was nosing its way into the red zone.

Without the noise of the interstate traffic to muffle it, the knocking in the engine sounded as if it would pound its way through the hood, and the headlights seemed to be fading as well.

"Keep going, keep going, keep going." Lainie couldn't hear her own whisper over the noise.

Out of the night, barely illuminated by the last glow of the fading headlights, a small square sign appeared. "WELCOME TO LAST CHANCE, POP. 743, YOUR LAST CHANCE FOR THE GOOD LIFE." On cue, the engine sputtered, wheezed, and died, and the car coasted silently to a stop on the empty road.

"No." Lainie began with a whisper and rapidly rose to full volume. "No, no, *no!*"

So much for sweet talk. She bounded from the car and heaved the door shut with all her strength. The resounding slam was satisfying, but Lainie was just getting started.

"You did it, didn't you?" She kicked the already dented door, then kicked it again.

Lainie slammed both palms down on the hood and jerked her hands away from the searing metal with a cry of pain. She sank to the ground in the dim glimmer of the dying headlights. "Stupid car. Stupid, stupid car. Stupid." She threw her head back and howled her anguish to the silent sky.

Finally, frenzy of wretchedness spent, she pulled herself to her feet and slumped against the bumper. "Now what?" She was weary, almost as if she had walked all the way from Long Beach to this deserted corner of desolation. "Wait till morning, I guess. Someone's got to come by here sometime."

Lainie slid behind the wheel and leaned back against the headrest. Her hand groped for the half-empty bottle in her improvised cup holder and raised it to her lips. The water had been icy when she bought it last time she filled the gas tank, but it had gone beyond tepid well into warm. She made a face and spat it out the window.

"Wonder how long before sunrise. And I wonder how hot it gets out here." Lainie had felt the heat of the Mojave Desert of California and the Sonora of Arizona as she traveled through. She was pretty sure she had been gaining altitude over the last few hours; nonetheless, the thought of sitting in her car while the desert around her heated up made her uneasy. She had heard gruesome stories of people stranded in the desert and how quickly they died of dehydration and heat prostration. Spitting that mouthful of water out the window suddenly seemed an act of foolhardy waste. She found the bottle cap on the floor and screwed it onto the bottle with an extra twist.

"I can't just sit here." Lainie got out of her car again and leaned against the door. She could hear the faint snarl of the big rigs gearing down as they roared through the night, full of power and purpose. She considered walking back to the interstate and trying to flag one down, but after only a few steps it was so dark that she could no longer see her feet on the road. She decided to stay with her car.

"Okay, you've rested. Let's give it one more try." Lainie got back behind the wheel and turned the key. The starter groaned and whined.

"It's all right. Take your time." She tried again, sat a moment, and tried yet again. The engine coughed to reluctant life. Lainie kissed her fingers and patted the dash.

"That's my good girl. Just take it easy."

Slowly, following the nearly nonexistent beam of her headlights, Lainie crept down the road. She was on top of the curve before she saw it, but her snail's pace made the turn easy to make. The night was so black she hadn't seen the huge outcropping of rock, but as the road curved around it, she found herself, not five hundred yards from where she'd broken down, in the town of Last Chance, population 743.

The town was as silent and seemed as deserted as the lonely spot she had just come from. But there were a few streetlights, some stores with darkened windows, and down the street she could see an intersection where a single stoplight blinked red. Just at that moment, with a loud clunk that sent steam and smoke pouring from around the hood, the engine quit one last time. Lainie fought the steering wheel into a turn and made it almost across the parking lot of the High Lonesome Saloon before the car came to a complete and final stop.

For a minute she just sat. This, she knew, was as far as this car was taking her. The beer sign in the window of the bar was still lit, and there were two pickups parked in front. Lainie opened her door and slowly got out. It was still hot, and her shirt stuck to her back. Her hair hung in strings down her neck, and she tugged at the hem of her shorts as she walked across the parking lot and pushed open the door.

The room was small and dark, with maybe four booths along one side and a long bar fronted by a few stools along the other. But it was cool, and the smell of stale smoke and sour beer was familiar and welcoming. The bartender and the bar's single customer looked up as she entered.

"Evening." The bartender glanced at his watch. "Barely made it. We close here in about fifteen minutes."

"Could you give me a beer? Or if not that, a soda? Just make it cold."

"I'm afraid this near closing it's going to have to be a soda. What can I get you?"

"Whatever's closest and coldest. Oh, my car's in the middle of your parking lot, and if you want it moved you're going to have to help me push it. Sorry."

The bartender craned his neck to look out the window. "Nah, it'll be all right, least till morning. Then you can get Manny from Otero Gas and Oil to give you a hand with it."

"Evenin', pretty lady." A wiry older man leaned on his elbows at the far end of the bar. Foam flecked his salt-and-pepper mustache, and his watery eyes narrowed with the effort to keep her in focus.

Lainie barely glanced at him. "What time does the station open, and where can I stay until then?"

"Manny gets there about eight, I think." The bartender rubbed the back of his neck. "But as to where you can stay, I'm not sure. There's only one motel in town, and it's closed."

"For good?"

"I'm just tryna be friendly, that's all." The voice at the end of the bar was aggrieved.

"No, it'll be back open in a few days. The owner's out of town till Friday, I think."

"Great." Lainie was too tired even to be surprised.

"Stranger comes to town, you oughta be friendly, that's all I'm tryna say."

"Les, that's enough. You go on and wait in the truck. I'll be done here in a little while."

"I'm not waitin' in your old truck. I'm gonna drive my own self home. And it'll be a cold day in the hot place before I come back here, you can bet on that." Les slid off his stool and stood swaying slightly before he began navigating toward the door. "Jus' tryta be friendly. Jus' try. World's a cold old place."

Lainie watched him find the door on his third try. "Should he be driving?"

"Nah, he's not going anywhere. I got his keys from him an hour

15

and a half ago. I'll drive him home when I close." The bartender glanced at the neon lit clock on the wall. "Which, according to the laws of this state, is right now."

He smiled at her, a nice smile, and walked from behind the bar to wipe down the tables and empty the ashtrays. Lainie liked the way his plaid shirt tucked into his jeans, and on him, the wide belt and silver buckle didn't even look hokey. She had seen worse, and maybe he was the Good Samaritan type. A furtive glance at his hands revealed surprisingly long and graceful fingers but no ring.

She tugged some of the snarls from her hair with her fingers and sat up straight on her bar stool, arching her back just a bit. "Don't suppose you have an empty spot for me tonight at your place? I'd be out of your hair in the morning."

The bartender gave her his nice smile but shook his head. "Sorry, every bed in my house has at least two kids in it now. And my wife's brother has been camped out on the couch since he got out of the service last month. Wish I could help."

Lainie stood up and stretched. "Well, I guess if the motel is closed until the owner wanders back, I'm sleeping in my car. How safe is that?"

"Oh, you'll be safer than you are comfortable. Not much happens here after dark. The diner across the road opens at six, so you'll be able to get some breakfast. Sorry about the motel, though. I hear it's comfortable. If it'll make you feel better, I could stop by the county sheriff substation and ask Ben Apodaca to swing by and check on you a time or two during the night."

"No." She didn't need some cop shining his flashlight in her window. "No, thanks anyway, but it's not the first time I've slept in my car. I'll be all right."

Lainie slid off her stool and walked back out into the hot night. Les had climbed into the passenger side of the newer of the two pickups and was slumped against the half-open window, asleep. Her footsteps crunched on the gravel as she walked to her car and opened the door. She threw everything from the back seat into the front except her pillow and climbed in.

The clouds had parted, and the little patch of sky she could see through the rear window held more stars than she knew existed. She watched them while the day's events played in her mind. Why did everything she ever tried to do get fouled up somehow? After a while, she heard a car door slam and an engine start, and she rose up to see the pickup pull onto the road with a spatter of gravel. The bar's neon lights were gray shadows against the black window.

Lainie squirmed to get comfortable. She tried to remember when she had ever heard such silence and could not. She was no stranger to loneliness, but she was to being alone, and it frightened her. Tomorrow she'd find a way to get to El Paso and the new start she knew was waiting for her there. What was it those signs said? Last Chance for rest, for the good life? She was still gazing at the stars when, enveloped by the hot smell of her cooling engine, she fell asleep. Maybe one more chance was all she needed.

2

Sunlight was pouring through the back window of Lainie's car when she opened her eyes. She was hot and sticky, and her mouth felt like cotton. Pain knifed through her neck and shoulder when she lifted her arm to check her watch, and she thought she'd never be able to straighten her legs again.

She slowly pulled herself into a sitting position and looked around. Last Chance looked no more encouraging than it had the night before; she was still stuck in the back of beyond. A promise in the air of searing heat to come reached her through the open window, but the early morning was cool. Long shadows still stretched west across gravel and asphalt, and the distant rocks and hills were blue and pink and purple against a vivid turquoise sky. A postcard with a view just like that had been what drew her to the Southwest in the first place, but for the life of her, at that moment, she couldn't remember what the attraction had been.

Lainie got out of her car and stretched, listening to the pop of each joint. "Okay, deep breath. You are going to get out of here somehow."

The High Lonesome Saloon was still closed, but in the window across the road three neon doughnuts progressively lowered their way into a large neon coffee cup while wafting neon steam formed the words *Dip 'n' Dine*.

18

"I need coffee." Lainie opened her trunk, hauled out a battered red backpack, and headed across the road. "And a place to wash up."

"Honey! You didn't sleep in that car, did you?" The waitress who greeted her when she came in was just too perky for 6:45.

Lainie turned and looked out the window. Her car was in plain view, and the waitress had obviously seen her get out of the car. She was in no mood for either idle chat or nosy questions. "Yeah. And I'd sure like to clean up. Where's the restroom?"

"Right through there. Oh, wait, I can do you one better." The waitress, who had a plastic tag over her pocket that read "Fayette," led Lainie past a door marked "Employees Only" and through a storage room to a small bathroom.

"How'd you like a shower? I use this sometimes when I have to work breakfast shift clear through supper. It gets so hot, and I don't have time to go home to freshen up after the lunch crowd thins out."

Lainie managed a real smile. "I would kill for a shower. Thanks."

"Well, that won't be a bit necessary. You just take all the time you want, and when you get done, I'll give you some breakfast."

Never had something as simple as a shower felt so good. The shampoo Lainie found on the shower shelf smelled like raspberries, and as the hot water sluiced around her shoulders and down her back, she closed her eyes and inhaled the fragrant steam, feeling her aches and stiffness slipping away.

Combing the tangles from her wet hair, she felt like a new woman. The shorts and tank top she pulled from her backpack were wrinkled but clean. She pulled her wet hair back, caught it with an elastic band, and smiled at herself in the mirror. *Just a touch of lipstick, and you're human again.*

As she searched the inside of her backpack, a bulge in the lining grazed her knuckles. Yanking the bag open wide, she held it to the light and discovered a slit just wider than her hand cut under the zipper. Her fingers felt numb, almost as if they didn't belong to her, as she worked her hand through the slit and down the side of the pack. She knew what she had even before she pulled the plastic bag of crystals into the light.

One of Nick's new friends had shown him a similar bag in their living room and bragged about what they could get for it on the street. She and Nick had argued after he left, and Nick had promised her he would never deal drugs. But he also promised he'd never see those friends again, and the day Lainie came home to see them pulling away from the curb, she knew she had to leave. She had put nearly a thousand miles between her and Nick, but when she pulled the drugs from her backpack, it was as if he had shoved his way into the room too. Her dream of him letting her go, of moving on, was over. Nick would already be looking for her, and he didn't give up.

Her hand was shaking as she shoved the plastic bag back behind the lining again, way down this time, clear to the bottom. She needed to get rid of the drugs somehow, but she'd figure that out later. That waitress would probably be checking on her if she didn't get out there soon.

"Feel better? You sure look like you do." Fayette gave her a smile.

Lainie climbed onto a stool at the counter and pulled a plastic-coated menu to her. "Yeah. I think I'll live. Thanks."

"Now. What can I get you? Want some eggs? Maybe a waffle?"

"Just coffee, thanks. And maybe some toast. I need to get going."

"Oh, you need more than just toast and coffee! No wonder you're so skinny. How about a couple of biscuits? I've got a pan just about ready to come out of the oven."

"Just toast."

"Oh, come on. Carlos is famous for his biscuits. You've got to give them a try."

Lainie sighed. She wasn't up to an argument and sometimes, though not often, she found it was easiest just to give in. "Okay, I'll have a biscuit."

"And some eggs? How do you like them? Over easy? And some sausage? I get it from a guy just over the state line who makes it himself, and it's the best you'll ever put in your mouth." Fayette smiled as she poured Lainie's coffee and pushed the cream pitcher over to her.

In the kitchen, Carlos must have pulled the biscuits from the oven, because the diner was suddenly filled with the aroma of hot bread. Lainie realized she was hungry. Her dinner had been a packet of peanut butter crackers and some beef jerky she bought at the gas station, and that had been some twelve hours earlier.

She returned Fayette's smile. "Okay, I'll take some eggs. Thanks."

"Carlos? You got that? Two eggs over easy, side of sausage."

Lainie sipped her coffee and gazed through the window at her defunct car in the middle of the High Lonesome's parking lot across the road. It had a dejected, abandoned look, and even though Lainie had yet to call Manny at Otero Gas and Oil, she didn't think he would be able to do much for her. "I really need to get to El Paso today. What's the best way to do that?"

Fayette stopped on her way to the kitchen and looked thoughtful. "Well, there's an eastbound bus that goes through San Ramon two or three times a day. That's about twenty miles from here, but someone's always heading up there, and I can try to find someone to give you a ride. If that fails, I can take you up myself after I close up here. But the only bus that comes that late doesn't leave until nearly midnight. Gets you into El Paso at about 2:30 in the morning."

Lainie thought a minute, then slid off her stool and picked up her backpack. "Do you have a pay phone I can use? I need to make a quick call."

"Right there by the front door. You walked right past it when you came in. Don't bother hauling that thing with you, nobody's going to mess with it."

"It's all right."

She pulled a phone card from her purse and punched in the numbers, turning her back to the dining room. "Come on, Lindsay, be home. Pick up."

When she heard the familiar voice on the line, she felt the weight on her shoulders ease. It was the first thing that had gone right since that light on the dash showed up last night.

"Hi, it's me. Listen, my car broke down, and I'm stuck in some hole off the interstate somewhere."

"Who? What?" Lindsay's voice came as a croak.

"Lindsay, wake up. It's Lainie. My car's dead. Like, really dead. I'm going to try to get out of here on a bus today, but it may be late before I get in. Do you think you can meet me?" She glanced over her shoulder at Fayette.

"Lainie, where are you?" Lindsay still sounded groggy. "I thought you were going to get here last night. They were only going to hold that job till this morning. What happened?"

Lainie rolled her eyes and was about to repeat herself when Lindsay continued. "Nick called."

Ice spread like fingers through Lainie's body. "Nick? When?"

"Yesterday. He seemed pretty sure he'd find you here. Did you tell him you were coming after all?"

"No, of course not. What did you tell him?"

"That I hadn't heard from you in months. Isn't that what I was supposed to say? I'm not sure he bought it, though. He kept asking for you. Why did he think you'd be here?"

"I have no idea. Listen, I'd better not come. Not for a while, anyway. If he calls back, do not tell him you talked to me. Just say you never heard from me. Do you hear me? You never heard from me."

She hung up and slowly sank, almost as if her knees were refusing to hold her up anymore, until she was sitting on her backpack. She sat with her face buried in her hands until she felt a hand on her shoulder.

"Honey? Is everything all right?"

Lainie took a deep breath, held it a moment, and blew it out in a gust. "Yeah, I'm fine. I don't know what I'm going to do, but I'm fine."

"Well, one thing you can do is come eat. Everything always looks better on a full stomach."

Lainie shrugged the hand off her shoulder and stood up. What planet was this woman from, anyway?

Fayette slid her arm back around Lainie's shoulders and guided her across the room to her stool. She went behind the counter, took a plate off the shelf, and placed it in front of Lainie. "Here you go. Here's some honey for your biscuits and some green chile for your eggs. Enjoy."

Lainie murmured a curt thanks. She needed to think, and Fayette looked like she wanted to chat. Lainie didn't look up again until the sound of her coffee cup being refilled brought her out of her reverie.

"There now. Feel better, don't you?" Fayette smiled down at her. Lainie saw that her plate was completely empty, wiped clean with the scrap of biscuit that she still held. She could not remember the last time she had eaten so much at one sitting. Truth be told, she didn't remember eating this meal either, and though she'd never admit it, she did feel better.

"I may be stuck here a little longer than I'd planned, and I really don't want to live in my car. Do you know when the motel is going to open again? The guy in the bar said maybe Friday?"

"That'd be about right. Rita's due back from the mayors' convention late Thursday."

Lainie just looked at her.

"She's at the small town mayors' convention. It's her one official trip every year, and she never misses it. That's the only reason she'd dream of shutting down the motel, even for a few days. Her sister, Coral Ann, usually takes over for her when she goes to the convention, but her daughter up in Phoenix went into labor three and a half weeks early and she was gone. Rita didn't have much choice but to close down for a few days."

"I'm sorry. Whose daughter?"

"Coral Ann's. Rita has two boys, but one's in the air force, and the other moved off to Dallas, I think. They neither one of them have kids."

Lainie tried not to roll her eyes. "So the motel is closed until . . . ?"

"I think you could check in Friday. But you don't want to sleep in your car till then. Let me think a minute."

A white-haired couple came in and claimed a booth by the window. Fayette picked up the coffeepot and crossed the room.

"Morning, Juanita, Russ. You need some menus, or you know what you want?"

"Well, you know Russ wants a pancake special with the eggs over medium. I've never seen a man for loving his old ruts." Juanita shot an exasperated glance at her husband.

Russ didn't look up from stirring cream and sugar into his coffee. "If something's good, don't mess with it. That's why I've stuck with you all these years, toots."

"Well, I'm glad to know I rate right up there with a pancake special." Juanita shook her head. "I'll just have toast and grapefruit."

"Right. Whole wheat, hold the butter. Be right back with that."

"I see Les Watson's truck is parked outside the bar at 7:30 on a workday morning." Juanita cradled her cup in both hands as she gazed out the window. "Think he's sleeping it off in the cab, or did Ray have to drive him home again?"

Russ didn't answer and Fayette had disappeared into the kitchen. In a moment she stuck her head back out again.

"I'm trying to think where someone might stay until Rita gets back. Got any ideas?"

"San Ramon? They have some motels up there."

All three looked at Lainie, still clutching her backpack. She shook her head.

"No, all my stuff is in my car. I need to stay nearby. Don't worry about it. If I can get some help moving it out of the middle of that parking lot, I'll just make that my base for a few days."

"Now that sounds awful. I know we can do better than that." Juanita clearly loved a project. "If Russ didn't have our spare room filled up with all that radio equipment, she could stay there."

"Really, I'll be fine. It's only for a few days."

They went on as if Lainie hadn't spoken.

"You know who might have a room? Elizabeth Cooley. She was just telling me that since her granddaughter went to college, she's rattling around like a BB in a boxcar. You know, she always did like a houseful of people."

"No, I'm fine. Really." Lainie spoke louder. They ignored her still.

"Elizabeth! Of course! Why didn't I think of her? She's perfect. I'll go give her a call right now. Think she'll be up yet?"

Lainie slid off her stool and slung her backpack over one shoulder. "Look, I truly appreciate all your help, but I don't need it. How much do I owe you?"

Fayette pulled her ticket pad out of her apron pocket and handed Lainie the top sheet. "Honey, are you sure? At least let's get that car over here somehow if Manny can't fix it, so you'll have someplace to be during the day besides the front seat of a broken-down car."

Lainie had never had so many people, strangers at that, show such concern for her well-being. And honestly? It made her want to run like the wind. Without a word, she slapped a ten-dollar bill on the counter and headed for the door, waving away Fayette's protest that she had change coming.

"Would you look at that?" Lainie pulled up short when Juanita's disapproving voice drew their attention to the window. A car even more beat-up than Lainie's had pulled into the parking lot of the High Lonesome Saloon beside the pickup Les had left there the night before.

Juanita pursed her lips. "How she puts up with that, I do not know. I wouldn't. Not for five minutes, let alone thirty years."

Russ hadn't more than glanced up from his breakfast. "Well, you don't have to. He's Evelyn's problem, not yours."

Les got out of the passenger side and climbed into the cab of his truck. The old car followed him out onto the road.

Juanita tore open another package of sweetener and stirred it into her coffee. "I know that. But it just doesn't seem right that such a sweet and godly woman should be called to bear such a heavy burden year after year."

She said more, but Lainie didn't hear. She was watching not Les but the county sheriff car that had stopped just outside the Dip 'n' Dine. The stocky silver-haired deputy stood by his car and waved a greeting that Les returned as he drove away. Lainie slipped into a booth by the door and slid her backpack under the table. Why was he staring at her car? Finally, after what seemed an eternity, he turned and walked in.

"Morning, Ben. On your way home?" Fayette poured a cup of coffee and set it in front of him.

The officer sat on a stool and helped himself to two chocolate doughnuts from the pyramid under a glass dome on the counter.

"Yep. Just got off."

"Rosalie out of town? Want some breakfast?"

"No, she's got breakfast for me. Some dang oatmeal and dang decaf coffee." He bit off half a doughnut and sloshed the other half in his coffee. "Know anything about the car with the California plates in Ray's parking lot?"

Everyone looked at Lainie. She tried to sound nonchalant. "That's mine. I had some trouble with it last night and that's as far as it got me. I'm just waiting for the gas station to open up. I'll be on my way as soon as it's fixed."

"And she's says she's going to sleep in it until it's fixed! Can you believe that?" Juanita seemed to feel every conversation included her. "Rita's out of town, you know."

Ben shook his head and bit into his other doughnut. "That's not going to happen. There's a vagrancy ordinance. I could find someone to drive you up to San Ramon, though. Got some motels up there."

"That's what I told her. But she doesn't want to leave her car. What do you think about her staying with Elizabeth Cooley?"

The deputy regarded Lainie with dark, hooded eyes. "Might work. For a few days, anyway."

"That's all we need. Rita's due back Friday. I'll go give Elizabeth a call."

Ben stood and picked up his hat. "Oh, by the way, the station's open. Saw Manny opening things up when I drove by." He tossed a few bills on the counter, waved to Russ and Juanita, and left. Fayette was already on the phone.

Lainie just put her head in her hands. It looked like Last Chance was it for her, at least for now.

3

Elizabeth says she'd love to meet you." Fayette sounded triumphant as she hung up the phone. "She just asks for a little time to get dressed and straighten up some. I'll draw you a map. You can walk anyplace in town in fifteen minutes, so you can have another cup of coffee, if you want one."

"No, thanks." Lainie had the uneasy feeling that custody of her own life was slipping from her grasp. She stood and slung her backpack over her shoulder. "If you can tell me where the gas station is, I'd better go see about my car."

"Just give me a minute here and I'll call over there for you. Maybe he can just meet you at your car. Save you a walk." Fayette was adding up Russ and Juanita's ticket.

Lainie did not want to wait a minute. She did not want Fayette back on the phone arranging her life for her. She really wanted to get in her car and get back on the interstate and head . . . where? El Paso was out. She couldn't go back to Long Beach. But all that was beside the point. The car was not moving out of the parking lot of the High Lonesome Saloon. And she wasn't going anywhere without a car. She sighed and sat back down to wait.

"What are you bringing to the potluck Sunday, Fayette?" Juanita fished her sunglasses out of her purse while Russ carefully scrutinized every item on the ticket Fayette had placed on the table.

"Oh, I thought maybe a chicken enchilada casserole. Folks seem to like that. Guess I don't need to ask what you're bringing."

Juanita laughed. "No, I wouldn't dare show up without my specialty." She stood up to leave, but her husband was still occupied with his accounting. "For Pete's sake, Russ, that tab is $10.45 plus tax. It's $10.45 plus tax every single time we have breakfast here."

She rolled her eyes at Fayette and headed for the door. Russ, after carefully counting out bills and change, followed her.

"There now, I'll call over to Otero Gas and Oil for you." Fayette reached for the phone and punched in a number. "Patsy? Hi, it's Fayette. What are you doing working this close to your time? . . . Well, I don't care. A half day is still too long for someone about to have a baby any minute. Manny needs to get you your own computer so you can do the books at home. Breathing all those fumes can't be good for you or the baby, and you can tell Manny I said so. Is he around? . . . Shoot. Know when he'll be back? . . . Listen, if he calls in, tell him to go on over to Ray's place. There's a car broke down in the parking lot . . . Yeah, California plates . . . Okay, sweetie, take care."

Lainie put her head down on her folded arms and closed her eyes. None of this seemed real. She didn't move as she heard Fayette cross the room to her booth and slide in across from her. She felt Fayette's warm hand on her arm.

"Honey? There's nobody in here right now but you and me. Tell me. Are you in trouble?"

Lainie did not raise her head or open her eyes. After a moment she mumbled into her arms, "Did you hear me when I was on the phone earlier?"

"Well, I didn't try to eavesdrop, but this diner isn't all that big."

"Do you remember if I mentioned the name of the town?"

"No, as I recall, you just said you were in some hole off the interstate."

Lainie sighed and sat up. "Well, that's something, anyway."

Fayette wasn't smiling, but her eyes were kind. When she reached across the table and took both Lainie's hands in hers, Lainie was surprised that she had no desire to withdraw them.

"Can you tell me what's wrong? I'd love to help you if I can."

Lainie took a deep breath. "Well, I had a job waiting for me in El Paso. I was supposed to get there yesterday, and I found out this morning that they didn't hold it for me. Now I don't have a job. I don't have a car anymore, so I don't even have a way to get someplace where I could find a job. And I have just about enough money to get me through the week. Then I don't know what I'm going to do."

Fayette didn't move. "Honey, I wouldn't wish what you've gone through on anybody. It must be awful scary landing in a little fly-speck of a town like this one with a broke-down car and no job. But we can help you with that. The thing I can't help wondering about is why you're so glad you didn't mention the name of the town. Please don't think I'm one of those small-town busybodies, but that conversation you had this morning was a lot less about what you had waiting in El Paso and a lot more about someone trying to find you. Now tell me, are you in trouble?"

Lainie couldn't answer. The lump that suddenly filled her throat warned that if she tried, her voice would come out about three octaves higher than usual, and the tears she was battling would give way in a torrent.

After waiting another minute or so, Fayette stood up. "All right, then. We'll just leave it at that for now. You go on and see Elizabeth. If Manny turns up, I'll give you a call there."

About ten minutes later, following the map Fayette drew on a napkin, Lainie found herself standing outside a small tan house protected on one side by a row of tall, skinny trees and surrounded by a short chain-link fence with green vines and wide blue flowers winding though. A garden hose trickled water into a planter with pink and white blossoms spilling over the side.

As she started up the walk, the warm aroma of something baking met her, and the low drone of earnest voices from the television came through the screen door. She wished herself anyplace but where she was, and only the memory of that deputy sheriff and his vagrancy ordinance kept her putting one foot in front of the other.

The lady who answered her knock was short with curly white hair, and she looked soft, like pillows. Her smile was friendly and generous.

"You must be Lainie. Come in here and have a seat." Elizabeth gestured toward a brown tweed sofa draped with a lavender-and-purple crocheted afghan. "Let me cut that TV off. I just keep it on for the company, and I've seen this episode about a hundred times anyway. The lawyer's ex-wife is the one who killed him." She turned from the television and smiled at Lainie. "Can I get you some coffee?"

Lainie shook her head. "No, thanks. I'm good."

"Are you sure? I've just made a pot, and I've got a coffee cake in the oven."

"No, really, I'm fine. I just ate."

"Well, maybe later." Elizabeth slid back into her chair and popped up the footrest. "The coffee cake should be done in about twenty minutes. Now, Fayette tells me you've had some trouble with your car and need a place to stay till you get it fixed. Well, I do have a room, and I long since promised the Lord I wouldn't turn away any stranger he sent my way, so you're welcome if you'd like to stay."

Lainie looked around the small living room. An old upright piano stood against one wall with a huge oil painting hanging over it, and a large flat-screen television dominated the wall across from it. Pictures, presumably of family, were everywhere. There was nothing to indicate that Lainie was walking into some kind of a cult, but she had never heard anyone casually talk about conversations with the Lord, and she didn't much like it.

"Thanks, but I'm not sure what I'm going to be doing. Manny hasn't even looked at my car yet, and as far as I know, he could have me back on the road this afternoon."

"Really? Fayette said you thought it had broken down for good." Elizabeth looked disappointed. "Well, even if you can get it fixed, it's bound to take at least a day or so to get the parts so Manny can fix it for you. You'll need somewhere to sleep. Here, let me show you the room." She struggled out of her recliner and led the way down a hall lined with even more framed family photographs.

The room was small and spotless, like the rest of the house. Elizabeth moved through the room with a proprietary air, smoothing the colorful patchwork quilt that covered the single bed, straightening the crisp white curtains on the window, picking an invisible piece of something off the chair. "I know it's probably not what you're used to, but it's clean, and you're welcome to it as long as you need it."

Elizabeth was right about one thing: the room surely wasn't what Lainie was used to. What she was used to was playing rent roulette in a series of roach-ridden apartments and residential motels. And unless her luck changed, she'd likely be back in those soon enough. It wouldn't hurt to stay here for a few days. She'd always dreamed of having a pretty room all to herself.

"I'm not sure how much I can pay. It took nearly everything I had to get this far."

"We can worry about that later. Let's just say that for the next week or so, you're my guest. After that, well, we'll see." Elizabeth led the way back to the living room, pointing out the bathroom and the kitchen as she went.

Lainie didn't bother to look. She had other things on her mind. Clearly, Elizabeth was a soft touch. If she could be talked out of a week's rent that easily, what else might she come up with if she were handled just right? Lainie smiled a sweet but tragic smile when Elizabeth turned around.

"I can't tell you what it means to me that you'd let me stay here. It's so beautiful. Everyone here is so kind to me. I'm just not used to it." Lainie thought about squeezing out a tear but decided that might be overdoing it. She sighed instead.

Elizabeth eased herself back into her recliner and smiled at Lainie. "I'm glad to do it. I've had some wonderful experiences with the folks God sends me."

Lainie knew she would feel a lot more comfortable if Elizabeth didn't keep dragging God into everything, but she smiled anyway and tried to answer in kind. "Well, I hope he doesn't disappoint you this time."

"Disappoint me? Honey, I've been disappointed by a lot of things in my time, but never, never, never has it been by anything God has done. Don't you give that another thought. Now, there are a few things we need to talk about if you're going to stay here, though. First of all, do you smoke?"

Lainie shook her head.

"Good. I can't abide the smell, and it comes in on your clothes even if you don't smoke in here. Do you drink?"

Lainie hesitated.

"Well, the one thing I ask there is that you don't come home having had too much. I have my great-grandchildren here from time to time, and that's just not something I want them exposed to. Not in my house."

Lainie nodded her agreement.

"Let's see. I have supper ready at 5:30 every night. You don't have to eat here, but I'd consider it a courtesy if you let me know before I start cooking. I stay up late, but I'd like to have my door locked by 11:00, and there's nothing around here to keep you out that late anyway. Oh, and my one hard and fast rule is that anyone under my roof on Saturday night goes to church with me on Sunday morning." She leaned back and smiled at Lainie. "I guess that about covers everything. Anything you'd like to ask me?"

Lainie had been nodding her agreement with everything, but the nodding stopped when Elizabeth mentioned church.

"Church? I'm not sure about that. The roof would cave in and God would have a heart attack if I went inside a church."

The timer on the oven sounded, and Elizabeth pushed down the footrest and struggled out of her recliner again. As she passed Lainie on her way to the kitchen, she smiled and patted Lainie's cheek. "Darlin', believe me, you just aren't that big a deal."

Lainie sat alone in Elizabeth's living room feeling as if she should be gravely offended and wondering that she was not. Okay, realistically, God probably wouldn't have a heart attack. She'd never killed anyone or anything. But church! She had a vague memory of going to Vacation Bible School with a neighbor when she was about seven, but never since then had she been anywhere near the doors of a church. But if Elizabeth made it a condition of her hospitality, she guessed she'd have to go. And if the roof came crashing in, it would be on Elizabeth's head, no pun intended.

When Elizabeth returned, Lainie was standing in front of the painting over the piano. The enormous landscape seemed somehow out of place in the fussy little room. She recognized the mountains and the desert around Last Chance, but it was the sky that dominated the painting—the sky and clouds that boiled and towered from iron-gray plates close to the ground high into sunlit billows dwarfing even the tallest mountain peaks below.

"Do you like that? That's the view from the front porch of the ranch. I must have watched a thousand storms blow up like that. And I'd be fibbing if I said I didn't miss it to this day, although moving to town was really the best thing for me to do. My grandson painted that. He's got a real gift, if he'd just use it." Elizabeth carried two plates, a lightly steaming square of coffee cake on each. "I know you said you weren't hungry, but this tastes so much better straight from the oven. Here, just take a bite. It's my mother's recipe. I'll go get us a cup of coffee."

Twenty minutes later Lainie was sipping her second cup of coffee and steadfastly insisting that she could not possibly eat another piece of coffee cake when Fayette called. Manny had turned up and was waiting for her at the Dip 'n' Dine.

Lainie set her cup on the maple coffee table and stood, shouldering her backpack. "I guess I'll go get this over with. I'll bring the rest of my stuff over this afternoon, if that's all right."

"Why don't you just put your knapsack back in your room before you go? There's not a reason in the world why you have to keep dragging it all over town."

Elizabeth was right, of course. If Lainie was never without her backpack, people would start to notice and wonder. But she wasn't quite ready to let it out of her sight. "I'll just take it with me. I don't know what I might need when I take care of the car."

—⁂—

Manny must have seen her coming. He was standing outside the Dip 'n' Dine with his hands in his pockets, smiling as she walked across the parking lot.

"Manny Otero?"

"Manny Baca. Frank Otero is my father-in-law."

Lainie really didn't care.

"Had yourself a little trouble, huh?" He was a bit younger than she and not quite as tall, but he had the air of easy nonchalance that mechanics always seem to assume right before they tell you the worst.

"What was your first clue?" The walk from Elizabeth's had not been long, but the day was already getting hot and the backpack weighed more with every step. Lainie didn't even try to hide her irritation.

"Why don't we take a look?" Manny's smile faded and he headed back across the road to her car. Lainie followed, wishing she had been a little nicer. The only thing she knew about cars was how to drive them. If she had to depend on whatever Manny told her, it would be good to have him on her side.

Manny raised the hood and peered under it. He poked at things, lifted other things, and occasionally said, "Hmm." Lainie just stood next to him feeling useless. She could see Ray through the window of the bar, though the sign still read Closed. When he smiled and waved, she just looked away. What did he have to be so happy about, anyway?

Manny slammed the hood down and wiped his hands on a rag. "How long have you had this car?"

"Maybe a week. Why?"

"Because whoever let a car like this get in this condition shouldn't be allowed to drive."

"Well, it wasn't me. Can you fix it?"

Manny shook his head. "Not for what you'd want to pay me."

The diagnosis was what Lainie had been expecting, but that didn't make hearing it any easier. She leaned against the door and looked at the sky. "Now what?"

Manny didn't seem to hear her. He was walking all around the car, running his hands over the dents and rust spots, getting down on his hands and knees to peer at the undercarriage. Finally he stopped in front of Lainie. "I'll buy it from you for three hundred dollars."

Lainie just looked at him. "Why? I mean, sure."

Manny's attention had returned to the car. He opened the front door and slid behind the wheel. "I've always wanted a classic Mustang to fix up, but the right one just never came along. Wait'll you see what I can do with her."

"Then it's yours." Lainie held out her hand to seal the deal. The last thing she wanted was for Manny to start having second thoughts about the junk heap he had just offered to buy.

"Manny!" Fayette stuck her head out the door of the Dip 'n' Dine and hollered across the road. "Patsy wonders when you're coming back."

"Ah, Patsy." Manny winced. "She's going to kill me when she finds out."

Lainie held her breath while she watched Manny struggle with his conscience. Finally, he patted the hood of the Mustang and hollered back. "She okay?"

"She's fine. Her mom just needs her to come get the girls."

"Tell her half an hour." He turned back to Lainie and grinned. "She'll come around. Once the baby gets here, she'll forget all about it."

"Oh, yeah. I gathered from Fayette that you guys are going to have a baby. Your first?"

"Third. We already got twin girls. But this one's a boy."

"Three kids, wow. You're not much more than a kid yourself."

"I'm twenty-five. Not that young."

"I think twenty-five's young. How many kids does Ray have?"

"Ray? None that I've ever heard him admit to. He's not even married." He laughed. "Although, now that I think about it, I have heard him pull a family out of the air late at night when some drunk and ugly woman starts getting a little too cozy."

His laughter died away at the look on Lainie's face. She held up an index finger.

"Just one minute. I'll be right back."

Ray looked up and smiled when she came through the door. "How's it going? Get everything taken care of?"

"Everything is fine, Ray. And how's the family? Are they fine?"

Ray stopped smiling and looked over Lainie's shoulder. In the mirror, she could see that Manny had followed her inside and was standing behind her. His face could barely contain his grin.

Ray returned to Lainie. "Yeah, well, let me explain . . ."

"Don't bother." Lainie's voice shook. "But let me explain a thing or two to you. All I was looking for was someplace to sleep. Period. And if that didn't suit you, all you had to do was say so. You didn't have to come up with some stupid story. As hard as it may be for you to believe, I probably would have managed to control myself."

She pushed Manny aside and strode to the door. Just before she slammed it she turned for one last shot. "'Cause darlin', believe me, you're just not that big a deal."

4

Lainie was tossing the contents of her trunk onto the gravel next to her car when she heard Ray crunching across the parking lot. She didn't look up, although she did consider heaving something heavy at his head.

"Look, about last night . . ." His words faded into silence.

Lainie leaned against the car, folding her arms and raising an eyebrow. "Yes? About last night?" She waited. "Well?"

"Yeah. It's just that . . ." While Ray struggled for words, Manny strolled up, still grinning. Ray turned on him. "You got one big mouth on you, you know that, Baca?"

Manny threw his hands up in mock surrender. "Hey, man, don't count on me to keep your women sorted out for you. I got three of my own to worry about."

"Forget it." Lainie jerked open the car door. She swept everything from the seats and floors out into the parking lot.

Ray backed out of her way. "Look. I have nothing to say for myself. I was a jerk."

"You got that right." Lainie pulled the case off her pillow and dumped the contents of the glove compartment into it.

Ray stood looking at the growing piles of debris in his parking lot. "What are you doing?"

Lainie shoved him aside. "I'm getting my stuff out of my car. Manny's going to buy it from me."

"But why here? What are you going to do with it?"

"I'm taking it to Elizabeth Cooley's. She has a big family too, but she found room for me anyway."

If Ray caught the "big family" barb, he gave no sign. He nudged an empty soft drink cup, straw still poking through the lid, with his toe. "Manny could have taken you by in the tow truck. How're you going to move all this stuff?"

That was it. The snap was almost audible as all the frustration she had been dealing with since she left Long Beach gathered itself together and blew.

—⁂—

Ray fell back a few steps and stared. All he had done was to ask a simple, logical question, and now here this woman was storming around his parking lot kicking her stuff all over creation, screaming like a banshee and cussing like a sailor. He shot a nervous look at Manny, but Manny had fled to his truck and was messing with the winch. Ray began easing toward the door of the tavern but hesitated. It just didn't seem right leaving her out here having a fit all by herself, especially after he made her sleep in her car. He looked up and blew out a gust of relief. The cavalry, in the form of Fayette, was on the way. She stopped to let a Ford 4x4 go by, waved at the driver, and ran across the road.

"What are you big bullies doing to this poor thing? It seems to me, after all she's been through, you'd be trying to help instead of causing her even more grief." She put her arm around Lainie's shoulders. Lainie tried to twist away, but Fayette was stronger than she looked and held firm. Lainie drew a ragged breath. She wiped her cheeks with the heel of her hand and sniffled.

"I swear, Fayette, I didn't do a thing. I just asked how she was going to move her stuff and she went nuts." Ray rubbed his shin where a low-flying flashlight had caught him.

Fayette looked at Lainie's belongings strewn around the parking lot. "What did you think she was going to do, Ray? Put everything in her purse? Someone's going to have to run her things over to Elizabeth's, and I think it would be real gentlemanly if you'd do that for her. I'll just take Lainie over to the Dip 'n' Dine with me while you put everything in your truck. I'll let Elizabeth know."

Before Ray could respond, Fayette turned Lainie around and guided her toward the road. She smiled over her shoulder at Ray and called out to Manny, who had begun hooking Lainie's car to the tow truck, "Better leave that for later, Manny, and go get Patsy. She called again."

—⁓—

There were people sitting in a couple of the booths when Fayette steered Lainie through the door. They had doubtlessly watched the entire incident in the parking lot of the High Lonesome Saloon, and they regarded Lainie with solemn alarm.

"Why don't you splash some cold water on your face while I pour you some iced tea?" Fayette gave Lainie a little push toward the restroom before she walked back behind the counter.

Lainie locked herself in the small room and turned the cold tap on full force. She cupped her hands under the gushing water and looked in the mirror at her blotchy red face and swollen eyes. "I just know I'm going to go out there and have a big old butterfly net dropped on me. And truthfully? If it will just keep the world out, a nice padded cell sounds pretty good." She bent over the sink and bathed her face and neck with the cool water.

When she gathered enough of what remained of her dignity, she walked back into the diner. One of the booths had emptied, but the people in the other looked much less troubled, almost friendly. Fayette must have eased their minds.

"Here's your tea. And here's someone I want you to meet." Fayette leaned across the counter and tried to tousle the dark hair of a tall, skinny kid of about sixteen. He leaned out of her reach and jerked his chin at Lainie in a gesture of silent greeting before returning his attention to the plate mounded with food in front of him.

"This is my son, Matthew, who seems to have forgotten his manners. Can you say, 'Good morning,' Matthew?"

The silence grew while Fayette waited. Finally, without swallowing his mouthful of food, Matthew mumbled a greeting. Fayette looked as if she had more to say but shook her head instead. Her cheer sounded forced.

"Matthew's going with the youth group from church today. They won't be back until supper, and who knows what they'll find for lunch, so he's stocking up before he goes."

Matthew had been sneaking glances at Lainie as he ate. She had nearly finished her tea before he spoke. "That's a cool tattoo."

Lainie glanced over her shoulder at the hummingbird caught there in midflight. "Thanks."

Matthew leaned back for a better look. "Got any others?"

"Matthew! That's none of your business." Fayette sounded shocked, but her son ignored her.

"I'm gonna get a tattoo as soon as I'm eighteen. Gonna start with a piece of barbwire around my bicep. I've got some other really cool ideas too."

"I've told you that you could get one now if it said 'Mom.'" Fayette brought another glass of milk. "A nice big heart with 'Mom' on it, and maybe some little cupids flying around? I'd even help you pay for that one."

Matthew rolled his eyes, drained his milk in one swallow, and stood up. He was even taller than Lainie thought, well over six feet, and after a big meal, he probably managed to tip the scale at 150. "I gotta go. Can I have some money for lunch?"

"Give me a kiss first."

"Mom, come on. I gotta leave."

"No kiss, no money."

Matthew rolled his eyes again and leaned over and kissed the air somewhere in the vicinity of Fayette's head.

"Nope, that's not going to do it." She tapped her cheek. "You want to eat before the sun goes down, you plant a kiss right here."

"Mom!"

Fayette just stood tapping her cheek. Matthew sighed, rolled his eyes yet again, and leaned down. Due to some quick maneuvering by Fayette, he actually made contact this time.

"There now, that didn't kill you, did it?" Fayette dug into her apron pocket for tip money. "Have a good time, sweetie. See you at supper."

Matthew didn't duck this time when Fayette reached up and brushed his hair out of his eyes, but he didn't look back when he left either.

"Nice kid." Lainie turned back to the counter.

"Yeah, he's a good boy at heart. But I worry about him. He's just busting to get out of this little town. There's not that much to keep a boy out of trouble, especially in summer. The youth group is taking a trip out to the desert today to look at a bunch of petroglyphs they've all seen a hundred times. But pull that old church bus around to the front of the building, and everybody just piles on. They'd go on a field trip to the dump, just to get out of town for a while."

Lainie had no idea what she was supposed to say. She didn't

know anything about kids, and furthermore, she didn't blame them for wanting out. She grabbed at the first thought that went through her head. "Oh, he'll be okay."

Fayette sighed. "I know. I guess moms just worry." She gestured at the window behind Lainie. "Looks like Manny's back. Do you need to talk to him?"

Lainie swung around and looked out the window. Her belongings were no longer spread over the tavern parking lot, and Ray's truck was gone. Manny had backed the tow truck to the rear of Lainie's car and was hooking it up. She had no desire to talk to him or to Ray for a long, long time. "He's buying my car from me, so I guess I'll have to settle that sometime, but I don't think I can deal with it today."

"You've had a day of it, haven't you? And it's not even noon. I think you should just go over to Elizabeth's and take a good long rest. There's all the time in the world to get everything else taken care of."

As Lainie watched, Ray pulled into the parking lot across the street and got out of his truck. He stopped to talk to Manny, and Manny was still laughing when Ray slapped him on the shoulder and went back into his bar. Lainie hoisted her backpack to her shoulder. "Sounds like a plan."

Heat pushed against the door of the Dip 'n' Dine and wrapped around Lainie like a blanket when she walked outside. The white sun had sucked all the color from the sky and the town. Even the single strip of blacktop that ran through was gray.

Manny, with her car in tow, pulled out onto the road. He rolled down the window and leaned out. "Want to ride with me down to the station and take care of all the paperwork?"

Lainie shook her head. She knew she should probably get that check before Patsy got wind of the sale, but she just couldn't. Not right now. "Think we could do it later? Maybe even tomorrow? I'd like to go get settled."

"Suit yourself." He waved and drove on. Lainie couldn't decide if his wide smile was because he wouldn't have a crazy lady riding in his truck with him after all, or if he was still thinking about the spectacle she had made of herself earlier. Either way, he was far too cheerful.

An old school bus with "Church of Last Chance" painted on the side rumbled by on its way out of town. A couple of young guys in the back hooted and waved their arms out the window to get her attention.

Lainie found herself wondering how serious Elizabeth was about making her go to church. She still hadn't decided if she would go, although she was leaning toward no. After all, what could Elizabeth do? Call the cops? Did Last Chance have church ordinances the way they had vagrancy ordinances? She wouldn't be surprised. Well, she'd give it till Sunday, then decide. If her luck changed, she might even be hundreds of miles away by then. Shifting her backpack to the other shoulder, she turned down Elizabeth's street.

A hot wind had begun to blow by the time she walked up the front steps. The row of trees to the side of the house danced in toward the roof and added a shushing whisper to the sound of the television gunfire pouring from the front door. Elizabeth looked up from the afghan she was crocheting when Lainie came in.

"Here you are! Get everything taken care of?" She started to struggle out of her recliner, but when Lainie waved her back, she returned to her crocheting. "I had Ray put everything back in your room. He sure was in some kind of mood, though. He wanted to dump every blessed thing you had in your car on the floor of your room, trash and all."

Lainie headed back to her room. As she passed the sofa, an

enormous gray-and-white tabby jumped off with a thud and padded behind her.

"That's Sam," Elizabeth called after her. "He thinks he owns the place. If you don't want him in there with you, just shove him on out. He's not the big shot he thinks he is."

Sam trotted past Lainie and led the way into her room. He rubbed his whiskers and chin against the two cardboard boxes and the suitcase that held all her belongings before he jumped up on the bed, stretched, and curled up in a patch of sunshine. Lainie could hear the deep rumble of his purr from where she stood in the doorway.

"This your space? Well, get used to sharing it."

It didn't take her long to unpack. She shook out the clothes in her suitcase and folded them away in the lined dresser drawers. She didn't have much else, just a few things that she carefully arranged and rearranged on the dresser—a snow globe with Mickey Mouse in a wizard's hat and robe that her father had given her for her eighth birthday, some makeup, a brush. When she finished, she clutched her backpack to her chest for a moment before crawling to the back of the closet, where she pushed aside the zippered garment bags hanging there and tucked her backpack into the corner. It disappeared into the darkness as the garment bags fell back into place.

Outside, the white clouds that had been boiling up took on a gray tinge, and the white curtains danced at the window. A sudden gust blew the door shut with a slam, and Sam jumped to his feet, blinked, and lay back down. Lainie opened the door.

"You want out? You better go while you can." Sam looked at her with half-open eyes and twisted to wash his stomach.

"This is your last chance." Sam closed his eyes and purred louder.

"Okay, cat, but don't think I'm getting up to let you out."

Sam offered the resistance of a fifteen-pound beanbag when

Lainie pushed him to one side and lay down next to him. The pillowcase was cool and crisp against her cheek and smelled fresh, like rain. Lainie closed her eyes. Sam oozed over until he was lying against her, but she was barely aware that the steady pressure down her side from hip to knee was him or that the soft rumble that lifted her into unconsciousness was the tremor of his purr.

5

Ray was squatting on his heels behind the bar the next morning checking his supplies when he heard the door open and someone step in. He waited for a voice, but there was only silence.

"Not open yet. Come back in an hour or so."

His hand closed around the baseball bat he kept under the bar and he stood up, keeping the bat out of sight under the counter. It was only that crazy California girl. He slid it back on its shelf.

"What can I do for you?"

"First of all, I want to say I'm sorry about yesterday." The girl smiled, and he noticed that when she wasn't screaming her head off, she wasn't bad looking. "I sort of lost it."

Ray shrugged. He sure wasn't going to argue with that.

"Anyway, can we start over?"

She was all over sugar, but that made Ray even more uncomfortable. He had heard about those split-personality people, and he was sure that if ever there was one, she was standing in his bar this minute. He had seen her all of three times and she had been a completely different person every time.

"I was hoping I could use your phone. I need to make some calls, and I don't need Elizabeth or Fayette hanging over my shoulder listening in."

"There's a pay phone in the hall there by the restrooms. Help yourself."

48

"Well, the thing is, my calling card is about out of minutes, and I'm about out of cash. Do you have a phone that isn't pay? I promise I'll keep it short."

Ray noticed she had a dimple when she smiled. He crossed the bar and opened the door to the storeroom that doubled as his office. "The phone's there on the desk. I'll ask you to keep the door open, though, if you don't mind."

Lainie sat on the desk with her back to the door. She kept her voice low and Ray couldn't hear what she said, even if he were interested, which he wasn't. But he could hear her tone, and Miss Sugar was giving way to Miss Ticked-off. Finally she yelled, "All right! Just forget I called!" and slammed down the phone.

He was actually kind of curious about which personality she would have when she came back in the room, although he made sure the bar was between them, just in case. But when she came in, climbed on a stool, and asked for a beer, she just looked scared. Ray found himself wondering if he could get that dimple back.

"Can't give you a beer. We're not open yet. But how about a soda? On the house."

She closed both hands around the soft drink Ray put in front of her but didn't drink it or even look up. She looked a lot smaller sitting huddled on that bar stool than she had looked in the parking lot yesterday.

"Everything okay?" Ray poured a bowl of peanuts and set it next to her.

She didn't look at him or at the peanuts, and when she spoke, it was more to herself than to him. "I am so stuck here."

Ray was good at assessing his patrons' moods, and usually when they didn't feel like talking he just left them alone, but something about the way she was hanging on to that soda like it was the only thing keeping her from falling off the stool made him stick his neck out even though he knew better.

"Nobody could help you out, huh? Well, there's worse places you could have wound up. And you're bound to figure something out eventually." He knew he had made a mistake as soon as the words left his mouth.

Lainie shoved her untouched soft drink at him, leaving it rocking in a pool of sloshed fizz. Her feet hit the floor with a thump. "Really? Do you even know what you're talking about? You may think there's worse places, but let me tell you, I have actually been out there, and there aren't. Not anywhere. And I am stuck here. Stuck with a bunch of nosy religious nuts and one bartender with an imaginary family."

"Look, lady." Ray had had enough of this drama queen. "Let me help you out of town. Just tell me where you want to go. I'll drive you to the bus station in San Ramon right now and buy you a ticket. It'll be money well spent, believe me. Come on, let's go." He slammed his bar rag down and snatched his hat off the rack by the door, giving the brim a good jerk over his eyes. He yanked the door open and stood in the shaft of sunlight that poured in. "Well? What are you waiting for? We can get your stuff and still get you to San Ramon in time to catch the 2:30 eastbound. And if you want to go north or west or just about anywhere, they have busses going there too."

"Fine!"

For a minute Lainie had the same scary look on her face that she had yesterday in the parking lot, but Ray stood his ground by reminding himself that he was a head taller and probably outweighed her by seventy-five pounds. She didn't come after him this time, though. She just seemed to sort of crumple, and her voice, when it came, was barely audible.

"I don't know where to go."

"Where's your people? Don't you have anybody back in California?"

Lainie shook her head and rubbed the heel of her hand across her cheek. "Nope. I think my mom might be in Wyoming somewhere, but I haven't seen her in a long time. And she wouldn't want me turning up, anyway."

"Friends?"

"Yeah, right, friends. I've got a boatload of really great friends."

Ray shifted his weight and shoved his hands in his back pockets. He had never known anyone who didn't have more family than they knew what to do with, or friends either, for that matter. He opened his mouth to say something but closed it again. Sometimes it was best to just shut up.

Lainie climbed back on her stool. She dragged her finger through the spilled soda and made little squiggly designs on the bar. Ray stood watching, but she seemed to have forgotten he was there. He closed the door, hung his hat back on the rack, and went on with his work. He was just about to turn the neon Open sign on when Lainie sighed and slipped off her stool again.

"Well, I guess I'll go on back to Elizabeth's. Thanks for letting me use your phone."

"Sure thing."

Lainie's shoulders slumped like she still lugged that backpack of hers. Ray made one more try.

"Hey."

She stopped at the door and looked at him.

"Don't bite my head off, but I meant what I said. Religious nuts and delusional bartenders aside, the people here are good folk. You could have done a lot worse. And I have been out there too."

Lainie pulled open the door. The sun made her hair look sparkly, almost white. "Yeah, sure."

Ray was still trying to think of something else to say when the door closed behind her.

6

Lainie woke to a vague sense of dread. It took a moment before she could identify its source. It was Sunday morning and Elizabeth expected her to go to church. She threw her legs over the side of the bed and sat up. No way. Lainie hadn't let anyone tell her what to do in a long, long time, and she wasn't about to start now. She squared her shoulders and headed down the hall in her bare feet and faded Dodgers T-shirt toward the kitchen and the smell of frying chicken.

"Got any aspirin?" Lainie leaned against the doorjamb and rubbed between her eyes with two fingers.

Elizabeth wiped her hands on the apron she had tied over her housecoat, her face a mask of concern. "There in the cupboard next to the sink with the glasses. What's the matter, honey?"

Lainie shook two tablets into her hand. She washed them down, poured a cup of coffee, and sank into a kitchen chair.

"I don't feel so hot this morning. I think I'll just stay home."

The concern on Elizabeth's face faded a bit. "What's wrong?"

"I just feel kind of crummy. Maybe something I ate. I'll just kick back this morning and I'll be fine."

Elizabeth's eyes were the color of the sky but not nearly as sunny. "It seems to me we had a deal. You're not backing out now, are you?"

Lainie avoided meeting Elizabeth's gaze by taking a sip of coffee.

"Deal? No, I remember that you said you'd like me to go to church with you, but I never said I'd go. I sure don't remember any deal."

"Well then, let me just remind you. When you came into this house, the one and only thing I asked of you was that you go to church with me on Sunday. And now you're trying to squirm out of our agreement. Is that all your word means to you? Why, I'm surprised at you."

She turned back to the chicken she was frying, shifted a piece or two with the fork she was holding, then fastened her gaze back on Lainie.

Lainie looked at the plaque that read "Bless This Mess" hanging on the wall behind Elizabeth's head. She looked out the window. And she bent down and gave considerable attention to Sam, who was rubbing his chin against her chair. But the silence kept growing, and she finally had to look up. Elizabeth stood watching her with folded arms, her mouth set in a straight line and her blue eyes shooting sparks. Lainie lifted her chin and returned the gaze. She managed four seconds before she had to drop her eyes again.

"All right then, I'll go." She snatched up her coffee cup and strode down the hall. "But don't think you're going to change me by making me go to church."

Elizabeth's voice floated after her. "I don't need to change you, honey. That's not my job."

Lainie slammed her door and leaned against it, considering her options. They came to two: packing her bag and leaving Elizabeth's, or getting dressed and going to church. Since she still had no place to go, she really had no choice. She yanked open a dresser drawer and began rifling through the contents.

"What am I supposed to wear to church? I don't even own any polyester."

She held up a short, sleeveless T-shirt and smiled.

"Okay, Elizabeth, you win. But I don't think you're going to like it much."

She was admiring the results in the mirror when a tap came on her door.

"Lainie? I'm sorry I got so put out. The last thing I want to do is start the Lord's Day with a tussle. Come on in and have breakfast and—"

Lainie threw the door open and stood back for effect. Elizabeth broke off in midsentence, and her eyes widened, though the smile never left her lips.

"Well. Don't you look . . . comfortable."

Lainie turned and preened before the mirror. The denim shorts showed nearly every inch of her long legs, and between the low-slung waist and the cropped shirt, at least six inches of torso lay bare as well. Tattoos peeked over the waistband. She turned back to Elizabeth with a smile and swept past her to the kitchen.

"Thanks." *Okay, church lady, let's see who comes down with the headache now. Something tells me we just may be staying home after all.*

—⁓—

Lainie first questioned the wisdom of her ensemble an hour later when the pan of hot chicken she was holding touched her bare leg as Elizabeth's pickup bounced down the dirt driveway and turned onto the road.

"Ow!"

"Sorry, Lainie. Just hold that chicken a little higher. It won't take a minute to get to church."

Elizabeth waited for a semi to roar past before she swung the truck onto the main road through town. She sat on a pillow to see over the dashboard and had another pillow or two nestled at her back so she could sit far enough forward to reach the pedals. Lainie braced her feet against the fire wall and tried to balance the hot pan over her lap.

"Why do you drive this thing? Wouldn't something smaller fit you better?"

Elizabeth laughed. "You know, that's exactly what I thought when I moved off the ranch. I couldn't wait to get me one of those little foreign jobs. But I guess I had been driving these things too long. I just felt like I was sitting on a roller skate at a tractor pull. Scared me to death."

"The ranch where the painting came from?"

"That's the one. My husband and I raised cattle about fifteen miles east of here, but when my husband died, I thought it was time for me to move to town and let the young folks take over. My son, Joe Jr., runs the place now. Hold on to that chicken. We've got one more little bump here." Elizabeth pulled into a row of pickup trucks parked in the shade of two old elm trees and switched off the engine. "Let's drop off this food, then I want you to meet Brother Parker before the service starts. He retired from a big church up in Albuquerque, but then we talked him into coming down here to God's country."

Lainie slid from the cab and looked around. Except for a tiny lawn, the two elm trees, and one of the pickups parked next to the church, there was nothing green between them and the purply mountains on the horizon. Just miles and miles of scrubby brown vegetation. If this was God's country, Lainie figured she knew even less about him than she thought she did.

"Elizabeth! Lainie! Wait!" Lainie turned and saw Fayette and Matthew hurrying across the parking lot. On her hip Fayette held a toddler with a head of dark curls, and Matthew carried an identical little girl on his shoulders. His eyes widened as they swept Lainie from head to foot, and his face split in an appreciative grin.

"You look hot!"

His mother glared at him before turning back to Lainie. "Well, she'll probably be the only cool person here today. I wish I had the nerve to wear shorts. Good for you, Lainie." She smiled, and Lainie tried to look as confident as she had felt in her own room.

"And here's Faith and Grace! What are you doing with Miss Fayette this morning?" Elizabeth patted the chubby leg of the little girl closest to her.

"Faith and Grace got a brand new baby brother last night, didn't you, girls? They spent the night with Patsy's mother, but first thing this morning she dropped them off and headed up to San Ramon to see that new grandbaby."

Fayette and Elizabeth chatted about pounds and ounces and hours of labor and Matthew gawked at Lainie until the sound of singing poured from the church.

Elizabeth stopped in midsentence. "Heavens! Church has started and I still have to get rid of this chicken."

"I'll take Lainie on in." Matthew swung the toddler from his shoulders and handed her to his mother with a little too much enthusiasm.

"No you won't, but you can take Miss Elizabeth's food to the fellowship hall for her while I take Faith and Grace to the nursery. And I better see you in that sanctuary when I get there. With your hat off."

Lainie returned Matthew's man-of-the-world leer with a drop-dead look of her own as she handed off the pan of fried chicken, then turned to follow Elizabeth up the wooden steps. The double doors stood open to catch any slight breeze, and as Elizabeth led the way through the vestibule into the church, Lainie felt every eye turn and follow their progress.

She knew the outfit had been a mistake, but she couldn't do anything about it now. She straightened her shoulders, lifted her chin, and followed Elizabeth down the center aisle to the third row on the left and slid in beside her. If the sixty or so people in the sanctuary had nothing better to do than to stare at her, then let them stare.

When the singing stopped, everybody sat down, and the curly-haired lady in the blue flowered dress who had been leading the singing stepped off the platform and sat on the front row. The choir in the loft behind the pulpit sat down too. A white-haired lady smiled and wiggled her fingers at Lainie from the front row of the loft. She seemed familiar, as did the sober-looking man sitting behind her and slightly to her left. After a moment's reflection, Lainie thought she recognized Russ and Juanita from her first morning in the diner.

A tall, thin man wearing the only suit and tie in the room mounted the few steps and stood behind the pulpit. His eyes were warm and his smile was welcoming as he looked around the sanctuary. When he spoke, his booming voice filled every corner of the small church.

"This is the day that the Lord has made!"

All around Lainie people responded, "We will rejoice and be glad in it."

He continued. "Good to see every one of you here in the Lord's house this fine morning. Elizabeth, I see you have a visitor. Would you like to introduce her?"

Elizabeth stood and turned around to face the rows of people sitting behind her. She held her hand firmly on Lainie's shoulder. "This is my friend Lainie Davis from California. She's staying with me for a while. I'm not going to ask her to stand up, but maybe she'll just give you a wave so you can see where she is."

Lainie glanced over her shoulder and lifted her hand in a half-hearted wave. Elizabeth sat back down and leaned over to whisper, "I'll introduce you to some folks at the potluck."

The service continued. There was more singing, wooden plates were passed up and down the rows, and then the curly-haired woman got up and faced the choir. She gestured with her hand, palm up, and they stood. When they began singing, Lainie was surprised at how good they were. She didn't much care for their choice of music, but for twelve people wearing tan bathrobes, they didn't sound half bad.

When they finished, the man in the suit got up and started preaching. Lainie had no idea what he was talking about and used the time to think about what she'd do when her money completely ran out. The three hundred dollars Manny paid her for her car wouldn't last forever, even in Last Chance. She thought of her backpack hidden behind the garment bags in her closet. Unbidden came the memory of those friends of Nick in her apartment talking about how much it was worth on the street. But she shoved that thought from her as soon as it surfaced. Whatever she did with it, it would never hurt anyone. She had seen too many lives destroyed that way.

Lainie's attention was drawn back to the service as the preacher closed his Bible and around her people shuffled to their feet. The pianist had slipped onto the bench and was playing softly, and everyone started singing again. The tune was haunting and wistful and reminded Lainie of something. She couldn't quite remember what it was, but it caused a fist-sized knot of sadness to settle in the pit of her stomach. She was glad when, after a few verses, the preacher raised his hand and the music stopped. With his hand still lifted, he looked out over the church and smiled his warm smile.

"And now, may the Lord bless you and keep you," he said. "May the Lord make his face to shine upon you, and be gracious unto you. The Lord lift up his countenance upon you, and give you peace."

The pianist started playing again, something happier sounding, and a buzz of conversation filled the room as people gathered their belongings and moved toward the aisles. Lainie stood where she was and looked around. Someone had claimed Elizabeth with a monologue that seemed to be about an upcoming circle meeting, whatever that was.

"Good morning, Lainie. I'll bet you don't remember me." Juanita, still in her choir robe and showing every one of her teeth in a big smile, leaned in from the other side of the pew and took one of Lainie's hands in both of hers.

"You're the lady from the diner, right?" Lainie pulled her hand back and tugged at the hem of her shorts.

"Bless your heart! You have a good memory. So glad you came this morning. I have to apologize for the choir, though. It's usually better than it was today, but one of the altos is out of town."

Lainie shrugged. "It was okay."

This clearly was not the response Juanita expected, because she stopped smiling and her mouth got a pinched look. She seemed to swell as she took in air though her nose.

Elizabeth finished her conversation and turned around. "Good morning, Juanita. Fine service, wasn't it?"

Juanita's teeth-baring smile returned. "Yes it was, even if the choir was only 'okay.'"

Elizabeth looked puzzled as she took Lainie's arm. "I hope you'll excuse us, Juanita, but Brother Parker is still greeting folks at the door and I want to introduce him to Lainie before he heads downstairs to the fellowship hall. Why don't we meet you down there?"

As Elizabeth led Lainie up the aisle to meet Brother Parker, Lainie wished she could pull at the hem of her shorts to lengthen them a bit before she met the pastor, but she could feel Juanita's eyes on her back and wouldn't for a million dollars give her that satisfaction.

7

W hat in the world did you say to Juanita to get her tail in such a knot? She was about ready to snatch you bald-headed."

"She apologized for the way the choir sounded, and I said it didn't sound that bad." A warm, mixed-up casserole aroma enveloped them, and Lainie could hear the sound of people talking and laughing in the fellowship hall.

"Oh, well, there you have it. That choir is the pride and joy of the church—of the whole town, really. They've won all sorts of competitions and gone on tours as far away as Oklahoma and Texas and I don't know where all. They even sang in Branson once."

"I'm not the one who said it sounded bad. She did."

"And that was your tip-off to fall all over yourself telling her how great it sounded." Elizabeth shifted her purse to the hand that had been clutching the stair rail and sighed. "Well, she'll get over it. Come on, if we don't get in there, there'll be nothing left but chili mac and Juanita's specialty."

It may have been Lainie's imagination, but the room seemed to get a bit quieter when she and Elizabeth entered it. A few people already sat eating at rows of long tables stretching the length of the room, but most still stood in a line that snaked toward tables laden with casserole dishes, platters, and slow cookers. Across the hall, under a high window, another table was well stocked with cakes, pies, and plates of cookies. Lainie had never seen so much food in one place before, and except for what was left of Elizabeth's chicken, a cake or two, and a large bowl of pale green Jell-O with cottage cheese, miniature marshmallows, and pineapple, she couldn't identify a single dish.

"Hi. Mom's got some places saved for you over there." Matthew skidded to a stop in front of Lainie and Elizabeth as they finished filling their plates and stood surveying the now crowded tables. "Here, Miss Elizabeth, lemme carry your stuff."

He led the way between the tables to the far side of the room where Fayette, flanked by Faith and Grace in high chairs, sat chatting with a small, wiry woman with auburn hair and piercing brown eyes.

"Here they are. Can I go now?" Matthew set Elizabeth's plate down and unfolded both chairs Fayette had leaning against the table with a single snap.

"Sure, go eat with your friends, but I'll need you to get these high chairs back to the nursery for me, so don't run off when you're done."

Elizabeth scooted her chair up to the table and leaned past Fayette to speak to her companion. "Good to see you back, Rita. How was the conference? Don't believe you've met Lainie Davis. Lainie, this is our mayor, Rita Sandoval."

Rita flashed a smile showing gold-rimmed teeth and stuck out her hand. Her grip was surprisingly strong for such a small woman. "Always good to see a new face in Last Chance." She turned back to Elizabeth, her voice growing even more animated. "The conference was absolutely tremendous! I got some great ideas about how to put this place on the map."

She sat back and took a sip of her iced tea, looking from one face to the other with a mysterious half smile.

"Well, what? Tell us about it."

"I'm afraid you're just going to have to wait a while. Good ideas have to incubate. If you break an egg open before it's ready to hatch on its own, all you've got is a mess. But I'll tell you right now, it's a winner."

Emphasizing the finality of her decision to remain mum, Rita turned to Lainie. "So, Miss Lainie Davis, tell me all about yourself. Where'd you come from? What brought you to Last Chance? Are you planning on settling down here?"

Lainie was poking something that had noodles and hamburger with her fork. She looked up and shrugged. "I'm from California. My car broke down. I don't know how long I'll stay."

Rita narrowed her gaze. "Yes, but why here? Last Chance isn't exactly on the beaten path. How'd you find us?"

"There were some signs on the interstate, I guess. Last Chance for gas, Last Chance for rest, stuff like that."

Rita slapped the table with her hand and sat back. "I knew it. I just knew it. Where's Russ?" She craned her neck and looked around until she spotted him at another table forking in chocolate cake and coconut pie. "Russ! Russ Sheppard!"

Russ looked up and Lainie would have sworn he rolled his eyes. But he put down his fork, pushed back his chair and ambled over to their table. "Afternoon, ladies. What can I do for you, Rita?"

"Lainie, tell him why you're in Last Chance."

Lainie looked from one to the other in confusion. "He already knows. My car . . ."

"No, no." Rita brushed Lainie's explanation aside as if it were a pesky fly. "Not why you're in this area, tell him why you are here in Last Chance and not, say, in San Ramon."

Lainie finally got it. "Oh. The signs on the interstate."

Rita smacked the table again. "There. Didn't I tell you those signs were what we needed to bring folks into town? And you fought me ever' step of the way. Now I want you to tell me that I was right and you were wrong."

Russ sighed. "Rita, those signs have been out there for two and a half years, and as far as I know, this is the only time they ever brought anyone to town. You know full well that if it weren't for me and a couple others on the town council, you'd likely drive this town into bankruptcy with all your schemes."

"I know no such thing!" Rita's brown eyes shot sparks, and she looked as if she had plenty more to say, but Elizabeth broke in.

"All right, you two. This isn't the council room. It's the Lord's house. You can save this for the town council when you're ready to share your new ideas, Rita."

Russ looked like he couldn't take much more good news. "Ideas? Good night, what are you up to now, Rita?"

"Never you mind. You just sit on that chile farm of yours and watch the town crumble to dust if you want to, but some of us believe in the future. You can help us grow, or you can just stay home. In fact, I'd rather you stayed home."

Russ heaved another sigh and turned back to his table. "Oh, I'll be there all right. Count on it."

Rita's eyes glistened with tears. "That man makes me so mad! I declare he'd audit a Sunday school picnic. 'How much did that watermelon cost? Were those the cheapest paper cups you could find?' Well, would someone tell me just exactly what's wrong with believing in the future?"

Elizabeth patted Rita's hand. "I wouldn't worry too much about it. Russ is who he is. And when you get down to it, that's probably exactly why he was elected to the town council. And why he's the church treasurer, for that matter. We need both types, I think— visionaries like yourself and the more practical types like Russ."

"I, for one, would not mind one bit if Last Chance got a little bigger." Fayette rummaged around in a diaper bag and pulled out some wipes. "I could use the customers, and I could use the help. Thanks to Carlos's big family, I can usually get help in the summer, but Tina goes back to college next week, and then I don't know what I'll do."

"What kind of hours are you talking about?"

All three ladies stopped talking and looked at Lainie.

"Why?" Fayette stopped scrubbing, and the twin she was working on took the baby wipe out of her hand and dropped it on the floor. "Are you looking for work?"

Lainie shrugged. "Maybe."

Fayette sat back in her chair and looked at Lainie. "Have you ever done waitressing?"

"I've done all kinds of things, including waitressing." Lainie waited while Fayette looked thoughtful. "So?"

"You know, Fayette, this could be just the thing," Elizabeth said. "You know you need the help. And here's Lainie needing a job. I call this more than coincidence."

"If it weren't for Matthew, I could keep on going just like I always have." Fayette still sounded like she was thinking about it. "But I just worry about him so. School's going to be starting soon, and it would make such a difference if I could be home after school."

"Worry about Matthew? Why, that's just silly. Not that you shouldn't lighten your load, but Matthew is one of the finest boys in this town. Always has been."

"He is a good boy, but he's getting awfully restless, Rita. Being tied to the diner like I am, I don't know where he is half the time. Up until this summer, he was in and out of the diner all day, mostly coming in for something to eat, bringing his friends with him. But I don't see him now till I get home. And when he does come in with

64

friends, half the time I don't even know who they are. They're not from around here. I know that much."

"Well then, it looks like you've got your problem solved." Elizabeth began gathering the empty paper plates around her into a stack. "You want to be home more. Lainie needs a job. And there you have it. By the way, I agree with Rita. You've done a fine job with Matthew. He's just feeling his oats."

Lainie had been just sitting and waiting. She was becoming accustomed to conversation concerning her circling around a bit before it came back to rest. Fayette still looked concerned, but she smiled at Lainie.

"All right, then. Let's give it a try. Why don't you come in at around eleven and help me through the afternoon for a while till you learn your way around. Then when school starts in a couple weeks, I'll go home after the lunch rush and come back later to close it down."

"Sounds good."

"I'll bring a uniform for you. I've worn about every size. I should have one small enough for you." Fayette looked around. The room had nearly emptied and Matthew was nowhere in sight. "Well, I guess my boy forgot about these high chairs."

Rita stood up. "Don't worry about it. Lainie and I can get them back."

"And I can hear my pillow calling me." Elizabeth brushed the crumbs from her pale blue slacks. "Nothing says Sunday afternoon like a nap."

—⚬—

Ray Braden threw his pencil down on the papers in front of him and pushed away from the table. The air conditioner lodged in the window of his tiny trailer did a good job of staving off the

Sunday afternoon heat, but its drone was putting him to sleep. He stretched and picked up the paper plate holding the remnants of the potluck dinner Matthew had run in while Fayette waited in the car with the Baca girls. He headed outside for the dumpster but stopped and grinned when he spotted Lainie Davis walking across the parking lot.

"Hey, Lainie! Still wearing your Sunday-go-to-meeting best, I see."

"Oh, shut up. Who broke their neck getting over here to tell you what I wore to church?"

Ray shrugged. "No secrets in Last Chance. Sneeze at one end of town, and someone at the other end will bless you before you get your hankie out. What are you up to?"

Lainie gestured at the Closed sign propped in the window. "Elizabeth is napping and I thought maybe I could get a beer, or at least some air-conditioning. And you're not even open."

"Nope, always closed on Sundays. But come on back. I can get you a cold drink."

Ray led the way back to the small travel trailer behind the bar. Lainie ducked to enter the low door and looked around. Except for a fan of papers spread across the tiny Formica table, the one-room space was immaculate. A neatly made bed took up one end of the room and a kitchenette stretched along one side. Ray was already squatting in front of the little refrigerator.

"It's pretty well stocked. What'll it be? Got a cola, coupl'a lemon-limes, some orange, and some grape."

"No beer?"

"No, I lost what little taste I had for it working in the bar. Don't keep it around. You ever have a grape soda?"

"No. It sounds awful."

Ray popped the tab. "You gotta try it. You'll never go back to beer."

Lainie took a cautious sip and made a face. "Well, it's cold. I can say that for it. And sweet."

Ray popped open another can and dropped in the chair across the table from Lainie. He scooped the papers into a single pile and pushed them to the side.

"I always put this stuff off too long. I'd rather do anything other than paperwork. That's why I'm still here instead of out at my place. It was either do the paperwork or shut down the bar for good."

"Don't you live here?"

"No, this is where I stay during the week. I go home after I close up Saturday night. I don't get there until after three, but I have all day Sunday and a good part of Monday morning to spend there."

"And where's home?"

Ray went to the door and opened it. "Come here. See that mountain way over there? Right where the land begins to rise, there's a pretty little box canyon that opens onto the valley. It's on my uncle's ranch, and I decided when I was about fourteen that I'd live there one day. I built a cabin during my summers home from college—just a couple of rooms, but it's mine. You can see the valley and everything in it clear across to the mountains on the other side from there."

"Wow. That's a long way to go for one day a week."

Ray's grin was a little sheepish. "Yeah. Well, it's where I live, and I always know it's up there waiting for me. I'll take you up to see it someday. You'll see what I mean."

"Sounds good, but it'll have to be on my day off. I suppose you also heard I was going to start work for Fayette tomorrow?"

"No, I hadn't heard. Well, good for you. Fayette needs a break. Sounds like you're thinking about sticking around a while."

Lainie shrugged. "I don't know. At least long enough to get

enough money to leave." She stood up and tugged at her shorts. "Well, I guess I better be getting back. You've got work to do. Thanks for the soda."

"Let me drive you. Truck's got air-conditioning too."

When they pulled up in front of Elizabeth's gate, Ray smiled at the sound of squealing tires and gunshots from the television. "Sounds like nothing's changed."

"I guess she's up from her nap. Want to come in and say hi?"

Ray shook his head. "Better not this time. If I'm going to give up a Sunday at my place to do paperwork, I'm dang sure going to get it done. Give her a hug for me and tell her I'll try to stop by to see her one morning this week."

"Okay." Lainie had turned to go into the house when Ray realized he wasn't ready to say good-bye.

"Do you want to do something some Sunday afternoon? It's about the only time both the High Lonesome and the Dip 'n' Dine are closed."

She stopped with one hand on the gate and looked at him. Man, she had long legs. "Don't you usually leave town on Sunday?"

Ray grinned and shrugged. "Usually, but not always."

A slow smile crossed Lainie's face. "Sure. Why not?"

After he pulled away from the curb, Ray waited till he got to the corner before looking into the rearview mirror to see if she was still standing by the gate. She was.

8

"Oh, my. That uniform just swallows you whole. Just tie the apron real tight around your waist." The air was still thick with the aroma of bacon and biscuits, but the diner had emptied of breakfast customers and Fayette had launched into her orientation lecture. Lainie only half listened. She let her gaze wander out the window. The High Lonesome Saloon was still closed. No sign of life anywhere.

"Come on in the kitchen. I want you to meet Carlos." Fayette slapped the swinging door open and led the way. Lainie followed. "Now, Carlos here is the reason the Dip 'n' Dine can open its doors each and every day. He is flat-out the best cook in this county, if not the whole state, and I'll defy anyone to say different. Personally, I think the title 'chef' suits him better, but he won't have it."

Carlos glanced up from the huge pot he was stirring. "Nothing wrong with being a cook. Fancy names don't change nothin'. Unless you want to throw a big raise in with it."

"Well, he's the king of this kitchen, and we try to keep him happy. He's got a special for every day of the week. Mondays it's green chile stew. We post it on the whiteboard by the door, but everyone in town has the schedule memorized. They won't let him change a thing. He usually has one of his nephews in here helping him." She gestured toward a kid of about twenty who was chopping onions.

"This is Pete. He's studying engineering at State. And as I say, we just try to stay out of their way."

She glanced back into the dining room. "Customers. Lainie, you go take them some glasses of ice water and menus, and I'll be right out."

Fayette took all the orders and served the food as the lunch crowd came and went, but she had Lainie running right behind her filling iced tea glasses, busing tables, and fetching menus. Lainie could barely get a table bused and wiped down before another group of two or three turned up to claim it. And to her increasing discomfort, everyone seemed to know her and to call her by name.

"Well, Miss Lainie, you sure look busy. How do you like working for Fayette? I imagine she runs a tight ship."

Lainie picked up the plastic tub of dirty bowls and glasses and turned to face a tall, thin man with white hair and a warm smile. It took her a minute to recognize him as the preacher from yesterday. He slid into one side of a booth and Russ Sheppard slid into the other side. Lainie had never said more than hello to a preacher before and was trying to figure out what to say when Fayette came up behind her carrying menus.

"Well, hi there, Pastor, Russ. I wondered if you two were going to get in here today. Y'all having the chile stew?"

"What else? And bring a few extra tortillas, would you?"

"You got it." Fayette handed the menus to Lainie "Don't know why I even bothered to bring these over. Lainie, honey, take these over to table two."

Lainie left Fayette chatting with the men and took the menus to two middle-aged women who beamed at her like she was their long-lost daughter. Then she fled to the kitchen. Carlos was hanging up the phone.

"That was Ray. Wonders if we can run a pint of stew over to him. He's all tied up. Lainie, you got a break coming?"

Pete was untying his apron before Lainie could speak. "No reason for her to spend her break working. I can do it. Be back in five minutes."

"No problem." Lainie spoke with studied indifference. "I've got a couple of seconds. I'll go."

"Nah. Don't worry about it. There's something I've been meaning to talk to Ray about anyway." Pete finished ladling the green chile stew into a carton, fitted the lid over the top, bagged it, and headed for the back door. As he reached for the knob, he glanced at Lainie's expression, and a knowing grin spread over his face. He held the white paper bag out to her. "Unless you got some reason of your own for wanting to go."

"Yeah, right. I love running around in all this heat. Go ahead, knock yourself out." Lainie pushed the kitchen door open and walked back into the dining room, furious that she could still hear Pete laughing as he let himself out the back door.

By 1:30, just a few tables held diners, and just before 2:00, the last two customers, ladies Lainie remembered from church the day before, had paid their check, gathered their purses, discussed the Bacas' new baby with Fayette, called their compliments to Carlos, and finally walked out into the heat of the afternoon.

Fayette brushed her hair from her face with the back of her hand and smiled at Lainie. "You had a real good first day, but I'll bet you're dead on your feet. I think that things have calmed down enough so that you can go on home. When we have a real busy lunch like we did, it's usually a pretty quiet afternoon."

Lainie took a quick look out the window. The High Lonesome was open, but the parking lot was empty. Maybe if she left now, she could stop in and see Ray for a bit before she went home. But as she watched, the old pickup that had been in the parking lot the night she arrived pulled in, and Les got out and made his way inside. No point in going now.

"I might as well stay till the end of the shift. Here come some customers anyway."

Fayette looked up as a utility truck stopped out front and three men in work boots piled out. She sighed.

"Shoot. I could have gone all day without him coming in."

The driver led the way, and Lainie could hear his raucous voice through the window. He was laughing when he pushed through the door.

"Fayette, honey, come here and give your daddy a big ol' kiss."

Fayette's smile didn't change when he grabbed her around the waist, but her eyes flashed as she pulled away. "Now, Chet, just sit down and behave yourself."

"Aw, you're getting too fat anyway." Chet grabbed a menu from her hand and slid into the nearest booth. "What you got that's not pure-D slop?"

Lainie could see that Fayette was struggling to keep her tone light. "You sure come in here often enough if all you can find is slop."

The other men in the group looked uncomfortable as they studied their menus. One sitting across the table from Chet looked up and muttered, "Give it a rest, Chet."

"Aw, she knows I'm just kidding around, don't you, Fayette? We go way back." He swatted at Fayette's backside with the flat of his hand, but she skipped out of reach.

"Chet, that's enough out of you." Fayette's smile and her bantering tone never faltered. "Now, can I bring you something, or did you just stop by to torment me?"

Chet chuckled and went back to his menu, not looking up again until Lainie appeared with glasses of water.

"Well, hello, darlin'! Where'd you come from?" He slapped his menu down on the table and looked up in pleased surprise. Lainie didn't bother to hide her contempt and set his water in front of him with such force that it slopped over the rim.

"Wait a minute. What's your hurry, darlin'?" He grabbed her wrist. "Fayette, you hire more little bits like this and you might actually get some customers in here."

Lainie jerked her wrist away. "If you want to keep that hand at all, keep it to yourself."

Chet recoiled in mock fear. "Ooooh, this one's tough. I'm all a-scared now." He laughed, and when Lainie turned to go, he ran his hand down her hip.

Before he could react, Lainie reached behind her and grabbed his thumb, bending it back to nearly touch his wrist. Chet's eyes flew wide open and his mouth was a frozen O of shock and pain. Giving his thumb an extra twist that caused his mouth and eyes to open even further, Lainie pushed her face within inches of his.

"Listen, Jack, if you ever, *ever* touch me again, I'll break your thumb right off." She shoved Chet's wrist into his chest and let go of his thumb.

The diner was silent. The men who had come in with Chet looked from him to Lainie and back. Fayette had come back into the room and stood frozen. Only Lainie acted as if nothing had happened. She put glasses of water in front of the other men.

Chet's silence lasted only a few seconds. "I'm outta here. You got so many customers you can let the help talk like that, Fayette, you don't need me." He stood and strode toward the door. "And unless you guys want to walk back to the site, you better beat me to the truck."

One of the men muttered "Sorry, ma'am" while the other dug through his wallet and placed a ten-dollar bill on the table before they followed Chet into the parking lot.

"What a jerk." Lainie picked up the untouched water glasses. "Who needs customers like him, anyway?"

"I do."

Lainie looked up and for the first time noticed that Fayette had not moved from her spot in the middle of the diner.

"Oh, come on, Fayette. He's a loser. Good riddance. Do you like being treated like that?"

"Of course I don't, Lainie. How can you even ask such a thing?" Fayette's voice was near enough to tears to break.

"Well, then I did you a favor. You're welcome."

"You don't understand, do you? You can just waltz off anytime you want to, but this diner is all I've got, and I've got a boy to take care of and hopefully send to college one day. You think I don't want to haul off and slap Chet's head off his shoulders? Of course I do. But that's a luxury I just don't have."

"I still think you're making a big deal out of nothing. He's just one guy."

"Just one guy." Fayette brushed her hair off her forehead with the back of her hand and crossed her arms across her chest. The lines etched around her eyes and mouth seemed deeper. "You know, Lainie, every month when I sit down to do my accounts, I pray that I'll have enough to pay my bills. And sometimes I don't. So I pray that the next month will be better. God has always met my needs, and I thank him every day for that. But I need to do my part, and that means seeing to it that every single customer who walks in that door walks out happy and ready to come back."

"Yeah, well, if you think God wants you to keep getting pawed by creeps like that, then go for it. But it's not for me."

Fayette closed her eyes and rubbed the vertical lines between them with two fingers. "You know, Lainie, it's been a long day. Why don't you go on home now? I can handle it from here."

"Whatever." Lainie untied her apron. "You want me to come in tomorrow?"

"I'll call you later. We can talk then."

9

"You're home early." Elizabeth hit the mute button on the remote control when Lainie walked in. "I wasn't looking for you for another couple hours. How'd it go?"

"Fine. I just got fired." Lainie walked through the living room to the kitchen without slowing down.

"Fired? Fayette's never fired a soul in her life. What in the world did you do to get fired the first day?" Elizabeth struggled out of her recliner and followed Lainie to the kitchen.

"Naturally it's my fault. Thanks for the confidence."

"Lainie, I'm sorry. You just caught me off guard, that's all. What happened?"

"Like you really care." Lainie tried to push past Elizabeth in the kitchen doorway, but Elizabeth wouldn't budge.

"I do care and I said I was sorry. So sit right down here at the table and tell me what happened."

Faced with the choice of knocking Elizabeth down or doing as she said, Lainie dropped into a chair at the kitchen table and filled Elizabeth in on the afternoon's events.

Elizabeth shook her head. "Poor Fayette. I feel so bad for her."

Lainie's feet hit the floor under her chair with a thump and she stood up. "I'm done. I'm going to go shower."

"For Pete's sake, Lainie, sit down. Sometimes I think you just go around waiting for someone to say the wrong thing so you can get mad and stomp off. As it happens, I think you did the right thing. No one should put up with behavior like that. It just breaks my heart that Fayette thinks she has to."

Lainie shrugged. "Her choice."

"Is it? That's mighty easy for you to say. You and I can just sit here drinking soda pop, talking about what Fayette should and shouldn't do, but she's the one trying to make ends meet in a diner that by all accounts should have closed down years ago." She looked up and smiled. "I'm just suggesting a little compassion and understanding for Fayette."

"Yeah, the one who fired me for not letting some jerk grope me? How am I supposed to understand that?"

The smile left Elizabeth's face as she got to her feet and reached for the phone. "Why don't I just give her a call and see if we can straighten this out?"

"No! Let it go. I can handle my own problems."

Elizabeth's expression softened. "I know you can, but I know Fayette like my own daughter, and I might be able to help."

Lainie shook her head. "Let's just drop it. I am so done with today, and I just want a shower."

Elizabeth sighed. "All right then. Dinner should be just about ready when you're done."

⁓〰⁓

After dinner Lainie stood by the sink drying dishes. Last Chance was not working out. How far could she get with the three hundred dollars she got for her car? Would it be far enough so Nick couldn't find her? Lainie was still lost in thought when she noticed that the television had gone mute and Elizabeth was talking to someone. She stuck her head around the corner and saw Fayette, still wearing her uniform, standing just inside the screen door.

Fayette's eyes met Lainie's over Elizabeth's head. Her smile was tired and didn't reach her eyes. "Hi, Lainie. Could I talk to you for a few minutes?"

Lainie threw her dish towel onto the kitchen counter and walked through the living room and out the front door without speaking. Fayette followed. The night wind gently tossed the branches of the cottonwood tree in the front yard, and a cricket in the corner of the porch added accompaniment to the rustling leaves. The air was rich with the fragrance of honeysuckle. Fayette eased herself to the top step of the porch.

"Oof. I'd better be careful about sitting down. I might not be able to get back up again. I can't remember the last time I was this tired."

She looked up at Lainie, who had yet to speak.

"Come on, sit here beside me. We need to talk."

Lainie shifted her weight to the other foot and crossed her arms. "I don't know what we have to talk about. It's done. I guess we could talk about what I think about your reasons for firing me, but I don't really think that's why you're here."

Fayette reached up for Lainie's arm and gently tugged. "That's exactly why I'm here. And I didn't fire you. I just said we'd talk later."

Lainie sat down next to Fayette. Sam appeared from under the honeysuckle vine with a cricket in his mouth. He dropped it and pounced again when it tried to hop away.

"Lainie, I've been thinking all evening about what happened this afternoon. I can't tell you how bad I feel about the whole thing. You shouldn't have had to deal with someone like Chet your first day. I just want to tell you that most of the folks that come into the Dip 'n' Dine are real nice people. You won't have to put up with the likes of Chet Babcock very often, I promise." She smiled at Lainie.

"I'm not putting up with the likes of Chet at all."

Fayette's smile faded.

"Look, Fayette, I'm not saying I don't need this job, because I do. But if Chet came in tomorrow, I'd do the same thing."

"Oh, Lainie, he doesn't mean anything by it. He thinks he's being cute. Just stay out of reach. That's what I try to do."

Lainie didn't say anything for a long moment. The struggle to subdue the pain and rage that had resurfaced that afternoon was almost more than she could deal with. When she spoke, her voice was hard. "You know, that's almost word for word what my mom said when I tried to tell her what her boyfriend was doing. *'He doesn't mean anything by it. Just stay out of his way.'* When staying out of his way didn't work all that well, I tried to talk to her again. That's when she threw me out. I was fourteen."

Fayette reached over and covered Lainie's hand with her own. "Oh, Lainie, I'm so sorry."

Lainie pulled her hand away and shrugged. "No biggie. Happened a long time ago. But I'm just saying you're not the only one who's had to deal. The difference is, I decided then and there that I call my own shots. No one lays a hand on me unless I say so. No one."

After a long silence, Fayette stood up and stretched. "Well, I should get home. Matthew didn't come in for dinner and I need to see what he's up to. Let's just leave it at this: I want you to work at the Dip 'n' Dine. I could tell today that you're going to be a great help. And if Chet, or anyone like him, comes in, just let me handle it, okay?"

"Wonder what Matthew thinks when he sees you letting men treat you like that." Lainie's remark, spoken to Fayette's retreating back, was almost offhand, but Fayette's expression, when she turned around, was shattered.

She opened her mouth to speak, then closed it again, and her eyes seemed to age ten years before she turned and drifted down the walk to the faded red sedan parked in front of the gate. Lainie sat on the steps stroking Sam and listening to him purr until the red taillights disappeared around the corner. "I don't know, Sam. Was I out of line? Does someone like me even belong here?"

———

Lainie wasn't sure what to expect when she returned to work, but Fayette met her with a hug and a warm smile, and within a day or two, their working relationship had settled into an easy routine. Lainie was placing a chef's salad and a tuna melt in front of two ladies sitting at table four when Carlos hung up the kitchen phone and called out, "That was Ray. He wonders if someone can run a hamburger over."

"Lainie, you go ahead." Fayette finished making a fresh pot of coffee. "But don't be gone long. If things get busy again, I'll need you."

The Closed sign was still showing in the window of the High Lonesome, but the door was unlocked when Lainie tried the latch.

"Hello? Anyone send for a hamburger?"

Ray appeared in the doorway of his office, and his face lit up when he saw Lainie. "Well, hey, look who's here! How's it going?"

Lainie shrugged. "Okay, I guess, once I made it through the first day."

Ray laughed. "Yeah, I heard about that. You're one tough cookie. Remind me not to get on your bad side."

Lainie handed him the white paper bag. "Like you've never been there. Here, you'd better eat this while it's hot."

"Now that you mention it, I have been on the wrong end of that stick. And I didn't much like it, either." Ray pulled the burger out of the bag and unwrapped it. "Can you stay and keep me company while I eat this? How about a soft drink or something?"

Lainie glanced out the window at the diner across the street. No new cars in the parking lot. "I guess so, for a few minutes, anyway."

"Another grape soda?"

"Um, no. A diet cola will be just fine."

Ray grinned as he poured her drink. "I didn't convert you, huh? Woman, you just don't know what's good."

He took a huge bite of his burger and shifted it to his cheek. "What are you doing Sunday?"

"Are you serious? If Elizabeth has her way, it'll be church in the morning. Then in the afternoon I'll watch paint dry."

Ray took another bite. He laughed. "Well, I can almost guarantee that she'll have her way. But why don't you come with me Sunday afternoon. I'd like to show you something."

"What?"

"A surprise. Are you in?"

Lainie shrugged. "Why not?"

Ray grinned. "Great. I'll pick you up about 1:00."

"Or you could just come to church and we could leave from there. We could have a whole day of fun."

Ray still smiled, but there was sadness in it. "I know you're joking, but the truth is, I miss that church. My mom had me there every Sunday of my life. In fact, I still have a couple perfect attendance Sunday school buttons somewhere."

"If you love it so much, what's keeping you from going?"

Ray gestured around him. "This. The bar. It just seems weird, serving drinks till 2:00 a.m. and then turning up at 9:30 for Sunday school. There's a disconnect somewhere that I can't get past. But this isn't forever."

"Why did you even buy the bar if it's not what you want to do?"

"I didn't buy it. It was my dad's. He had a stroke about five years ago, and I came back to Last Chance to help him out. He died last year, but before he did, he made me promise to keep it for my brother who's in the Marines. Steven always loved this place. He and my dad used to talk about how the two of them would run it one day. Steven should be getting home next spring, so as much as I'd rather be elsewhere, I'm here till then."

"So you and your mom went to church and your dad and your brother had the bar? How'd that work out?"

Ray laughed.

"Well, Steven went to church too, until he got my dad on his side. But after that, yeah, you've about got it right—me and Mom at church and Dad and Steven here."

"Sounds like your mom and dad were kind of mismatched."

"Everybody in town thought so when they got married, from what I hear. Sweet little girl from a prominent ranching family running off with a rodeo bum. Then when he messed up his leg, he took his insurance money and came back and opened this bar. The family liked to never get over it, especially since it was my granddad who bought the policy in the first place so my mom would have some security. I guess Granddad didn't think rodeoing provided all that much of it. Anyway, since Mom's family were all nondrinkers and pillars of the church, it caused a big scandal. But the truth is, they were crazy about each other. They were sweethearts until the day she died."

Ray set his empty soda bottle down on the bar. "But that's enough of my family skeletons. How about you? You grow up in a soap opera too?"

"I wouldn't say that. But I wouldn't call it pretty either."

The phone in the office rang, and Lainie looked out the window. Three cars and a pickup were parked in front of the Dip 'n' Dine. She jumped off her stool.

"That's got to be Fayette. Don't answer until I get out the door."

Ray laughed. "I'll tell her you left a long time ago. See you Sunday. And wear jeans."

10

Lainie was sitting on the top step scratching Sam's chin when Ray's pickup pulled up at Elizabeth's gate. She smiled at the pale and well-worn Stetson pulled low over his eyes.

"Hey, cowboy, that's some getup you've got there. Going to a rodeo?"

He tipped his hat back with one finger. "No ma'am. Just dressing up to make a Sunday call. And may I say you look mighty fine yourself?" His smile widened as he took in her well-fitting jeans and white cotton shirt.

"So where are we going? I hope it's someplace air-conditioned. I wore jeans because you told me to, but it's hot out here."

Ray helped Lainie climb into the truck. "Nope, no air-conditioning where we're going, and no more questions. It's a surprise."

Lainie leaned back and watched the handful of stores and businesses, silent behind their Closed signs, give way to open country. Ray picked up speed and clicked on the radio. A man who sounded like he was about to cry was singing about walking into his empty house. Lainie giggled, and Ray glanced at her.

"What?"

"Well, look at you. You're sitting here in your pickup wearing boots and a cowboy hat, listening to country music. Is that song even for real? He's singing about a dusty rocking horse!"

Ray glared in feigned offense. "Have some respect, woman. The man's suffering. His wife's taken the kids and dog and gone off and left him. Didn't even dust the rocking horse first. And for your information, boots and a hat are required apparel for appreciating serious music like this."

Lainie laughed out loud. "Maybe that's my problem. No boots. No hat. Don't get the music."

She rolled down her window and let the hot wind rush in. Leaning her head back against the seat and closing her eyes, she could almost be flying. In her mind, she watched the dry land with its clumps of sagebrush and rabbit bush drop farther away until even the blue mountains on the distant horizon flattened into shadow on the desert floor.

"Look." When she opened her eyes, Ray was pointing to half a dozen birds circling one over the other in tight formation on fixed wing. "Hawks. They've caught a thermal. They're supposed to be looking for food, but I think they're just having a good time."

Lainie leaned forward to peer from under the windshield. "See the one at the very top? That's me."

"Is it?" Ray sounded impressed. "What's the world look like from up there?"

"Big. And empty. This truck looks like a speck on a licorice whip. And there are no people anywhere. Just me and a bunch of other birds, and they're way down there. No one can touch me."

"I don't know about that. Some of those other hawks are moving right up there." He pointed to another bird, tiny in the heavens. "See that one? That's me, so you'd better watch out. You're about to get some company."

Lainie laughed as the bird Ray indicated peeled away from the thermal and swooped toward the sagebrush below. "Don't think so. Scared of heights?"

"Shoot, I'm just getting us some lunch. What's your pleasure, ground squirrel or kangaroo rat?"

"Yuck!" Lainie's nose wrinkled in disgust. "If that's all you can come up with, I'll do my own hunting. Maybe if I go a little higher, I can spot a Starbucks."

Ray shook his head. "Nope. This is the one place on earth that not even Starbucks can find. But don't worry. I packed us a lunch. You just didn't seem like the ground squirrel type."

He slowed the truck and bounced over a cattle guard as he turned off the highway. "You might want to close that window. It's going to get dusty."

The eager anticipation in Ray's voice was infectious, and Lainie found herself looking forward to whatever Ray had planned.

"All I see is cows and those hills up ahead."

"That's the San Ramon Range. It runs from just north of here down into Mexico."

They bumped along in silence until Ray crested the last hill, drove past a long, low adobe house with a deep shaded porch facing the valley below, and finally pulled up next to a corral by a barn and turned off the ignition. Two saddled horses stood leaning their weight on three legs, munching hay from a feed box and swishing flies with their tails.

Ray opened his door and pulled some bulging saddlebags from behind the seat. "Here we are."

Lainie did not move. Her eyes were fixed on the horses.

"Come on, I want you to meet some friends of mine." Ray stopped at the fence and rubbed the nose of the nearest horse.

Lainie stuck her head out the window. "I can meet them from here. Hi, horses."

Ray laughed. "Come on, you're not afraid of these babies, are you? I always thought of you as a girl who'd take on anything that came her way."

"Well, horses have never come my way, okay?" Lainie slid out of the truck, keeping the open door between her and the horses. "Those saddles don't have anything to do with your surprise, I hope."

"Good grief, woman. I can't believe that anyone who'd bring Chet Babcock to his knees is hiding in a truck from old Belle here. Two-year-olds ride her."

A whip-thin, white-haired man, slightly stooped and bowlegged, ambled out of the barn. Ray raised a hand in greeting. "Hey, Billy. Thanks for saddling up for us."

Billy returned the wave. "No problem. Everything all right?"

Ray shook his head and laughed. "We've got a little tenderfoot fever going on. Lainie's never been this close to a horse. Not sure she likes it."

Billy shifted his direction and ambled toward the truck. He placed his hand lightly between her shoulders and steered her toward the corral. "Come on, sister. Nothing to be scared of. Grab hold'a the horn, left foot in the stirrup there, and up and over. There ya go." He handed her the reins and adjusted the stirrups. "You can let go of the horn now. It's not gonna fall off."

Lainie wasn't quite sure how it had happened, but she was on horseback, and the ground looked a long way off.

"Ready?" Ray mounted in one smooth move. "Hold the reins in one hand and nudge Belle with your heels. Lean the reins against her neck to the left or right to turn her, and gently pull back to stop. She doesn't need more than a light hand. We'll take it easy." He clicked his tongue and his horse moved out at a slow walk. Belle tossed her head and followed. Lainie grabbed the reins and the horn in both hands and hung on.

A light breeze blew the hair from her face, and somewhere nearby a bird whistled from a low branch. Belle's gait was slow and rocking, and Lainie felt the tightness between her shoulders ease. Ray looked over his shoulder and grinned.

"How you doing?"

"So far, so good. Don't go any faster, though, okay?"

"We're not in any hurry. But you can let go of the saddle. Hold the reins in your left hand, and rest your right hand on your leg. You'll be fine."

"Easy for you to say. I want a steering wheel—and some brakes." Lainie loosened her grip on the saddle horn and lowered her right hand to her side, keeping her left hand with the reins close to the horn, just in case.

The trail was narrow, and Belle seemed content to plod along behind Ray's horse. The sun was warm on Lainie's shoulders, and to her surprise, she found herself enjoying the ride. She leaned forward and patted Belle's neck. "You are a sweet baby, aren't you? You wouldn't buck me off, would you?"

Ray laughed. "Belle's too fat and lazy to buck. She's the horse the kids learn to ride on."

"Did you hear that, Belle? He called you fat and lazy. When I get off, you can go kick him if you want to."

Ray laughed again. "Come up here, I want to show you something."

Lainie came to a stop beside him on a wide ledge. The valley fell away before them. A single black ribbon of highway wound through it, and dirt roads like scars in the earth wandered from the main road through the sage. Towering clouds billowed on the horizon and floated across the sky, casting moving shadows on the valley floor. Far to the west, a blue veil of rain reached for the dry earth.

"This looks just like the painting in Elizabeth's house."

"Yeah, that was painted not far from here. You know, I haven't been everywhere on earth, but I sure haven't seen any place I think is more beautiful than this country right here."

Ray turned his horse back to the trail, and without any urging from Lainie, Belle followed. They rode in easy silence for another half hour until they arrived at a small cabin tucked between two huge cottonwood trees. A trickle of water moistened the rocks of a streambed that emerged from a pile of boulders behind the cabin.

"Here we are. This is my place." Ray swung from the saddle and tossed his reins over a rail next to a water trough before loosening the girth of his saddle.

"I knew that was where we were going." Lainie sounded smug.

"City girls. You can't put anything past them." Ray grinned up at her and pulled the saddlebags from the back of his saddle. "Come on. Aren't you hungry?"

Clutching the saddle with both hands, Lainie threw her right leg over the saddle and slowly lowered herself to the ground. Her legs felt rubbery and nearly buckled under her. Ray caught her waist.

"It'll take a minute to get your land legs back. You're going to feel it tomorrow, though."

Lainie glared up at him. "Now you tell me. You do know I have to work tomorrow, don't you?"

"Oh, you'll be able to move all right. You'll just look funny doing it."

Lainie took a careful step. "You laugh and you're a dead man."

Ray's expression was careful deadpan. "Wouldn't dream of it. Come on, let's see some hustle. I want to show you something."

"You are really asking for it, aren't you? If I could move, you'd be so sorry."

She stopped inside the door. Paintings lined the walls and were propped up on easels in the middle of the room. The air was thick with the sharp aroma of oil and turpentine. She whipped her head to look at Ray, still standing behind her in the doorway with an expression of eager uncertainty on his face.

"What is this? Are these yours?" She stepped inside and wandered from painting to painting. In every painting sky and towering clouds dwarfed the desert below—the orange and purple sky of sunset, a dark sky filled with storm clouds, a pale blue sky dotted with lofty white billows casting shadows on the desert floor.

"Well, say something." Ray took off his hat and ran his fingers through his hair.

"These are amazing. And you did them? I didn't know you were an artist. I thought you were just a . . ." Her voice trailed away.

"Bartender? Nope, I told you that wasn't my idea. I'm just stuck there for now. *This* is my life." His sweeping gesture took in the room.

Lainie stopped in front of a large painting hanging on the wall. She gazed at it a long moment before turning to Ray in confused recognition. "This looks like the one at Elizabeth's."

Ray grinned. "Yeah, she was my first customer. She bought that at my senior show. I tried to give it to her, but she said she wanted to be known as the first person in the world to buy an original Ray Braden."

"But she said her grandson painted that."

Ray looked bewildered. "Yeah. I'm her grandson."

"What? I don't believe it. Why didn't you say something? Why didn't she?"

Ray shrugged. "It never occurred to me that you didn't know. I guess I thought she must have said something. She probably thought I had, or Fayette. Everyone around here has known everyone else for generations. I guess it just doesn't occur to us to explain relationships."

"But you never come around."

"Oh, I've dropped by a time or two. You've been at work. Things are a bit, well, awkward." He fell silent and dug into the saddlebags. "Come on, I'm starved. Let's have some lunch. Why don't you get us a couple of drinks from the fridge?"

Lainie opened the door of the refrigerator and found it well stocked with grape soda and diet cola. Grabbing one of each, she joined Ray on the front steps and handed him his drink.

"Thought you didn't like diet cola. Bring a lot of girls up here?"

Ray shrugged and took a long pull of his drink. "Actually, I think you're the first one who's been here. This is where I go to get away from people so I can do my work. Not too many folks get up this way."

"And all that diet cola?"

Ray grinned at her over the top of the bottle. "I brought those up last week. You want to be prepared in case someone does drop by."

"Pretty sure of yourself, aren't you?" Lainie took a bite of her sandwich. "What if I'd said no? Or more likely, what if I had flat refused to get on that horse?"

"Oh, I have powers of persuasion. You didn't stand a chance."

Lainie choked on her cola. "Get real! If that guy down there hadn't practically thrown me on Belle, we'd be back in town by now."

Ray looked offended. "You just didn't get the full dose, that's all. I wasn't even in first gear when Billy showed up. And besides, I guess we could have come in the truck, but where's the fun in that?"

"Now you tell me." Lainie stretched her legs out in front of her and gazed out over the valley below. "Who is Billy, anyway? Your uncle?"

"No, Billy's the foreman. He's worked here for as long as I can remember, long before my granddad died. I called to say we were coming, so he said he'd saddle the horses for me."

Lainie took another sip of her soda. "So why are things awkward between you and Elizabeth? Is it because you don't go to church?'

"Yeah, I guess, in a way. Mostly it's the bar. She's hated it since my dad opened it. And she really hates that I'm working there instead of painting."

Ray fell silent. The only sound was the sudden whisper of the scrub pines when a gust of wind caught them.

"See, she was my champion when I was a kid. You can probably figure that art isn't high on the list of admirable pastimes for boys around here, and I took some flack at first because I liked to draw. But Gran stuck up for me. She's the one who bought me my first paints. She drove me to the community center in San Ramon for art lessons when I was in grade school. Then when I was in junior high, she sent me to art camp in Santa Fe. Man, that was a different world—one I knew I never wanted to leave. Gran was so proud. When everyone else in the family went to State to study ranch management and I wanted to go to the University of New Mexico in Albuquerque to study art, Gran flat said I was going. And that was pretty much that. It takes a brave man to cross Gran when she gets her feet planted."

"Tell me about it. I don't even know how it happens, but I wind up doing everything she wants me to before I know I'm doing it."

Ray's laugh sounded sad. "Yeah, well, things were going pretty well for me after I finished graduate school. I was represented in some good galleries and was selling fairly well when Dad had his stroke and I came home. Gran didn't much like it, but she understood. Family is really important to her. But after Dad died and I stayed on at the bar, she just blew up. She saw me giving up everything I had worked for to pour drinks, and that broke her heart. And that broke *my* heart. Even telling her that it was only till Steven came home didn't help. She doesn't think he needs to run a bar either."

"But you haven't given up your art. That's some gorgeous stuff in there. Doesn't that prove that you'll go back to it full-time someday?"

"She doesn't know about it. Oh, she knows I've built the cabin and that I come up here, but we don't talk art anymore. It just causes too many problems." He stood up, dusting his hands on his pants. "Now do you see why I don't come around much?"

Lainie looked up at him "Well, you know your grandmother better than I do, but she doesn't seem like someone who'd hold a grudge all this time. Are you sure she's the problem?"

When Ray didn't respond but turned his silent gaze over the valley, she continued. "I mean, cutting her completely out of your art after all her support seems kind of like you're trying to punish her somehow. Is that what you're doing?"

Ray was quiet so long that Lainie was afraid she'd really made him mad. Finally, he blew out a gust of air and shook his head. "I don't know. Maybe you're right. Maybe I am taking all this out on her. I'll think about that." He held out his hand. "Let's go for a walk. I'll show you around."

Her hand felt easy in Ray's as they walked up the trail behind the cabin. The sun on the scrub pines that clung tenaciously to the rocky slope filled the air with a spicy scent. A lizard skittered across their path. Every few paces Ray stopped to show a view he had painted or intended to paint. He clambered up a boulder and reached a hand to pull her up. As she reached him, she lost her footing on the gravelly granite, and he caught her and pulled her close. For a moment they stood gazing into each other's eyes. It was Ray who broke the spell.

"Look." He pointed over her shoulder. "You're even higher than you were before."

She turned within the circle of his arms and saw the hawks wheeling lazily in their thermal, the topmost bird still far above the others. Leaning back against Ray's chest, she rested her arms on his and felt them tighten around her.

"Independent Lainie," he whispered into her hair. "Always keeping everyone else so far away. Doesn't it get lonely way up there?"

"I like it that way." Her murmur was so low she could have been talking to herself. "I learned how to take care of myself a long time ago. I don't have to look out for anyone, and no one has to look out for me."

"And you never need anyone?"

She turned again and looked up at him, sliding her arms around his neck. "Sometimes."

He searched her face as if it were a country he longed to explore, then slowly lowered his lips to hers.

The kiss was long. Gentle and passionate at the same time. When he drew away, it was only a few inches. He smiled into her eyes and brushed the hair from her face before pulling her more tightly to him and moving in for another kiss.

The sun was low in the west, and wisps of western clouds were beginning to show pink when Lainie and Ray strolled back around the cabin. The mountain's shadow crept across the desert floor.

"This is the part of the weekend I hate—when it's over. We need to get those horses back and get them fed." The energy and enthusiasm that had fired Ray all afternoon seemed to drain away.

"Oh, they won't starve if they have to wait a little longer." Lainie caught his hand and drew him toward the cabin door, her smile rich with meaning.

Ray followed only a step or two before he stopped. His eyes were tender when he took her in his arms. He kissed her nose and her forehead and finished with another light kiss on her lips. "It's getting late. We need to get going if we're going to get back to the barn before dark."

Lainie pulled away and looked at Ray. "What's wrong?"

"Nothing's wrong. We just have a long ride ahead of us, and going down isn't as easy as coming up."

"Don't give me that. I know you didn't bring me up here just to look at some pictures. What happened?"

Ray picked up Lainie's hand. He kissed it and held it against his cheek. "You know what? I did bring you up here to show you where my heart lives—in this place, in my art. I want to know you better, and I want you to know me. But this is moving a little fast. Let's just take it easy."

Lainie jerked away. "Right. My mistake. Don't mind me. I'm a tramp."

Ray reached for her hand again, but she had moved out of reach. "Come on, Lainie, be fair. You think I don't want to go inside with you? I'm human, you know, and you're beautiful. But it's because I do want to see where this goes that I want to go slow. I don't want to rush into something and ruin it."

Lainie folded her arms. She wasn't quite sure she was ready to forgive him yet. His smile was coaxing, and she allowed him to draw her into his arms again.

"And for your information"—he kissed her lightly—"I would flatten anyone I heard using that term about you, and I'm not a violent man. I don't want to hear you say it about yourself, either. Ever."

"I was being sarcastic."

"I don't care. No one, not even you, can disrespect Lainie Davis and get away with it."

"You make it sound like people are coming from miles around to take their shots. Is it that bad?"

Ray laughed. "No, and that's my point. If everyone in Last Chance sees you as someone special, maybe you should give them some credit."

"Maybe no one in Last Chance really knows me."

Ray took her face in both his hands and looked into her eyes. "Lainie, despite what you may think, you're not the only one in town with a past. Everyone in Last Chance has something in their life that they're not proud of. And in a town this size, it's more than likely that everyone else knows about it. We—most of us anyway—have learned to just overlook the bad and to concentrate on the good. Otherwise Last Chance would be the blackmail capital of the Southwest."

"Even you?"

"Yep, even me."

"Even Elizabeth?"

Ray threw back his head and roared with laughter. "Well, maybe not her, but everybody else. Now, come on. We really do have to get going. It'll be dark soon." He took her hand and led her to where the horses were tied, and this time she didn't pull her hand away.

11

Elizabeth waved from the front porch when Ray's pickup pulled up. "Did you all see that sunset? You know, I've been out here sixty years and more and they still take my breath away. Are you staying for supper, Ray? I know you can't have eaten yet." She opened the front door and Sam, who had been keeping watch with her, led the parade into the house.

"Depends. Are you having waffles?"

"It's Sunday night, isn't it?"

Ray grinned and gave her a one-armed hug. "Then I wouldn't miss it."

In the kitchen, Elizabeth put them to work making coffee and setting the table while she whipped up the waffle batter. Lainie couldn't remember seeing her so happy.

"Ray, you need to come around more and that's all there is to it. Lainie and I would love the company, wouldn't we, Lainie?" If she noticed Lainie and Ray exchanging smiles over her head, she didn't say so. "It's been a while since I've had anyone over in the evening. It's like a party. In fact, I think I'll call Fayette and Matthew and see if they'd like to come over and join us."

"You heard the lady. I've been ordered to come around more. And I always do what my grandmother says." Ray kept his voice low while Elizabeth chatted on the phone.

Lainie made a rude noise and handed him a stack of plates. "Here. Go put these on the table."

Elizabeth hung up the phone and turned around. "Matthew's still out with friends, but he's due home any minute. I told Fayette just to leave a note telling him to come on over and bring his friends with him. He always did love my waffles."

"Who doesn't?" Ray put the syrup pitcher in the middle of the table.

The first waffles were ready to come off the iron when Fayette came in alone.

"Matthew's not home yet?" Elizabeth gave her a peck on the cheek.

"No, and I'm getting worried. He said he'd be home by dark."

"Honey, it's barely dark now. You know how boys can be. He'll be along soon. Did you mention in your note that his friends are welcome too?"

"Yes, but they don't even come into our house when they come to pick Matthew up. These aren't boys from around here. I don't know their families, and, well, they just don't seem like they were raised right, if you know what I mean."

They sat around the table in the kitchen and Elizabeth held her hands to Fayette and Lainie. Ray completed the circle. "Ray, darlin', will you offer thanks?" She smiled across the table at her grandson, and Ray bowed his head and in simple, easy phrases thanked God for the day, for the food, and for their many blessings, adding a prayer that his brother Steven come home safely.

Lainie would have sworn that she saw tears in Elizabeth's blue eyes after Ray said amen, but her voice was as strong as ever as she passed the butter and syrup.

Ray forked a sausage onto his plate. "I found out Lainie didn't know till this afternoon that you were my grandmother."

"Really? Didn't we talk about that painting in the front room the day you got here?"

"You said your grandson painted it."

"I didn't say which one? Are you sure?"

"Yep, I'm sure. I did not know until this afternoon when I saw paintings like that one at Ray's cabin and put two and two together."

"Well, forevermore," said Elizabeth.

"You rode clear up there?" Fayette raised an eyebrow. "I thought you kept that place off limits to us mere mortals."

"She forced me." Ray grinned at Lainie. "She said she had to see my etchings."

"Ray!" Elizabeth sounded shocked.

"Just kidding, Gran. I was a perfect gentleman, wasn't I, Lainie?"

"Well, I'll thank you to be a perfect gentleman in this house, as well."

"Yes, ma'am." Ray ducked his head like a chastened little boy.

Lainie was glad that the conversation drifted to other things as they finished their waffles and lingered over another cup of coffee. She still felt a prickle of humiliation when she thought of Ray's rebuff at the cabin. The second rebuff, actually, if she counted the night she got into town. She looked at Ray, who gave her a wink over his coffee cup. This dude needed some figuring out. She began stacking the sticky plates, and when Fayette tried to help, Elizabeth stopped her.

"No. This is your time to just sit. You go on in the living room with Ray. Lainie and I'll just dump these dishes in the sink."

When they joined Ray and Fayette a few minutes later, Ray was straddling the piano bench looking at the hymnbook open on the piano and plinking a tune with one finger. He vacated the bench and gestured for his grandmother to be seated.

"Why don't you play for us, Gran?"

Elizabeth sat down and flexed her fingers. "These old hands of mine are so stiff now. I don't know that I can, but I'll give it a try."

Her hands flew over the keys as she played a hymn Lainie remembered having heard at church. When Elizabeth finished, she didn't turn around but flipped through the pages looking for another.

She began to play and to sing, "On a hill far away, stood an old rugged cross . . ." Ray joined in, adding bass harmony. By the time they were singing, "So I'll cherish the old rugged cross," Fayette was singing too. And when Ray took the hymnbook off the piano and handed it to Lainie, pointing out the place, Elizabeth didn't miss a note.

After they finished, Elizabeth sat back and put her hands in her lap.

"Don't stop now." Ray headed for the hall. "Is your guitar still in the closet?" He brought out the battered case and tuned the old instrument. His soft chords added to the piano notes as they sang hymn after hymn.

"Okay, I'm warmed up now." Ray settled the strap more comfortably on his shoulder and shook out his fingers. "Let's do 'In the Garden.'"

He played the old hymn flawlessly. It was clearly a guitar solo with Elizabeth accompanying him on the piano. Lainie found the page in the hymnbook and tried to follow along. Even without the words, the melody was haunting. But the words touched Lainie in a place deep inside she had long guarded. What would it be like to have someone tell you that you were his own? That you were his own in a loving, protective way—not like you were his property. A crushing ache swelled in her chest until she felt she couldn't breathe.

With a flourish, Ray finished and took an elaborate bow. "And that was my first solo at church. How old was I, Gran, fourteen?"

"About that. I remember how proud your mama was." Elizabeth's smile was sad.

"Yeah, she was pretty sick by that time. I thought sure my mind-blowing musical talent would bring Dad to church for her at least that one time, but nope. He was a pretty tough old bird."

"Yes, well . . . That was his loss, I'm afraid, because you play beautifully."

"Oh, he liked to hear me play, all right, just not hymns. But I did get to play 'In the Garden' for him before he died—minus the accompaniment, of course."

"Well, that's a surprise. Brother Parker went to see him in the hospital but Buck wouldn't even acknowledge his presence. Just lay there with his eyes closed like he was asleep. He was awfully stubborn right to the end."

"He didn't have much choice but to listen to me play. He could lie there with his eyes closed all day long. I wasn't going anywhere. So I played and talked to him all I wanted to."

"Well, who knows? It may have done some good." Elizabeth didn't sound as if she believed it had.

"I think I know." Ray's voice was husky, and he cleared his throat to continue. "Right at the last, when we both knew he wouldn't be here much longer, I told him we had to get serious. I told him he was about to step out into eternity, and if he ever wanted to see Mom again, he'd better do some serious think-ing. So we talked, or I did, and I told him it was about a whole lot more than seeing Mom again. I took his hand, told him that Jesus had died even for an old reprobate like him, and asked him if he wanted to tell God he was sorry for all the shenanigans he had pulled, and he squeezed my hand for yes. Then I asked him if he'd like me to pray and tell God so. Squeezed again. So I did and then asked if he meant it. One more squeeze. That's about all either of us could do. So I have to believe he's with the Lord and Mom right now."

"You never told me that." Elizabeth's voice dropped to just above a whisper.

Ray shrugged. "I should have, but I'm my father's son, I guess. I can be every bit as stubborn, sorry to say."

The tears in Elizabeth's eyes ran over and rolled down her cheeks. She pulled a lace-trimmed handkerchief from her sleeve and blew her nose. "I'm sorry. It's just that your mama's deepest regret, other than leaving you and Steven, was that she was never able to reach Buck. But eternity being as it is, it probably didn't seem to her that she was there five minutes before she turned around and there he was." She dabbed her eyes and stuffed her handkerchief back into her sleeve.

Ray put his arm around her for a quick squeeze. "Well, on that note, I'd better take off. It's nearly ten, and I've got at least a couple hours of paperwork to do tonight. This has been great. Let's do it again soon."

"Heavens, is it really ten already?" Fayette jumped to her feet. "Where is Matthew? Something's happened. I just know it."

Ray put his hands on her shoulders and gently pushed her down into a chair. "Look, before you rush off, let's call Ben and see if there's been any trouble anywhere. We'll ask him to tell Matthew to go on home if he runs into him."

Fayette sank back on the sofa, clutching her purse. "Thanks, Ray. I'd appreciate it if you called, but then I'd better get home, because when I do see Matthew, it'll be best for everyone if no one else is around." Her smile barely turned up the corners of her mouth.

In just a couple minutes Ray came back in from the kitchen. "Well, Ben says all's quiet. Not so much as a speeding ticket. But he did say he'd keep an eye out."

Elizabeth hugged Fayette good-bye. "He's fine, sweetie, just being a boy. I can't tell you the number of nights I sat up waiting for the boys—well, for Steven mostly, but they always got home."

Fayette paused on her way out the door. "Well, thank you so much for having me over. If I'd had to sit home all evening wondering where he was, I think I'd have gone nuts. And I did love the music."

As Ray prepared to follow her, Elizabeth hugged him too. "I want you to know just hearing you play and sing tonight blessed my soul more than you'll ever know. And the news about your dad, well . . ." Her voice choked off and she reached for her handkerchief.

Ray put his arms around her and kissed the top of her head. "We'll do it again sometime soon." He held his hand out to Lainie. "Walk me to the truck?"

A cool night wind was blowing when Lainie and Ray stepped out onto the porch. He slid his arm around her and pointed into the sky. "Big Dipper. See?"

"Mm-hmm. Wow, there are a lot of stars. I had no idea there were so many."

"That's 'cause the lights blotted them all out when you were in California. See that pale swath of stars that goes right across the sky? That's the Milky Way."

"You know a lot about the stars."

Lainie could feel his smile against her hair. "I've just always loved the night sky. When I was a kid, I used to spend most summer nights outside in my sleeping bag. I would more or less doze all night long, and every time I woke up the sky was different."

Lainie leaned her head against Ray's shoulder and looked at the sky. It made her feel small and unimportant, but somehow that was okay. She felt a tension she couldn't remember ever being without slide from her neck and shoulder, and she closed her eyes as a soft sigh escaped.

A tightening of Ray's arm around her shoulders and his soft breath on her face prepared her for the touch of his lips on hers. When he drew away, it was only far enough to gaze into her eyes. He brushed a strand of hair from her face with one finger. "See you tomorrow."

The screen door opened and Elizabeth stuck her head out the door. "Fayette just called. Matthew's home."

Ray raised his hand over his head in a wave. "Glad to hear it. Knew he'd be okay." He got in his truck and leaned out the open window. "Thanks for coming with me today. It meant a lot to me to get to show you what I'm really all about."

Lainie smiled. "Yeah, well, you really owe me big time. I'm already getting so sore I can hardly move."

"It'll be easier next time. Promise." Ray started his engine, and Lainie watched till the red taillights turned the corner. The street settled into the night sounds of crickets and rustling leaves. Lainie looked up at the sky, white with stars. It was hard to believe that this sky arched over the lights and the noise of the life she had left behind.

A slither of dread settled in her stomach, reminding her that her old life was not entirely behind her. A remnant hid like a snake in the backpack in her closet. For two weeks she had tried not to think about it, but now she just wanted it gone.

She turned and ran up the steps. Elizabeth smiled from her recliner and opened her mouth to say something. Lainie beat her to it.

"Could I borrow your truck? There's something I need to do."

"Now? It's past ten."

"I won't be gone long, but it's really important."

"Well, of course, honey. The keys are on the hook in the kitchen, but—"

"Thanks." Lainie didn't stay to hear the rest. She ran to her

102

room, grabbed the backpack from the closet, and snatched the keys off the hook on her way out the door.

Not until she was on the road did she stop to consider what she was going to do. Disposing of the drugs in Last Chance was out. The town was just too small. Even if no one saw her, someone was likely to find them. She turned toward San Ramon.

The plan came to her before she got to the highway. She'd find a trash barrel and shove the package deep inside. It would wind up buried in a landfill somewhere. Or, better yet, she'd drop it in a mailbox. It might actually get to the proper authorities that way.

Up ahead, she could see the small portable building that housed the county sheriff substation. Ben Apodaca's patrol car was parked alongside, nose pointed toward the highway in case he got an emergency call. Her mouth was dry as her truck, almost under its own volition, slowed and pulled off the highway and stopped next to Ben's patrol car. Through the window she could see him at his desk, bent over some paperwork.

Closing her eyes, she tried to compose a prayer, but all that came was, "Help, please, help." Taking a deep breath, she grabbed the strap of her backpack and got out of the truck.

Ben looked up when she walked in. Lainie hadn't seen him since that first day at the Dip 'n' Dine, but she could tell he recognized her. "Evening. What can I do for you?"

Lainie took a deep breath, opened her mouth to speak, closed it again, cleared her throat, and then plunged in. "I . . . I just need to talk to you." There. If she had second thoughts now, it was just too bad.

"Then come in and have a seat and we'll talk." Ben gestured with his chin at a chrome and worn red vinyl chair across from his desk and reached for the stained carafe simmering on a hot plate behind him. "Want some coffee? It's been sitting here a while and it'd probably be easier to eat it with a fork than drink it, but it's hot."

Lainie accepted the chipped white mug and held it in her hands. The acrid, burned aroma of the over-brewed liquid assailed her nose and wafted around her. Across the desk, Ben waited in silence.

"I'm not sure where to begin." She looked from the opaque black brew in her cup into Ben's brown eyes.

"Well, you know what they say." A half smile lifted a corner of Ben's mouth.

Lainie nodded at her coffee mug. "Okay, well, when I left California, I was sort of running." She glanced quickly up at Ben. "Not from the law, but from . . . a person."

She waited for Ben to say something, but he was silent.

"There was this guy who I knew, who I'd been with for a while, and he was getting into some serious stuff. Stuff I wanted no part of."

"Stuff? What kind of stuff?"

Lainie hesitated. "Drugs. Using at first. Then I think he was getting caught up in dealing."

"And how do you fit in with this?"

"I didn't fit in at all. That's what I'm trying to say. I've never used, and I sure never sold any. I hated that Nick—that was his name—was hanging out with those dirtbags. They scared me, and he started to scare me too."

Silence filled the small office again as Lainie gazed into her coffee mug like she was reading her past there. Finally she looked up. Ben had leaned back in his chair and crossed his arms over his chest. She couldn't tell if he believed her or not.

"So I started saving my money, and the day I had enough to buy the cheapest car on the lot, I threw everything I had into this old backpack and hit the road."

"And you got as far as Last Chance."

Lainie nodded.

Ben leaned his arms on the desk. "Why do I think there's more to this story?"

Taking a deep breath, Lainie pulled her backpack onto her lap. "Because there is."

She reached into the depths of the battered pack and pulled out the ziplock bag and placed it on the desk in front of Ben. "When I got here and I was unpacking, I noticed the lining was torn, and I found this tucked way down in the bottom."

Ben picked up the package and looked at it. He passed it from one hand to the other and held it to his nose. When he looked at Lainie, all warmth was gone from his eyes.

"Is this what it looks like?"

Lainie shrugged. "I don't know. You tell me."

He placed it back on his desk. "You say you found this when you got here. Why didn't you turn it in right away? It's been what, nearly two weeks?"

"I was scared! I had hoped Nick would just let me go, but when I found this I knew he'd be looking for me. And even though everyone here seemed nice, I didn't really know them. That first day at the diner, you just looked at me like you wanted to run me out of town. I'm surprised you didn't do a background check on me."

Ben's hooded brown eyes met hers in a level gaze, and one eyebrow rose.

"You did. You checked up on me."

"You bet I did. Elizabeth Cooley has a heart as big as all outdoors, and I wasn't about to let some stranger off the interstate come in and take advantage of her."

Lainie fought down indignation. He had a point. "And?"

"You're still here, aren't you? The report came back as clean as a hound's tooth. Although, now that I think about it, I never have seen any California ID."

Without saying a word, Lainie opened her purse to retrieve her driver's license and handed it across the desk. Ben looked closely. "Yep, that's the name I looked for, all right." He handed it back to her and pulled a yellow pad from his desk drawer. "Okay, here's what we're going to do. You're going to tell me everything you can about where this came from, and then you're going to stay right here in Last Chance till we get this sorted out. Okay?"

Lainie nodded.

"And one more thing. I guess it's only right that you tell Elizabeth what's going on, but no one else needs to be involved in this."

He looked at Lainie, and she nodded again.

"Good. Now, let's start with this Nick. He have a last name?"

It was a little past midnight when Lainie pulled back into Elizabeth's driveway. In one sense, nothing had changed. Whether or not she actually had the drugs, she knew Nick was looking for her. But on the other hand, he seemed farther away and she felt safer than at any moment since she first discovered the bag in her backpack.

Light poured through the screen door and lit the walk. Elizabeth was waiting up, of course. Lainie sighed and threw her lightened backpack over one shoulder. It was going to be a long night.

12

Fayette was already busy when Lainie got to work the next morning. She barely glanced at Lainie as she passed. "Table two needs coffee."

Lainie grabbed the coffee pot. "Matthew okay?"

Fayette's lips tightened into a straight line. "Depends on who you ask. He's mad at me because Ben stopped the car, checked them all for alcohol, and then told him to get on home because his mama was worried about him. Said the other guys laughed at him. Well, I'm sorry, but if he'd been home when he said he would, he'd have spared himself all that."

Lainie watched Fayette stomp off and decided it might be a good idea to stay out of the way herself—not easy since she was stiff from her long ride.

But when Carlos answered the phone in the kitchen and it became clear he was agreeing to send Ray's lunch over, Fayette slapped her order book down by the cash register and hit the door to the kitchen with one hand. She kept her voice low, but there was no mistaking her tone when she grabbed the receiver from Carlos.

"Ray? We're just a little bit too busy over here to do delivery today. But if you want to come get it, I'll have it waiting for you at the cash register." She paused. "No, I'm not mad. I'm just busy. And so is everyone else. So do you want to give me that order?"

She caught Lainie's eye and snapped her fingers, pointing at the order pad by the cash register.

When Ray crossed the road a few minutes later, Fayette was waiting by the cash register. "That'll be eight ninety-five." She punched the amount into the cash register and stood unsmiling while he counted out his cash.

Clutching his white paper bag, Ray met Lainie's eyes as he headed out the front door with a questioning "What gives?" look. She answered with a "Who knows?" shrug. But when the diner finally emptied, she cornered Fayette by the pie safe.

"Are you sure Matthew's okay?"

"He's fine. He's not speaking to me at the moment, but he's fine. Why?"

"Because you've been a witch all day, that's why. You've yelled at me, you've yelled at Ray, you've even yelled at Carlos. And what's worse, the customers noticed it. Juanita even asked me what's wrong. You want her noticing that you're yelling at everyone? She's not exactly the type to keep things to herself."

Fayette slammed her rag down on the table she was washing. "That's just what's wrong with this place. Every blessed person in town knows what every other blessed person in town thinks, says, or does. And I, for one, am just sick to death of it. I don't know what possessed me to buy this place anyway. I was this close to opening a French bistro in Albuquerque." She held up a thumb and forefinger about an inch apart.

Lainie raised her eyebrows. "French bistro? In Albuquerque?"

"Well, why not? You think slingin' hash is the best someone like me can do? Is that it?"

"Hey, take it easy. You can do what you want to. But you have to admit, there's a big difference between those two choices. And why Albuquerque?"

Fayette finished wiping down the table and slid into a chair. "Because I like Albuquerque. Bud and I went there on our honeymoon, and we stayed near Old Town for a few days. They have the cutest little restaurants there, and ever since I dreamed of having one." Her smile was wistful. "The French bistro just sort of made itself part of the daydream. I thought I'd call it Lafayette. Don't you think that'd be cute?" Lainie nodded and Fayette went on. "Anyway, when Bud was killed, I got a pretty good-sized insurance check, and that's when I had to decide whether to put feet to my dreams or not. But the insurance money was the only thing in the world I had to take care of Matthew with, and I just couldn't take the risk."

Lainie looked around the empty diner. "This place was less of a risk?"

"Oh, I don't know. At least it's here where I grew up. People care. And if I do fall flat on my face, there'll be people to help me back up. And do you know what the deciding factor was? I thought since I was bringing up Matthew alone, this would be the safest place to do it. Great decision, huh?" Her laugh was bitter.

"I guess you can find trouble anyplace you look for it. And I'll tell you this, in the city, you don't call the local cop and ask him to tell your kid to get himself home."

"Maybe not. But I get so scared sometimes that I'm not up to raising a teenage boy." Fayette put her hands against the edge of the table and started to push herself to her feet. "Sorry I took it out on you and Carlos and everyone else who crossed my path this morning."

A service truck came to a stop just outside the door, and Fayette watched the driver get out and hitch up his jeans. "Great. Now my day's just perfect. Lainie, that coffeepot's about empty. Make us a new pot, would you? I'll take care of this."

As Lainie stepped behind the counter, she heard Fayette mutter, "Chet Babcock, you picked the wrong day to mess with this mama bear."

"Hey, Fayette, I've decided to let bygones be bygones. Came in to kiss and make up." Chet was alone this time and grabbed his own menu from the rack before he slid into a booth by the window.

"Afternoon, Chet. What can I get you?" Fayette placed a glass of ice water on the table and stood back, unsmiling, with her order pad ready.

"Aw, come on, Fayette. Lighten up. Used to be we could have a little fun in here. Don't go getting all stuck up on me."

Fayette waited without saying a word, and Chet tossed the menu on the table. "Shoot, only thing in here worth eating is the green enchiladas. Gimme some of that."

"You got it." Fayette turned toward the kitchen.

"And put a fried egg on it."

"You got that too."

Fayette disappeared into the kitchen, and Chet slumped back in the booth. He glared at Lainie, and she returned his gaze until he dropped his eyes and looked out the window.

In a few minutes Fayette was back with a plate of green chile enchiladas and a basket of golden pillows of fried bread.

"Here you go." Fayette was smiling now. "And I brought you some sopaipillas too. Both of them are on the house."

"Well, now, that's more like it." Chet grinned as he picked up his fork. "Apology accepted."

"Just a minute. Don't think this is an apology. We don't have anything to apologize for here."

Wariness replaced the grin on Chet's face. "Then why's it on the house?"

"That's up to you, Chet. It's either the last thing you'll ever eat in my restaurant or it's an agreement between the two of us that you'll behave like a gentleman when you come in here. And that means keeping your crude comments and your hands to yourself." Her smile was cheerful and warm. "So what's it going to be?"

"You keep your enchiladas, and your sopaipillas too. I don't need this." Chet threw his fork down and began to push out of the booth.

"Your choice, but you know no one makes green enchiladas like Carlos. And Russ tells me this year's chile crop is going to be especially fine. You don't want to go cutting off your nose to spite your face."

Chet hesitated. Finally he grabbed a sopaipilla and tore off a corner with his teeth. While Fayette waited, he drizzled honey into the warm hollow interior and stuffed half of it in his mouth.

"Well, what's it going to be?

Chet gripped his fork like it was a hammer and dug into the steaming enchilada. The yolk of the egg on top broke and spread like warm sauce through the green chile. "You're worse than my wife, you know that?"

"Friends, then. Good. I was hoping that was the choice you'd make. Now we have just one more thing to take care of and we're good. Lainie, come here a minute, would you?"

Lainie, who had been watching the confrontation with undisguised fascination, jumped when Fayette suddenly called her name. She crossed the room and Fayette slipped her arm around her waist. Chet's expression showed he wasn't any happier about what Fayette might have in mind than Lainie was.

"Chet, I'd like you to meet Lainie Davis. She lives here in Last Chance now, and she works for me. I think that as a gentleman, you'd like to apologize for the way you acted last time you were in here."

Chet threw down his fork again. "Me apologize? She like to broke my thumb off."

"And you know you had it coming. Now, you prove that you intend to show the same respect to every employee of the Dip 'n' Dine that you've promised me, and I'll throw in a piece of pie with the enchilada and the sopaipillas. I've got lemon, coconut, apple, and pecan. Your choice."

Chet's brows met low over his eyes and he stared out the window a long moment before throwing a quick glance at Lainie and muttering, "Sorry. I was out of line."

Fayette's smile widened, and she gave Lainie's waist a quick squeeze. "There, that didn't hurt a bit, did it?"

Chet picked up his fork again and shoveled in a huge bite of enchilada. When he could get it shifted to his cheek, he said, "I'll take pecan."

—⁂—

After Chet finished his meal and ambled back to his truck, Lainie held up her hand for a high five from Fayette. "Not bad! Even if you did have to bribe him with free food."

"Oh, I don't see it so much as a bribe as a treaty. I had to say some things he didn't want to hear, and the food made it easier for him to listen, that's all."

"Well, I'm impressed, anyway. I don't know why you're worried about handling Matthew. You're a natural."

Fayette's smile was sad. "The difference is, I don't care that much about Chet. It's pretty easy to say 'my way or the highway' to him."

She glanced out the window as Matthew scuffed across the parking lot. "Well, speak of my darling son and here he comes. I told him he has to come in here directly from school for the next two weeks, but with all the back talk I got . . . Well, I'm just glad he got here."

Fayette forced cheerfulness as Matthew slumped in with his backpack slung over his shoulder. "Hey, honey, how was school?"

He glared at her without saying a word.

"Now you can take that back booth if you want, or you can go to my desk in the kitchen if you don't touch anything on it. I'll bring you something to drink."

Matthew gave Fayette a look that would curl paint and shoved his way through the kitchen door.

Lainie smiled in sympathy. "Want me to take care of this?"

"Please. One more mouthful of attitude from him, and I'm liable to boot him out that back door—which is exactly what he wants me to do."

Lainie walked into the kitchen where Matthew was pulling books and notebooks out of his backpack and slamming them down on an old desk already crowded with ledgers and invoices.

"Hey, Matt. Need a cola or something?"

He didn't look at her. "What I need is for you guys to get out of my face."

"Just asking." Lainie turned to leave, but Matthew called after her.

"Wait. You can bring me a root beer, I guess."

Lainie raised an eyebrow and left without saying a word. When she returned a few minutes later with a cold drink and a straw, Matthew ignored her. Lainie stood by his chair holding his drink until he looked up. "What?"

"I'm not your servant, dude. And I'm not your mother either. If you want this drink you're going to have to ask for it. And I want to hear a 'please.'"

Matthew curled his lip. "Keep it."

"You got it." In one smooth move, Lainie dumped the drink down the drain and set the glass in the sink. Without looking back, she pushed through the swinging door back into the dining room.

Fayette looked up from cutting a piece of coconut cream pie. "How's he doing?"

Lainie shrugged. "He's being a jerk. But that comes with being a kid, I guess. I mean, I never had one, but I sure remember being one."

"A jerk?" Fayette scowled and headed toward the kitchen. "Was he rude to you? He better not have been. That's one thing I will not put up with."

Lainie put out a hand to stop her. "It's okay. He's just being a kid. Cut him a little slack on this one. Compared to the people I used to hang out with, he's an angel. At least he didn't use any four-letter words."

"He'd better not!"

A little later when Lainie clipped an order to the turntable in the window to the kitchen, Matthew called to her.

"Hey, Lainie, may I PLEASE have a root beer?" He grinned when Lainie raised her eyebrow again.

When Lainie brought it to him, his thanks were as elaborate as his request. She set the drink next to him. "Don't overdo it. If you find some happy medium there, we'll get along just fine."

"Lainie, wait." She turned to see what he wanted. "I heard you talking to my mom in there. And, um, thanks for sticking up for me. She just gets me so crazy sometimes. She thinks I'm three years old or something."

Lainie pulled a kitchen stool over to the desk and perched on it. "Look, Matthew, I'm not trying to pick sides here. Yeah, I think your mom could cut you some slack, but at least you've got a mom who cares what happens to you. And that brings some baggage with it. So deal. When I was sixteen, I had been on my own for two years. My mom truly did not know if I was dead or alive. So believe me, there are worse things than sitting in here with Carlos, doing your homework and having people serve you stuff on a tray."

Matthew looked impressed. "Wow. You really walked out when you were fourteen? And you never went back? That's awesome!"

"I didn't walk out. My mom threw me out, and it wasn't awesome. I went hungry a lot of times. I slept anywhere anyone would let me for as long as they let me, and that was never very long. I wound up dropping out of school. So excuse me if I don't get real upset for you, Matthew. I happen to think you have a pretty plush setup."

"Why did your mom throw you out?"

Lainie stood up and put her hand on his shoulder. "That is none of your business. Now, I'm going back to work. You need another root beer, you know where they are."

13

Lainie heard the hymns pouring through the screen door out into the night air as she opened the gate to Elizabeth's yard. Elizabeth looked up when Lainie walked in, but her fingers never missed a note.

"You know, I had forgotten how much I love playing these old songs. I must have played through the whole hymnbook today." She followed Lainie into the kitchen. "How are things with Matthew?"

Lainie poured herself a glass of iced tea and slipped out of her shoes. "He's okay. Fayette's a good mom. I think they'll get through it."

Elizabeth plopped onto a kitchen chair. "Pour me a glass too, would you, honey?" She smiled her thanks. "I got a call this morning from Lurlene, she's the choir director. Nadine had to go over to El Paso, so Lurlene asked me if I could come play for choir practice Wednesday. Why don't you come with me? You have the sweetest voice, and I know you'd add so much."

"Choir practice? You've got to be kidding, right? Like Juanita's going to let someone like me join in."

"Oh, don't let Juanita get to you. She doesn't have as much say as she thinks she does. And besides, I'm not even talking about joining, just coming Wednesday night and singing with the choir.

116

I have to confess, though, I did tell Lurlene what a nice voice you had. She's the one who told me to bring you with me."

"I have to work Wednesday night."

"But choir practice doesn't start till after prayer meeting. You should be done in plenty of time."

Lainie got to her feet. "I don't know. I'll think about it, but no promises. Right now I'm going to grab a shower."

—⁓—

Prayer meeting was over and the choir members were making their way to the choir loft when Lainie walked through the front door. Elizabeth was already seated at the piano with Lurlene looking over her shoulder and pointing out something on the music. Elizabeth looked up and beckoned Lainie forward with a smile.

"There you are. Come up here and meet Lurlene."

Lainie walked to the front of the church and was pulled into the warm embrace of the choir director.

"Welcome! I'm so glad you came. So Elizabeth tells me you're a soprano."

Lainie shrugged. "I haven't a clue."

"Well, if Elizabeth says so, you are. She is one woman who knows her music. Now why don't you take that chair on the end of the first row there?"

For the next hour Lainie was lost in the music. She had no idea what the notes on her sheet music represented, but Lurlene was easy to follow as she deftly led each section of the choir through their parts. When she finally put the whole together, the anthem made Lainie's arms break out in goose bumps.

Finally, Lurlene stepped back from her lectern. "Well, I guess that'll have to do. Lainie, I'm so glad you came. We gather in the adult Sunday school class as soon as they let out on Sunday for a quick run-through before the service. If you'd like to join us then, we'd love to have you." She smiled at Lainie and closed her music folder. "Russ, close us in prayer, would you please?"

As Russ's drawling bass filled the room, Lainie found herself listening instead of tuning him out. When he prayed that the efforts of the choir would glorify God, she wondered if God would even notice such a small group, and at the same time she felt a pleasure that she had not experienced since she was a little girl listening to her father praise a carefully colored page from a coloring book.

Each member of the choir took the time as they left to tell her how much they loved having her sing with them. Even Juanita squeezed her arm and bared her teeth in a smile as she passed. "Well, how about you? Wasn't it nice having you sit in with us this evening."

Not sure who it was supposed to be nice for, Lainie just nodded. Juanita swept past her up the aisle, calling for Russ to come on. He finished his conversation at his own pace, then ambled up the aisle after her.

Elizabeth gathered her music from the piano and joined Lainie. "Whew. That just about did me in. I remember now why I retired from this."

Lainie smiled at Elizabeth's bright eyes and rosy cheeks. "Oh, I think you had a pretty good time tonight. It's lucky that you spent all that time playing hymns this week. You were good to go."

"Oh, luck didn't have anything to do with it. It never does, you know. The Lord knew I was going to need to get my fingers all warmed up, even if I didn't."

Lainie fell silent. Elizabeth seemed to turn every conversation to what the Lord did, or wanted, or was going to do, and it still made Lainie uncomfortable.

The silence lasted until Elizabeth got herself settled on her cushion behind the wheel of the pickup and pulled out onto the highway.

"So what'd you think of choir practice? You looked like you were enjoying it."

Lainie reached for the bored mask she wore on such occasions, but a smile made it to her face first.

"It was fun. When we finally put it all together, it sounded amazing. I've never done that before. It was cool."

"I've always been on the piano bench and not in the choir, but to me it's a tiny foretaste of what heaven's going to be like. Just countless voices raised in praise." She smiled at Lainie and pulled into the drive. "And you, sweet girl, have the voice of an angel."

Elizabeth led the way into the house, still humming. "Let's have a glass of tea."

"You're sure in a good mood. You really miss this, don't you?"

"I guess I do, but I know these old fingers can't keep up like they used to. It's time for someone else to take over. It's nice to help out once in a while, though. But the reason I'm singing is Steven! I just can't stop praising God. Why don't we take this tea out on the porch."

"Steven?"

"Oh, my goodness, I forgot you weren't in prayer meeting. Steven's coming home. He should be here by Thanksgiving. And if that's not a reason to give some thanks, I can't think of one." Even in the dim light of the porch, Lainie could see the tears sparkling in Elizabeth's eyes. "I've just prayed nonstop since the day he left, and of course the rascal hardly ever called or wrote, so I just had to count on no news being good news. Every now and then, he'd write to Ray on the email and Ray would make a me copy, but I never did learn to use those computers, so I'd just have to wait till Ray would tell me something."

"So Steven will take over the High Lonesome, and Ray . . . ? I guess he'll leave, right?"

Elizabeth set her glass down on the table with a little thump. "If you ask me, and nobody does, more's the pity, both those boys can find something better to do with their lives than run a honky-tonk. Not one good thing's ever come from there. And a whole lot of hurt just pours through those doors."

"Hey, don't feel like you have to hold back. Tell me what you really think."

The rocking chair slowed a bit. "Well, you just pushed one of my buttons. Last Chance got along just fine for years without a bar, and I've just never gotten over the fact that it was my own son-in-law who brought one in. I thought I'd never be able to lift my head again."

"But won't it be nice to have Steven back in town? I mean, what else is there to do here?"

"Well, if the only choices were selling spirits or going hungry, some folks would just as soon go hungry. But fortunately, Steven's got a few other options. There's the ranch, for one. Joe Jr. is always looking for reliable hands."

"Oh, that's sounds exciting. He'll probably jump at that."

"Now you're just pecking at me to see if you can ruffle my feathers. Well, not tonight, Miss Lainie. My boy is safe and he's coming home, and that's all that matters to me. The Lord has taken care of him this far, and he doesn't need me, or you either, to figure out what comes next. Now I'm going inside. *Matlock* is fixing to come on. You need another glass of tea?"

Lainie shook her head. "I'm good. I'll just stay outside a while. It's been a long day."

"Is that Ben? I wonder what he wants." Elizabeth stood with her hand on the latch as the patrol car came to a stop at her gate and Ben Apodaca got out and ambled up the walk.

"Evening, ladies."

"Evening, Ben. Come sit down. Can I get you a glass of tea?"

"No thanks, I'm not staying." He tipped his hat back and looked at Lainie. "I assume you had a good talk with Elizabeth."

Lainie nodded, afraid to trust her voice.

"Good. Well, I just stopped by to tell you your story held up."

"Well, of course it held up, Ben. Lainie didn't track you down in the middle of the night to lie to you."

"Be that as it may, I thought you'd like to know that those guys you told me about are all in custody."

"Even Nick?"

"Nick's in the hospital. I guess he got messed up pretty bad when those drugs went missing. But they're keeping tabs on him, and he's sure not going anywhere for a while. Just thought you'd like to know."

"Thank you, Ben. We appreciate it." Elizabeth had to speak for her, because Lainie couldn't say a word. Her face was in her hands, and wrenching sobs wracked her body.

Russ held his cup up for a refill when Lainie brought the coffeepot over during breakfast the next morning. "Didn't know you could sing, girl. We need to see you up there in the choir."

Juanita cleared her throat and tried to catch Russ's eye. But if he remained oblivious to Juanita's telepathic message, Lainie caught every word. *Over my dead body.* She poured Juanita's cup. "Well, it was a lot of fun, but I don't know about joining."

"We don't want to rush Lainie into anything, Russ. You know what a commitment that choir takes. And besides, as far as we know, she's not even a . . ." Juanita's voice trailed off.

"Not even a what, Juanita?" Russ's voice took on its usual irascibility. "We're not asking Lainie to lead the women's missionary society or teach junior high Sunday school. We just get up there and make a joyful noise. Why shouldn't Lainie join us?"

"Well, it may be just noise to you, Russ Sheppard, but it's a ministry to the rest of us. And anyone who joins us needs to have their heart right before they set foot in that choir loft." She turned to Lainie and bared her teeth in a smile that never reached her eyes. "I'm sure you understand that, don't you, Lainie? It's not that you don't have a lovely voice, because you do. It's just that, well, you need to really be able to live out what you sing. Otherwise it's just a performance. I'm sure you understand that, don't you?"

"Sure. I understand perfectly. I just sang last night because Elizabeth talked me into it. It was fun, but I don't need anyone checking me out all the time to see if I'm good enough. So don't worry about it, okay? Now, do you need anything else, or should I bring the check?"

As Lainie returned the coffeepot to its stand, she heard Russ's muttered, "Well, that was real nice, Juanita."

Juanita stopped to talk to Fayette when they got up to leave, but Russ held back a moment.

"You know, Lainie, I wouldn't be too put out by what Juanita says. She doesn't mean things to sound the way they come out sometimes."

Lainie shrugged. "No big deal."

Russ placed the exact change, including tip, on the table. "Probably not, but I wish you would think about joining the choir. We're starting our Christmas music pretty soon, and we could sure use you."

Lainie smiled. "I'll think about it."

"You do that." Russ took his hat off the rack by the door, walked outside, and got behind the wheel of his truck. Juanita didn't stop talking until the pickup slowly started backing out of its parking place.

"So you're thinking of joining the choir, huh?" Fayette began making another pot of coffee.

"No, actually, I'm not. I went to practice last night, but that's it. But if Juanita wants to get all torqued over it, that's her problem."

"Oh, Juanita. No, everyone who heard you last night has commented on what a nice voice you have. Lurlene stopped in for a minute before you got here, looking for you. I know she wants to talk to you about it."

Lainie raised an eyebrow. "Really? Are they that desperate?"

"Desperation has nothing to do with it. She said you have an outstanding voice and wonders how long you're planning to stay in town.

Lainie shrugged and began clearing Russ and Juanita's table. "I guess I don't know myself. I'm just taking it as it comes."

"Well, you'll give me some notice if you decide to take off, won't you?" Fayette gave her a look. "I'd like to know I can count on you being here if you're on the schedule to work."

Lainie walked past Fayette with the bin of dirty dishes and shouldered her way through the kitchen door. She didn't need to be afraid of Nick anymore, and things in Last Chance were getting complicated. She didn't usually stick around for complications, but this one might be different. At any rate, she was making no promises.

14

The crisp cool of dawn stretched further into the morning as summer faded into early fall, and by the time the sun crested the hills and warmed the windows of the Dip 'n' Dine, the diner hummed with customers.

In the weeks she'd been working with Fayette, Lainie had learned the ebb and flow of the diner, and after the breakfast crowd had thinned, there was usually a minute or two for a break and a cup of coffee. She had just grabbed a cup when she saw Rita's car sliding into a parking space with a spatter of gravel. Rita started waving before she got out of the car, elaborately mouthing something Lainie couldn't begin to decipher. She gave a weak wave in return.

"So what do you hear from Steven?" Rita was already talking as she pushed through the front door.

Lainie shrugged. "Nothing, as far as I know."

"Well, that's just the strangest thing I ever heard. It's been weeks since we heard he's on his way home. You'd think a boy would let his own family in on his plans."

"Oh, you know Steven." Fayette joined them from the kitchen. "He always did dance to his own tune. He'll turn up."

"I'm just saying it would be a whole lot easier to plan a big ol' 'welcome home' parade for him if we knew when he'll get here. That's not the kind of thing we can pull together in an hour, you know."

"Tell you what. Why don't you just go on and make your plans? Pick a day, say between Thanksgiving and Christmas, and go for it. Even if you find you have to move the date around a little bit, you'll still have all the hard part done."

"Well, you sure make it sound easy. Do you know how much work is involved in doing something like this? I'm talking about a full-blown parade—Boy Scouts, FFA, 4-H, mounted sheriff's posse, and I don't know what all."

"Rita, I've seen you work. You can do this kind of stuff in your sleep."

Rita shook her head and rolled her eyes before she left with the same whirlwind of bustle with which she had entered. "You call me the absolute first minute you have any news from Steven, you hear me?"

Lainie threw her hand up in a mock solute. "Yes ma'am!"

Fayette winked at Lainie. "Now you're catching on."

The autumn sun had already dipped below the horizon when Lainie slipped her arms into her sweater and stepped out the door of the Dip 'n' Dine. She watched a pickup pull into the parking lot across the road and two cowboys she didn't know get out and go into the High Lonesome. Ray still had said nothing about leaving Last Chance. And truth be told, she had avoided the subject as well. It was so much easier to take each day as it came, to just enjoy a Sunday drive to Silver City, or a movie in San Ramon, or even a quiet talk on a slow night at the High Lonesome. The future, with all its complications, could wait in the shadows. But with Steven coming home soon, that future was getting harder to ignore.

"Okay, Ray, what are you thinking? Are you going to let me know your plans, or will you just be gone one day?" Lainie shoved her hands in her pockets and started home.

She was about a block from Elizabeth's when a pickup pulled up alongside her.

"Hey, pretty lady, need a ride?" Les Watson brought his battered truck to a near stop in the middle of the road and leaned out the cab window, squinting red-rimmed eyes in an effort to focus.

Lainie kept walking. "I'm good, Les. Nearly home. You just come from Ray's?"

"Naw, I been up to San Ramon. That nanny-goat Ray's gonna lose hisself his best customer if he don't watch out. I don't need a wet nurse when I stop by to unlax a little after work. If I wanted someone to nag me half to death, I'd just go on home." He laughed. "You sure I can't give you a ride? You gotta be dead on your feet."

"Tell you what, Les. Scoot over and let me drive and I'll take you home."

"Shoot, Lainie, not you too. You been spending way too much time with Elizabeth, or Ray, one. You're gettin' to be as bad as they are."

Lainie stopped at Elizabeth's gate. "Well, I'm home now anyway. Are you sure you can make it the rest of the way?"

Les flapped his hand toward Elizabeth's door. "You go on in. It'll be a sorry day when Les Watson can't get his own self home and it's not even Friday night." He gunned the engine and his truck sped toward the corner. Lainie watched the pickup disappear in the distance, clipping a hedge and narrowly missing a stop sign as it careened around the corner. For the first time she was grateful that Last Chance rolled up its sidewalks at sundown. No one needed to be on the streets till Les was safely home.

Elizabeth stuck her head out of the kitchen when Lainie came in and smiled. "Just in time. I'm about ready to put dinner on the table.

As Lainie headed to her room, she called over her shoulder. "Does Les Watson live far from here?"

"About three blocks. Why?"

Lainie called down the hall as she unbuttoned her uniform. "I just saw Les on his way home and he was in no shape to be driving." She dropped her voice as Elizabeth appeared in her bedroom door. "I'd like to think he got home okay."

"Tsk. I think I'll go call Evelyn, just to make sure."

Lainie snapped her jeans and pulled a T-shirt over her head, still mulling her future in Last Chance. Did she even have one? And what did it look like if she did?

Elizabeth was hanging up when Lainie joined her in the kitchen. "Well, Les got home okay, thank the Lord. He's already in bed asleep." She put a bowl of creamed corn on the table. "Grab the tea from the icebox, will you, Lainie?"

After Elizabeth offered thanks, Lainie picked up a platter. "If it's all right with you, I think I'll walk on over and see Ray after dinner."

Elizabeth placed her napkin in her lap in silence.

"Don't worry. I just need to talk to him a little. I'll be back before you go to bed."

Elizabeth looked up and sighed. "I just wish you didn't have to find him at that place. You can take my truck if you want to. Of course, I'll have to ask you to park across the street at the Dip 'n' Dine. I can't have my 'Follow me to Sunday school' bumper sticker sitting outside a honky-tonk."

"Thanks anyway, but I'll walk. It will feel good to stretch, and it's a nice night."

"Well, you be careful. You know better than I do what kind of drivers are out there. Wear a light-colored wrap and walk against traffic."

"Yes, mother." Lainie leaned over and kissed Elizabeth's cheek before she knew she had done it.

Elizabeth smiled. "Well, that was nice."

Lainie felt her cheeks warm as she busied herself filling her plate. *Where did that come from? I must be getting soft.*

—⁓—

The sound of Waylon Jennings poured out the front door as Lainie walked into the High Lonesome. There were only a couple pickups in the parking lot, and she was pleased to find no one at the bar and only a few quiet groups huddled in booths. Ray looked up when she walked in, and his smile lit up the dim room.

"Well, hey there. Haven't seen you in a while."

Lainie grinned as she climbed on a stool at the bar. "Like maybe two days?"

Ray leaned across the bar on his elbow, bringing his face inches from hers, his smile never fading. "Only two days? Seems a lot longer."

Lainie held his gaze for a moment before the frank interest of the other patrons caused her to lean back. Ray followed her lead.

"So what can I get you? Or did you just come in to distract me?"

"A diet soda, I guess. I made the mistake of telling your grandma I saw Les on the way home tonight totally plastered. She's none too happy about me coming over here and all but made me promise not to drink anything."

"A wise decision, however it came about." He set the glass in front of her. "And I even found a straw for you."

Lainie took a long sip from her soda. "So, everyone's asking. Have you heard anything from Steven?"

Ray shrugged. "Not much. Just that he ought to be home by Thanksgiving."

"And you? Are you still going to be here Thanksgiving?" There. It was out in the open.

Ray took a large can from under the bar and scooped peanuts into a bowl sitting on top before he said anything. "Oh, sure. I'll still be here then. I wouldn't miss Steven's homecoming for anything. And it'll take me some time to get him up to speed here before I can take off. If I do go back north, it wouldn't be before the first of the year, anyway."

"*If* you go back north?"

"I don't know, Lainie. It's a good six, seven weeks before we'll see Steven, and another six weeks after that before I can even think about leaving town. That's a long time. It's way too early for me to start making plans. Anything can happen between now and then."

Lainie's smile was a small one. "Haven't you been counting the days until you could go back to painting full-time? I'd have bet money that you'd have your bags in the car when he got here."

"Oh, I'm going to paint again, that's for sure. I contacted some galleries as soon as I heard that Steven's coming back, and they want to see some digital shots as soon as I can put a slide show together. It's the moving I'm thinking twice about. Since I've been working at my cabin, I think I've done some of my best work. Most of my stuff is from photos I've taken right around the ranch, and working from life is even better. I'm thinking about how that might work. What about you? You made any more plans to leave town?"

Lainie shrugged. "And go where? It's not like I have any kind of life I need to get back to."

"Oh, come on. No family? No friends anywhere? Someone somewhere must be wondering why you dropped off the face of the earth. You're not on the lam, are you?"

Ray's bantering grin slowly faded as he studied Lainie's face. She dropped her eyes and took a long sip of her soda.

"That was supposed to be a joke." Ray waited while Lainie drained her glass to the slurping bottom.

"Well, it wasn't very funny. Half the people in the town look at me like they expect to hear sirens in the distance. I just didn't expect that from you."

Ray put his hand over hers. "Okay, it was a poor joke. Sorry. But there's more to this than just me hurting your feelings. Want to tell me what's going on?"

Ray's hand on hers was warm, and his brown eyes made her feel safer than she had felt since she could remember. Lainie hesitated. She was filled with the longing to place her burden on his broad shoulders. It got so heavy sometimes. She shook the feeling off and squared her shoulders. Not a good time to start counting on anyone.

"Nope, nothing's wrong. I'm just touchy tonight, I guess. Sorry I overreacted."

Lainie looked down at the hand covering hers. She could feel his long gaze on the top of her head. Finally, he squeezed her hand and straightened up. "Okay. Have it your way. But I'm here if you need me."

He moved from around the bar and Lainie watched him cross the room to clear a table, stopping to trade a quiet joke with another group. Their easy laughter made Lainie feel even more the outsider. She picked up her purse and slid off her stool as Ray walked back to the bar.

"You're not going? You barely got here." Ray seemed genuinely disappointed.

"I told Elizabeth I wouldn't stay long. She'll be looking for me."

"I'll walk you out." Ray placed his hand in the small of her back and moved through the doorway with her. When they were outside, he pulled her into a shadow and slipped his arms around her waist. He smiled into her upturned face. "Sunday's all I've got. Let me pick you up after church. Maybe we could go over to Hatch. The chile festival is this weekend, I think."

"Wow. Chile, huh? That's original."

"Hey, don't knock it. The whole world knows about Hatch chile. People come from everywhere for this festival." He dropped a soft kiss on her nose and another on her lips.

"Then I don't see how we can pass it up." Lainie smiled up at him.

Ray didn't answer. His arms tightened around her waist and his mouth covered hers. Lainie stood lost in his arms and the scent and the taste of him. Vaguely, as from a long distance, she became aware of an approaching vehicle, but only when the jeers and coyote howls began did she pull away.

"Get a room!" The long, low Chevy screeched to a stop in the parking lot. Two boys fought for window space from the backseat, and Lainie could see the shadows of several more in the darkness of the car. When Ray turned around, they spun out, still hooting and laughing.

"Was that Matthew?" Ray sounded incredulous.

Lainie took a deep breath and held it before slowly exhaling. "I don't know. It's awful dark. The one making all the noise wasn't Matthew. I don't know about any of the others."

Ray watched the taillights disappear in the distance. He was still scowling when he turned back to Lainie, but a slow smile spread over his face as he pulled her to him again. "Now, where were we?"

Lainie put her hands against his chest. "As Elizabeth would say, we're standing out here in front of God and I don't know who all, that's where we are. And I need to get home."

He leaned in for another light kiss. "Okay then, see you Sunday."

"After church, or during?"

"I'll pick you up at Elizabeth's about one."

"Still hiding from the church ladies, huh? Ray Braden, you're a chicken."

He grinned. "You got that right. But one of these days I might just surprise you."

Lainie headed across the parking lot, but when she reached the road, she looked back. Ray was standing in the doorway with his hands in his pockets, watching her.

She was almost to the street that turned off toward Elizabeth's when she saw the headlights of the approaching car. It slowed to a stop next to her.

"Hey, honey, want a ride?" One of the riders in the same Chevy she had seen earlier leaned out the window and made kissing noises while the driver shoved the gear shift into Reverse and slowly backed down the road, keeping pace with her quick step.

"Come on, baby. If you think that old man was good, you ought to try me."

He opened the front door and started to get out. With one swift kick Lainie slammed the door shut.

"Hey, watch out! You coulda chopped my hand off."

"Then count yourself lucky. It could have been worse. Now get lost."

"C'mon, guys. Let's get outta here," one of the boys, hat pulled over his eyes, muttered from the backseat.

Lainie leaned down and peered into the car. "Matthew, is that you?"

The others hooted in laughter. One called in falsetto, "'Matthew, is that you?' Oooh, Matthew, you're busted."

The road out of town was long and straight, and she watched the taillights even after she could no longer hear the laughter, the catcalls, or even the souped-up engine.

15

As the days till Thanksgiving grew fewer and fewer with still no word from Steven, Elizabeth's jubilant mood was replaced by a nonstop bustle, as if by working hard she could put the silence and the longing from her mind. It was still dark on Thanksgiving morning when faint sounds from the kitchen woke Lainie. Elizabeth was in the kitchen, of course, where she had been baking and peeling and stirring for the last three days. A tiny twinge of guilt nudged Lainie as she turned over and snuggled back beneath her covers. She really should get up and go see if Elizabeth needed help, but the diner was closed today, and a day to sleep in was so rare. Surely, if Elizabeth really needed her she would have come to wake her. She didn't need to come up with another excuse because by the time she had recited these to herself, she had drifted back to sleep.

When Lainie woke again, the sun was up, and this time she slipped into the robe Elizabeth had given her and wandered to the kitchen looking for a cup of coffee. She stopped in the doorway. Every surface in the kitchen was covered with serving dishes containing who-knows-what nestling under plastic wrap; baking pans full of rolls, some hot and golden brown, some pale and awaiting their turn in the oven; and pies—lots and lots of pies.

"Wow. Got enough food?"

Elizabeth jumped and turned around to face her. She brushed

a white curl from her forehead. "My lands, Lainie, you scared me out of five years' growth. Grab a couple of rolls off that tray there and get yourself some butter and jam out of the icebox. I'm afraid that'll have to be breakfast this morning. The coffee's on the stove."

Lainie pulled a mug from the cupboard and reached for the coffeepot. "How many people did you say were going to be there?"

Elizabeth counted on her fingers. "Well, I guess anything up to about twenty-seven or twenty-eight or so is a good possibility." She looked at the table and her forehead furrowed. "I hope I made enough pies."

"Are you taking the whole meal?"

"Heavens, no. This is just the baking. And I made a few other things just to fill in—ambrosia, scalloped corn, cranberry relish— just in case." She dropped into a kitchen chair and surveyed the bounty spread around her. "Pour me a cup of coffee and hand me a plate, would you, sweetie? I believe I'll join you in a bite of breakfast. I'm at a good stopping place."

Lainie cleared a spot at the table and pushed the butter and jam to where Elizabeth could reach them.

"This is a lot of stuff to get up to the ranch."

"Fayette's going to come by. Between her big old trunk and her big old backseat, we ought to be able to get it all in. And if we have any that won't fit, I'll just send it along with you and Ray. When's he coming?"

Lainie shrugged and reached for another roll. "He said he'd call this morning and see what's going on. I think he had some paperwork he was hoping to get done this morning before we left."

"Well, I hope he doesn't work too long. This is a day for giving thanks for all God's many blessings, not for working." Elizabeth got up to pull another pan of rolls out of the oven.

"And you've been working since what time? Long before dawn,

134

anyway. And that's just this morning. I'm not even talking about the rest of this week."

"This? This is just feeding folks, and I love doing it. It's one of the things I miss most about living on the ranch."

"Well, feeding folks seems an awful lot like work to me."

"I can see how it would, since that's what you do every day at the Dip 'n' Dine, but this is a labor of love, and I look forward to it."

Lainie stretched her legs out in front of her and cradled her coffee cup in her hands. The early morning sun poured through the windows, and Sam stretched out in a patch of sunlight on the kitchen floor and half closed his eyes. The smell of freshly ground coffee mingled with the yeasty aroma of hot bread and the fragrance of the spicy pies. Lainie leaned down and rubbed a finger under Sam's chin, and his purr filled the kitchen. She got to her feet and gave Elizabeth a hug before she headed back to the bathroom.

Elizabeth looked up and smiled. "What's that for?"

"Nothing. Just feeling thankful, that's all. I'm going to go get a shower if you don't need me for anything."

"No, you go on. Oh, there's the phone. Get that for me, will you? Now that I'm sitting down, I don't want to get up."

Lainie answered the phone and smiled when she heard Ray's voice.

"I'm not calling too early, am I?"

"Are you kidding? Your grandma's been up since way before dawn cooking."

"Sounds like her. Listen, things here are a little more complicated than I thought they'd be. Do you think you could catch a ride to the ranch with Gran and I could meet you there? I should be there by dinner, but I don't want to hold you up."

Disappointment settled like a lump in Lainie's stomach. "I don't mind waiting for you. Is there something I could help you with so you could finish up sooner?"

"No, I wish you could. I'm the only one who can deal with it and it needs taking care of right away. If you waited I'd just feel bad about keeping you, so I'll just meet you there this afternoon."

Lainie turned to Elizabeth, who sat listening to her side of the conversation with an ever-darkening scowl on her face.

"Can I ride with you? Ray's tied up till later."

Elizabeth pursed her lips and held out her hand. "Let me have that phone." Lainie handed it over without a word.

"Raymond Joseph? What's so important that you can't spend Thanksgiving with your family? . . . I don't care about your paperwork. I care about having my family together, and this is as near to my whole family as I've had in nearly a year. And now you say you're not even coming . . . When? We're sitting down about 2:30, you know . . . Okay, but I'm about as put out as I've been in I don't know how long. Bye-bye. I love you too."

She handed the phone back to Lainie and sat puffing like a steam engine and batting back tears. "That blasted bar. Not one good thing has come from having that place in Last Chance. Not one."

Lainie returned the receiver to its cradle, a little shocked at the force of Elizabeth's language. "Well, I guess I need a ride. Think there'll be room for me and all this?" She swept a hand around the kitchen.

Elizabeth put her hands on the table and pushed herself to her feet. She blew out a sigh and gave Lainie a resigned smile. "Of course there'll be room for you. It's all this food we need to figure out how to carry. I just pray I've cooled off by the time I see Ray this afternoon or I'm liable to snatch him bald-headed. Missing most of Thanksgiving Day because he decided to work instead. I've never heard of such a thing."

Truth be told, Lainie's Thanksgiving had been colored by Ray's phone call too. Ray wasn't moody and unpredictable, was he? She didn't want moody and unpredictable, not now, not ever again.

By the time Fayette's old car pulled up in front of Elizabeth's house later that morning, Elizabeth's mood had turned sunny again, and she was humming to herself in the kitchen.

"Don't worry about Ray. I'm sure he'll turn up when he said he would and you can ride home with him. If his worst failing is that he's too responsible, I guess we can forgive him."

By carefully fitting some pans together like pieces of a jigsaw puzzle in the trunk, balancing others on their laps, and holding still others between their feet, they managed to get all the food and themselves squeezed into the car.

"Here, be real careful with this. I don't want it sloshing all over." Fayette handed a bowl to Matthew, who was slouched in a corner of the backseat with a sullen expression on his face. He rolled his eyes and gazed out the window while the dish wobbled precariously on his lap.

"Matthew! I said be careful!" Clearly, she and Matthew had exchanged words before they arrived.

"I said I've got it, okay?" Matthew muttered something under his breath.

"What's that?"

"Nothing."

When they passed the church, Elizabeth broke the silence that shrouded the car.

"You know, I sure was sorry when they stopped having a Thanksgiving morning service. I never could come, of course, since I was up at the ranch trying to get dinner on the table, but now that I'm in town and could go, they up and stopped having them. Last night's service was nice, though. It did us all good to think about all our blessings."

She looked at the sullen faces around her and broke into laughter.

"Well, I have to say this is the sorriest group I've ever been around on Thanksgiving. Here we are with more to be thankful over than you can shake a stick at, and we sit moping like our last friend just took the dog and stole the car. Now, I for one am thankful I have a car full of good food and I'm going to my family. What about you, Fayette? Tell me something you're thankful for."

Fayette didn't say anything for a moment. Then she sighed and glanced in the rearview mirror. "Sometimes I want to just shake him till his teeth rattle, but I thank God every day that he gave me Matthew."

"Lainie? What about you?"

Lainie thought about all that had happened since her car started overheating out on the highway last summer. She surely wasn't grateful then, but gradually, almost without her noticing, things had begun to change. And this morning, in the warm comfort of Elizabeth's kitchen, for the first time she had recognized gratitude.

"I don't know. That I met you guys, I guess." Just because she was aware of it didn't mean she felt comfortable talking about it.

"Well, we're thankful we met you too. What about you, Matthew?"

Matthew grunted something unintelligible and continued looking out the window.

Elizabeth acted as if he had spoken. "You're right, Matthew. You have a good roof over your head, plenty of food, and a mother who loves you and cares how you turn out. You have a basketful of blessings to be thankful for."

"I didn't say any of that." Matthew brought his attention back to the conversation.

"Didn't you? I'd swear that's what you said. That and the music lessons you've taken in my living room for the past eight years? Didn't you mention them too?" Laughter spilled from Elizabeth's voice.

"No." An unwilling smile tugged at the corner of Matthew's mouth.

"Well then, what about this?" Elizabeth reached down, plucked a cinnamon roll from the pan at her feet, and tossed it over her shoulder into the backseat without looking. Matthew almost grinned as he caught it in the air. He stuffed it into his mouth.

"I'll take it that you're thankful for cinnamon rolls."

"Matthew . . ." Fayette sounded tired and exasperated, but Elizabeth reached over and patted her arm.

"We're doing fine here, Fayette. Let's not go back to where we started. Now, why don't you give us something else that you're thankful for?"

Fayette thought a minute, then laughed. "Well, there are times you'd never get me to admit it, but I'm thankful I have that old diner. I don't know what Matthew and I would do without it. And I'm thankful for all the people who come in and keep me running my feet off all day." She caught Lainie's eye in the rearview mirror. "And I'm thankful the Lord brought Lainie to Last Chance. I don't know how I managed without her."

"Now, that's just what I was going to say. I'm thankful the Lord brought Lainie into my life too. And not just because I seem to be seeing more of my grandson, either. Lainie, you want to add anything?"

Lainie ignored the bantering tone. "I'm thankful I've got a job, I guess. And that you took me in." She nudged Matthew's foot with her own. "Come on, Matthew. You need to come up with something too."

"I'm thankful I'm not a turkey."

Lainie grinned at him. "Well, that's a matter of opinion."

Fayette hooted in laughter. "I am so thankful for Matthew's sense of humor. He can make me laugh like nobody else." She pulled the car up under the trees that in summer shaded the long, low ranch house and turned off the engine.

Elizabeth headed for the front door, balancing a pie on each hand, and Fayette opened her trunk. Lainie filled her arms with more dishes and followed her. Behind her she heard Matthew mutter, "Sorry, Mom," and she smiled to herself. She had never thought much about Thanksgiving being all about giving thanks, but it did add a whole new dimension.

"Come in this house!" Nancy Jo, Joe Jr.'s wife, met them at the door wearing an apron that covered her brown pants and autumn print blouse. "My gracious, how much food did you bring? I thought you were bringing a couple pies and the rolls."

Elizabeth turned up her cheek for a kiss. "I did. But as long as I was at it, I made a couple other things too. I don't think it will go to waste."

"Not with this crowd. I'm just hoping they'll last till dinner's ready. They've already eaten just about all the dip and whatnot I put out for them." A roar erupted from the back of the house, and Nancy Jo looked over her shoulder. "Sounds like somebody must have scored a touchdown. Matthew, you can go on back and join the men after you drop that off if you want to."

Lainie stood in the wide entry holding her pans. The house was redolent with the aroma of roasting turkeys and full of people, most of whom she had never met. A boy of about seven pursued by another a year or so older raced by and bumped against her, nearly knocking her off balance.

"Jacob! Michael James! If you're going to run, go outside." Nancy Jo watched them disappear out the front door and turned back to her guests with a shake of her head. "Welcome to the zoo." She peered out the open door. "Where's Ray? Didn't he come with you?"

"He'll be along later. And don't get me started on that." Elizabeth led the way to the kitchen, where she was greeted with hugs by three young women who were peeling potatoes and cutting vegetables.

"Well, hello, sweet girls. I don't know if you've met my friend and housemate, Lainie. I know you've heard a lot about her. Lainie, these are two of my granddaughters, Kimberly and Sarah, and my granddaughter-in-law, Bethany. You met Kimberly's boys, Jacob and Michael James, in the hall, and Bethany here is going to be giving me my first great-granddaughter just after the first of the year. How you feeling, sweetie?"

The two blue-eyed blondes and the petite, curly-haired brunette smiled and murmured greetings, but Elizabeth didn't even pause for breath.

"I made some cinnamon rolls thinking folks might like a bite this morning to tide them over till dinner this afternoon." She gestured toward a pan Matthew had left on the kitchen table. "But I don't know how well they'll go with dip. Maybe you want to save them for another time."

"Are you kidding?" Nancy Jo pulled a platter out of the cupboard and began piling it with still-warm pastries. "Your cinnamon rolls? Why don't you carry these out to the guys and I'll put the coffee on. We can have ours in here where it's a little quieter and we can keep an eye on dinner. Kimberly, grab some mugs out of that cupboard, and Sarah, why don't you and Lainie carry those pans on the table out to the service room? I've set up some tables out there for the overflow."

With the coffee brewed and the turkeys basted, the women gathered around the well-scrubbed table, chatting and laughing over their coffee and rolls. Lainie listened to them talking about events that she had never heard of and people she didn't know, but their eyes and laughter and the occasional explanation for her benefit drew her into their circle, and she found herself feeling one of the family.

Nancy Jo got up and peeked at the two turkeys roasting side by side in the huge oven. She ladled a few spoonfuls of drippings over the browning birds and returned to the table with the coffeepot.

"You know, I don't care what anyone says, I just love this part of the holidays, when all the women are in the kitchen and the men are entertaining themselves somewhere, watching TV or something. I know it's not a bit up-to-date, but there you have it."

Sarah caught Lainie's eye behind her mother's back and rolled her eyes. "So Gran, what do you hear from Steven? Any idea when he's going to get home?"

"No, I haven't heard word one. I guess he'll just get here when he gets here. Rita calls me every blessed day to ask what I know."

Sarah got up and bent to give her grandmother a squeeze. "I'm sorry, Gran. I didn't mean to upset you. I won't ask anymore."

Elizabeth patted the hand Sarah rested on her shoulder. "It's okay, baby girl. I think I'm just worried. I didn't mean to snap."

At 2:30 exactly, Nancy Jo went to the den to call the men to dinner. The turkey had been carved and lay in neat slices on large turkey-shaped platters. Casseroles of candied sweet potatoes and green beans in mushroom sauce were brought golden and bubbling from the oven, and bowls of mashed potatoes, gravy, cranberry sauce, cornbread-sausage stuffing, ambrosia, scalloped corn, and several things that Lainie didn't recognize covered every inch of the two long tables in the spacious dining room.

Joe Jr. extended both his hands, and one by one every family member and guest took the hands of another until all were standing with heads bowed in a circle that ringed the large room. He offered a prayer of thanksgiving, and everyone joined in the "amen." Ray still had not come.

When everyone was seated, Lainie found herself halfway down the table headed by Joe Jr. and Nancy Jo's oldest son, Justin. Ray's empty chair was on her right, and one of the ranch hands sat on her left.

"Man, this is good turkey. I don't know how anyone can eat those farm ones." James, Joe Jr. and Nancy Jo's youngest, speared another slice of dark meat. "Where'd you bag this one?"

"Out by Rio Seco. Got him the last day of the season. Here, need some more gravy?" Justin passed the gravy boat down the table.

Lainie stopped eating and looked at the food on her plate with dismay. She had admired the wild birds she had seen while out riding with Ray. She had no idea people actually killed and ate them.

James caught her look and guffawed. "What's the matter? Never had wild game before?"

Lainie tried to smile. "I'd just rather look at them than eat them, I guess. I mean, why kill live turkeys when you can buy them in the store?"

The ranch hand at her left shifted his mouthful of food to his cheek and, without looking at her, spoke to his plate. "You think them store birds started out in plastic bags?"

Everyone laughed, and Lainie felt her face flush hot.

"Come on, you guys, leave her alone. Not everyone's crazy about hunting, even those of us who appreciate the game." Bethany smiled down the table at Lainie. "Don't pay any attention to these guys. Squeamish girls make them feel manly. They're really just a bunch of third graders."

The indignant protests at her statement were cut short by the sound of crunching gravel, and Lainie looked up to see Ray's pickup disappear around the house.

At the other table, Elizabeth's eyes narrowed and her lips tightened. Ray's absence at his promised arrival time had not gone unnoticed. Lainie turned her attention back to her plate, refusing to look up as the door opened.

She heard a second of absolute silence before the room erupted in a riot of pushed back chairs and cries of welcome. Glancing up, she saw Elizabeth moving across the room at a pace Lainie didn't know possible, and a tall, blond young man take three steps into the room and sweep her off her feet in a whirling hug. Behind them in the doorway, Ray stood grinning and watching the scene play before him.

"Well, somebody call Rita." Kimberly crossed the room with outstretched arms. "She can plan that parade now, 'cause look who just came home."

16

After the rest of the family claimed Steven's attention, his grandmother wiped her eyes and turned to Ray, still standing in the doorway.

"Is this where you were? Here I've been worried about him for weeks and so mad at you this morning I wanted to shake you, and you had this planned all along?"

Ray shrugged, but his grin never left his face. "Don't blame me. This was all Steven's idea. He wanted to surprise everybody and didn't even let me in on it. He landed in El Paso early this morning and called and said he was catching the bus for San Ramon. I drove up and got him. I thought for sure we'd be here earlier, but the bus was late."

Steven, with Jacob hanging off one hand and Michael James hanging off the other, looked over the heads of all the family members gathered around vying for hugs and handshakes. When he found Lainie, his eyes lit with interest and his smile widened. He made his way over to where she still sat in her chair at the dining room table. He held out his hand, and when she took it, he held it in both of his and leaned in to kiss her cheek.

"Hi, I'm Steven. I know I haven't met you, but if you're here you must be family, or just about."

He was taller than his brother and bigger, with broader shoulders.

Lainie felt the cool roughness of his cheek against hers and inhaled the slight muskiness of his presence. He pulled back just enough for her to be taken by the striking blue of his eyes. They made Lainie think of the way the ocean looked early on a morning when the sun wasn't shrouded by fog.

"And you are?" He gazed down at her as if she were the only person in the room, and when he smiled, his white teeth were dazzling.

"This is Lainie." Ray appeared at her side. "I've told you about her."

Steven stepped back, but his eyes never left Lainie's. "Don't think so, brother. I would have remembered." He cocked his head to one side and smiled his blinding smile.

Ray placed both hands protectively on Lainie's shoulders. Steven broke the tension of the moment by laughing and looking away. "Hey, James, how's State doing this year? That new quarterback any good?"

Lainie became aware again of the bustle of the room. Everyone was going back to their chairs and full plates, and Nancy Jo was busy directing the addition of another chair and plate at her table.

"Here's a place right next to Gran, Steven. Come get some turkey. When's the last time you had a home-cooked meal?"

"One like this? Not since the last time I sat right here. No one can set a table like you and Gran."

Ray took the empty chair next to Lainie's. Steven, at the next table, still held the attention of nearly everyone. Only the ranch hand on Lainie's other side was more interested in his dinner than he was in the returned warrior.

"Well, you are just full of surprises." Lainie passed Ray the turkey. "How long have you been keeping this secret?"

"I didn't hear a thing till this morning. He's been back in the States for about three weeks, visiting some friends in California."

"Three weeks? And he didn't call your grandma? She's been afraid to even go to the grocery store for fear he'd call while she was gone."

"Well, that's Steven. He doesn't mean to be inconsiderate. It just never occurs to him that the rest of us aren't suspended in time when he's not around."

Lainie looked over at Steven sitting next to his grandmother. Elizabeth was handing him dish after dish and urging him to take larger portions of each. He looked up and caught Lainie's eye and winked. She quickly looked away. Why did her face feel so warm? He certainly wasn't the first full-of-himself guy she had ever met.

"You guys don't look much alike. I would never have thought you were brothers."

Ray looked up from spooning stuffing onto his plate. "Nope, he looks just like my dad—and has Dad's personality too. I take after the Cooley side of the family. They say I look more like Uncle Joe Jr. than my own dad."

"Did you get a chance to talk on the way here about him taking over the bar? Do you have any more of a timeline?"

"Nope. He's been through a lot and I didn't want to rush him. I've kept up with the bar this long. A few more weeks won't make any difference. I'll give him to the first of the year, anyway."

The sun had slipped behind the rocky hills by the time the last of the platters had been passed and passed again and finally sat empty on the long tables. The conversation slowed.

"Anyone ready for pie?" Nancy Jo stood up and was met with a chorus of groans. "Okay, we'll wait a while. Joe Jr., why don't you throw another log or two on the fire, and we'll get some of these leftovers under wraps."

Everyone slowly got to their feet, and the men moved off toward the den while the women grabbed empty platters and stacked plates. Lainie shot Ray a look.

"So you guys go sit like slugs and the women keep working? What kind of deal is that?"

Ray shrugged and grinned. "Hey, who am I to buck tradition? Here, don't forget this." He tried to hand her a casserole dish that had held scalloped corn, but she shoved it back in his hands.

"Come on, you can help bring this family into the twenty-first century." She grabbed his sleeve and pulled him into the kitchen. "Nancy Jo? Do you have an extra apron? Ray feels so bad about holding up dinner that he really wants to help with the dishes."

Nancy Jo looked over her shoulder and laughed. "Yeah, that'll be the day. No, we're doing fine. It won't take us fifteen minutes. We can do this in our sleep. We got most of the pots and pans washed before dinner. Why don't you two go walk off some of that dinner?"

On the back porch, Lainie drew deep breaths of cold piñon smoke–scented air. She could still hear the sounds of laughter and conversation behind her in the warm, brightly lit house, but it was muffled and seemed a world away. A gust of wind blew up and rattled the bare branches of the cottonwoods overhead, and Lainie shivered. Ray pulled her close and rubbed her arms.

"Cold?"

She nodded. "A little, maybe."

"I'll run and get you a jacket. Be right back." Ray ducked back through the kitchen door.

When the door opened again, Lainie turned around expecting to see Ray and found herself face-to-face with Steven.

"Hi. I thought I saw you come out here. Where's Ray?"

"Right here." Ray followed him out holding a warm oversized jacket. "This might be big—I think it's Uncle Joe Jr.'s—but it was the first one I found." He draped it over Lainie's shoulders and wrapped her like a cocoon, pulling her close.

Steven grinned. "You're going to wind up falling on your face like that." He took the jacket and held it while Lainie slipped her arms into the long sleeves. "There. Now you can move."

Ray pushed a sleeve back to find Lainie's hand and enveloped it in his own, and the three stepped off the back porch and started across the yard to the road that led to the corrals. Steven fell in on Ray's other side.

Steven took a deep breath. "Man, I missed the way this place smells. I didn't even realize it till I got out of the car this afternoon—the smoke, the horses, something else I can't even name. It's just home."

Ray clapped his shoulder. "Glad you're home, bro. And you're here to stay this time."

Steven didn't say anything.

"So what are your plans now? You want to bunk with me? I don't have a lot of room, but we can manage somehow."

"Nah, thanks anyway, bro, but I don't want to crowd your space. Gran said I could use the daybed in her sewing room. In fact, Gran *told* me I was using the daybed in her sewing room. Seems someone else has the guest room." He grinned at Lainie.

"There's no rush, but you know the bar's ready when you are."

"Yeah, thanks for that. I know you had to put your own stuff on hold. It'll seem weird without Dad, though. He and I always planned to run it together."

"Well, he wanted you to have it, anyway. I'll bring you up to speed as soon as you're ready. Maybe sometime in the next week or so?"

"Yeah, sounds good. Sometime next week."

They walked to the end of the road before heading back to the house. Lainie turned the collar of the jacket up to block the wind. Warm lights shining from the windows of the ranch house beckoned, and she tried to move Ray and Steven on a little faster.

The pie had been served when they stepped back into the cavernous living room. Everyone held a plate with a whipped cream–topped slice, and mugs of steaming coffee rested on every convenient surface.

"There you are!" Nancy Jo appeared in the kitchen doorway. "Gran called Rita to tell her you were home, and she's called back three times trying to reach you. Here's her number." She handed Steven the cordless phone and a slip of paper.

Steven peered at the number and started slowly punching in numbers. "Why am I calling Rita now?"

"Didn't Ray tell you? She's going to declare Steven Braden Day and give you a big parade and everything. Now, do you all want pumpkin, pecan, or mincemeat?"

Light poured from the windows of the Dip 'n' Dine and the smell of coffee and sausage enveloped her when Lainie got to work early the next morning. Fayette was carrying a tray laden with steaming plates across the room toward a table where four men in work boots sat cradling mugs of coffee. Lainie glanced at the clock. The diner wasn't due to open for another twenty minutes. Fayette caught her glance.

"I know. But they were here, I was here, and Carlos was here. I didn't see any need to keep them sitting out in the cold when they could be inside with a cup of coffee. Now run and get your uniform on. Another truck just pulled into the parking lot."

It was nearly eleven before Lainie was able catch her breath. She ducked into the kitchen and found Fayette hanging up the phone.

"I had to put in an emergency order up to San Ramon. I don't know why I didn't see this crowd coming. Seems everybody is taking the day off and coming in here for breakfast. How's it looking out there?"

Lainie craned her neck to look. "Pretty quiet. Rita's still in her breakfast meeting with Steven, but I think he quit paying attention an hour ago."

She walked up to their table with the coffeepot and put the check on the table. "Need another refill?"

"None for me. I've got to get going." Steven got to his feet and held out his hand to the mayor. "Rita, it's been a pleasure. I've gotta say, though, I'm blown away by all this. I sure don't deserve it."

Rita jumped to her feet and reached up to give him a hug. "What do you mean, you don't deserve it? You bet you deserve it! And you represent all the other young men and women out there fighting for us. If you don't want this for yourself, take it for them."

Steven grinned at Lainie over Rita's head. "Well, if you put it that way . . . Hey, there's Ray. I need to see him about something."

Across the road Ray slammed the door of his truck and waited for Steven to catch up. Lainie could see the smile light Ray's face. Steven was a charmer, all right. Lainie just wished he didn't make her feel so uneasy.

17

At the end of the long day, Lainie stood on the sidewalk outside and rolled her shoulders to ease the ache that had settled there sometime in the middle of the afternoon. It was as dark outside as it had been when she got to work that morning, and cold gusts of wind blew dried leaves and bits of trash around her feet. Across the street, a lone truck sat in front of the High Lonesome. Lainie waited for an eighteen-wheeler to roar by, then ran across the road.

Ray looked up when she pushed her way through the door, and his smile warmed her.

"Hey, Lainie! Come on in. I thought you'd be on your way to Steven's welcome home party."

Lainie climbed on a stool at the bar. "I just thought I'd take a break before I go. From what Elizabeth said, the whole town is going to be there, and I've had about all the people I can take for a while. She looked down at the cup Ray put in front of her. "What is this?"

"Hot chocolate. Sorry, I'm out of whipped cream."

"Yuck. Got any coffee?"

Ray leaned across the bar and grinned at her. "Try my cocoa. You'll love it."

"Yeah, well, that's what you said about the grape soda, and that was nasty." She took a tentative sip and shrugged. "Not bad. Could use some whipped cream, though."

A gust of wind rattled the windows, and Lainie watched a tumbleweed the size of a beach ball blow across the parking lot and slam against the fence.

She shivered. "I'd better run. It's getting bad out there."

Ray came out from behind the bar. "Tell you what. I've seen ghost towns with more going on than this place tonight. Finish your cocoa, and I'll just lock up and run you home. Won't take ten minutes."

He reached for his hat but stopped when the song changed on the jukebox and a slow, gravelly voice began a song of regret and loss.

"Oh, there's my man Willie. You've got to dance with me before we go." He took her hand and slipped his other hand around her waist, drawing her into the tiny space in front of the jukebox. He gently rested his cheek against her hair and led her in the first steps while Lainie closed her eyes and smiled to herself. Following had never been one of her strengths, but following Ray was easy. She was glad he was holding her close, because the longer they danced and the longer she felt his breath gentle on her face, the weaker her knees became. Finally, the last aching notes died to silence and Ray let go of her waist, twirled her once, and drew her close again. Lainie blinked, drew a deep breath to clear her head, and looked up at him.

"Oh."

Ray just smiled and slipped his other arm around her waist. As he bent his face to hers, the crunch of gravel interrupted them and a flash of headlights slid across the bar and came to rest on the back wall.

Ray sighed as they pulled apart. "Company. Guess I'll have to take back my offer of a ride—unless you want to wait a while. Or I could call over to Gran's and get Steven to come get you."

Lainie shook her head. "No." She gestured at the suddenly

darkened windows of the Dip 'n' Dine. "Looks like Fayette's about ready to go. If I hurry, I can catch a ride with her."

A blast of wind caught the door and tried to slam it against the wall as four men with hats jammed down around their ears and jacket collars pulled up stamped into the room.

"I tell you what, it's fixin' to blow up a storm worth writing home about out there." The first one through the door took off his jacket and hung it on the rack by the door.

"I'll say. There was five of us got out of the truck, but the wind just up and took Shorty. He oughta be passin' into Mexican air space 'bout now." He stopped when he saw Lainie. "Hey there."

Lainie buttoned her coat. "Hi and bye." She paused on her way out the door. "Oh, I was going to tell you. Guess who's got a solo at church on Sunday."

Ray's face split in a grin. "You're kidding! Good for you. What are you singing?"

"Some of the Christmas music we've been working on. I've never sung a solo before and I'll probably pass out in the middle of it."

Ray turned her coat collar up against her neck, his hands lingering on either side of her face. "You'll do just fine. I know it."

"Hey, you two, shut the door, would you? It's getting as cold in here as it is outside, and ever' bit as windy."

"And Fayette's getting in her car. I need to run." Lainie sprinted across the parking lot, waving over her shoulder at Ray and calling out to Fayette to wait.

Finding a spot to park Fayette's old Dodge anywhere near Elizabeth's house wasn't easy. Pickups, SUVs, and just a few sedans lined both sides of the street.

"Wow. Elizabeth wasn't kidding when she said she was having some folks over." Lainie took the pan of enchiladas Fayette handed her.

"Well, these things can take on a life of their own." Fayette started down the narrow path between the cars and the side of the road, with Lainie close behind. "Private parties are unheard of here in Last Chance. Everyone just assumes that they're included. But they all bring food too."

The house was definitely standing room only. People had even spilled out onto the front porch and stood hunched into their heavy coats, but the air of celebration permeated even the cold. Inside, the chairs and sofa were occupied by older people holding overladen plates of food. Younger folks stood in small groups chatting and eating while children threaded their way through the crowd, pausing only briefly when someone caught them by the shoulder and told them to slow down. A quick glance into the kitchen told Lainie that Elizabeth had more help than she knew what to do with, so she escaped down the hall to her bedroom. The door was closed and she expected to find it empty, but two little girls stood at her dresser holding her Mickey Mouse snow globe. She managed to smile as she held her hand out for the trinket.

"I didn't break it." The little girl who handed over the snow globe looked scared.

"No, I can see that." Lainie turned the globe over so the girls could see the shower of glitter fall around Mickey in his Sorcerer's Apprentice wizard costume.

"Can I try?"

"If you're careful." Lainie handed the globe back to the little girl, who received it with great care and held it in both hands. "This is very special to me. My dad bought it for me at Disneyland when I was about your age."

"I'm seven."

"Well, I was eight. He took me to Disneyland for my eighth birthday. And this was my birthday present."

The girl gently turned the globe back and forth to start the glitter shower. "Wow. This is really old. My mom likes antiques. Can I show it to her?"

Lainie held out her hand for the globe. "Maybe another time. Right now I'd like to change my clothes, so you girls need to go back to the others."

Lainie turned the lock when the girls left and leaned against the door. The sounds of the party were a muffled roar. Even after she changed clothes, she couldn't make herself open the door and go out to join the party. She was tired, but it was more than that. She didn't know what to make of a place where everyone was so much at home that they could invite themselves to a house and know they'd be welcomed like family, where the whole town could turn out to welcome someone home because he belonged to them.

She picked up the snow globe again. How special she had felt that day. Her dad had made a point of taking her and only her to Disneyland. Not even her mom was invited. He had called her his princess and bought her a Cinderella dress that she wore all day. He bought the snow globe on the way out. She tossed it lightly in her hand. Maybe this *was* an antique. That was all so long ago. She had worn the dress so often that it was pretty much in tatters within a few months. The snow globe had become her most prized possession. Her father, though, left two days after her birthday, and she had not seen him since.

She was lying on her bed listening to the clock radio on the nightstand when a tap on her door pulled her to her feet. She expected to see Elizabeth coming to check on her, but it was Steven who ducked in when she unlocked the door.

"Thought I might find you back here. Hiding out?"

"I guess I am. No one's going to miss me, anyway."

Steven cocked his head to one side and smiled a slow smile. "I did. I saw you come in with Fayette, and next thing I knew you were gone. I kept waiting for you to turn up, but you never did, so I came looking for you."

Lainie laughed. "There are fifty people out there who came just to see you, and you noticed I wasn't among them. Yeah, right."

"Seriously! I had been watching for you." He sat cross-legged on the floor with his back against the door. "Mind if I take a seat?"

Lainie sat on the bed and pulled her knees up under her. "Suit yourself. Isn't your public waiting, though?"

Steven grinned and cocked his head toward the rumble on the other side of Lainie's bedroom door. "Good people. Right now they're either arguing about Last Chance High's recently concluded football season, its upcoming basketball season, or whether the state'll go up in flames when the new governor takes office in January. I don't think they'll miss me."

He stopped talking and gazed at Lainie with a half smile long enough to make her shift uncomfortably and search for something to say. "So, are you looking forward to taking over the bar?"

Steven's smile slowly widened as if he knew of her discomfort and had no intention of easing it. "Yeah. I need to get over there when Ray's not so busy and talk to him about that. He told me to take a couple weeks to decompress first, though, and I appreciate that. It is a little weird being back, even though I grew up here. And there's that crazy parade and stuff that Rita's been going on about. But Ray's done his bit. Fair's fair."

Lainie raised her eyebrows and shrugged. If Steven was looking for sympathy, he was looking in the wrong place. Ray had put so much of his life on hold for his brother, willingly and without complaint, but it was time he got it back.

The door opened a crack behind Steven and stopped as it hit his back. Elizabeth's voice wafted through the opening. "Lainie, are you all right, honey?"

Steven got to his feet and opened the door. Elizabeth's eyes widened at the sight of him. "Steven!" She glanced over her shoulder as she bustled into the room, closing the door behind her. "What are you doing in here?"

"Just talking, Gran. I came back about five minutes ago to say hi."

Elizabeth's voice was barely more than a whispered hiss, and her face was pink with indignation. "I don't believe you two! Here we have a houseful of company and you lock yourselves in the bedroom. What are people supposed to think?"

Steven put both hands on her shoulders. "They probably didn't even notice we were gone, and we weren't locked in, by the way. But I'll come on back out to the front room."

"Well, people are starting to leave. You need to come say goodbye."

Steven draped his arm around her shoulders and led her from the room.

Lainie lay back down on her bed and stared at the ceiling. How did you know when to care about what people thought and when to dismiss it? Elizabeth obviously had it all figured out, but Lainie wasn't sure she'd ever get it.

The sanctuary of the Church of Last Chance was fragrant with evergreen when Lainie filed into the choir loft Sunday morning. Steven sat next to Elizabeth in her usual pew. Lainie had half expected him to try to get out of church, but there had been no question, either on his part or on Elizabeth's. Elizabeth had just rapped loudly on the sewing room door and called that it was time for him to get up, and a half hour later he had appeared in the kitchen dressed and ready to go.

The door of the church opened quietly during the opening prayer, and when Lainie sneaked a peek, she saw Ray slip in and take a seat on the back pew. Her eyes flew open and she nearly choked, but he just bowed his head and joined the congregation in prayer. If Lainie had had a little fluttering in her stomach at the thought of her solo before, she had a whole bird sanctuary going on now.

The announcements and the first two hymns went by in a blur, and all too soon the ushers were standing in front of the altar holding offering plates while the pastor prayed. Lurlene faced the choir and raised them to their feet. Lainie's heart seemed to follow Lurlene's graceful upward gesture and lodge in her throat. Over and over throughout the last few weeks, she had stood at Elizabeth's piano and practiced to Elizabeth's accompaniment. So why couldn't she remember the first word of her song?

The choir finished the first verse and the sopranos and altos began singing "ooooo" in two-part harmony. Lurlene smiled at Lainie and raised both her hands and her eyebrows. Lainie opened her mouth and nothing came out. If asked, at that moment, she could not have given her name. Her mind was a complete blank. Lurlene didn't bat an eye. She just led the sopranos and altos through a chorus of "ooooo's" and circled round again to Lainie's solo while mouthing the words "Truly he taught us." Lurlene nodded at Lainie again, and Lainie opened her mouth again, and this time sounds came out. Lainie knew words were coming out, and perhaps Lurlene could even hear them, but Lainie was sure no one as far away as the first row even knew she was singing. Lurlene jerked her thumb upward to indicate more volume, but no volume was to be had. Lainie simply didn't have enough breath left in her chest to push out her song.

Finally, with a sweeping gesture, Lurlene brought in the rest of the choir, and as the music swelled with "Christ is the Lord! O praise his name forever," Lainie drew a full breath. She realized her hands were clutched together so tightly that her fingers ached, and her legs felt as likely to hold her up as the tinsel she could see shimmering on the Christmas tree to the left of the organ. After what seemed an eternity, Lurlene brought thumbs to fingertips to end the last note and lowered her hands to seat the choir.

Lainie sat facing the congregation and feeling the heat crawl from her collar and prickle her scalp. Tears tried to fight their way past her batting eyelashes. She raised her eyes from the hands twisting in her lap and caught Elizabeth's encouraging smile. It didn't help. In fact, she felt even worse. Elizabeth had been so proud and had practiced with her so long, and not even the most charitable listener could say she had done anything but make a mess of it.

When the service finally came to a close, Lainie filed out with the rest of the choir, slipped out of her robe, and headed for the door as fast as she could. The other choir members either smiled weakly at her or assured her she had done just fine. All Lainie wanted, though, was to get away. And she almost made it.

"Lainie!" Juanita's sharp voice caught up with her as she reached the door.

With no way out, Lainie turned to face the guardian of the choir's reputation and was enveloped in a hug. When Juanita pulled back she said, "Don't you worry about this. You only have to sing your first solo once in your life, and it's behind you. From now on it's smooth sailing, and you have a lovely voice."

Lainie just looked at her and blinked. "I'm not singing again. That was my first and my last solo. I stunk."

"Well, I'll be honest with you. It wasn't the way we rehearsed. But everybody falls on their face one time or another. It's the getting back up that counts. And you always struck me as that kind of girl. I have to say I'm surprised at your attitude."

"Well, surprise!" Lainie tried to walk around her, but Juanita blocked her path.

"Now, Lainie, you listen to me. Does the term 'get back on the horse' mean anything to you?"

Lainie shifted her weight from one foot to the other and cocked her head, waiting for Juanita to get out of her way.

"Well, around here, everyone knows exactly what that means, because every one of us, at one time or another, has found ourselves eating dirt when we thought we were sitting on a horse. And those of us who thought we could get some sympathy by running to mama got ourselves turned right around and sent back outside to get back on that horse. Now, you've got to get right back up there and sing, or you're going to let this thing grow way past its importance. And let me tell you, wasting your God-given talent is a sin, pure and simple."

Lainie shook her head. "I was so lousy."

Exasperation tinged Juanita's voice. "Oh, for pity's sake, Lainie. This is not about you, it's about worship. And you are not the first person to flub her first solo, or even the one who flubbed it the worst. I sang my first solo when I was twelve years old, and I was so scared I stood up there and wet my pants in front of the whole church."

"You're kidding."

"I am not kidding. I just stood there in a puddle staring at my mother in the second row and worrying that I was going to get in trouble for ruining my new lace-trimmed socks and my Easter shoes. Finally, someone took me by the hand and led me off the podium."

"So did you get in trouble?"

"No. The socks washed clean, so did the shoes, and my mother and I came over one afternoon during the next week and did a little spot cleaning on the carpet. I begged her to let me go join the Methodist church in San Ramon, but of course she wouldn't hear of it, and the next Sunday, I was up there again and sang my solo. And, I might add, I've been singing ever since."

"And none of your friends gave you a hard time for wetting your pants?"

Juanita just looked at her. "Honey, we were twelve years old. What do you think?"

"Ouch. That must have been rough."

Juanita waved a dismissive hand. "Oh, it was for a few days. But then someone ripped the seat of their britches on the playground or threw up in the lunch line, and we all had something new to talk about."

They walked together into the sanctuary where Elizabeth still waited for Lainie. Juanita waved a greeting and continued down the aisle to the door. Elizabeth watched her go.

"What did Juanita have to say? She wasn't giving you a hard time, was she?"

Lainie gave Elizabeth a one-armed hug as they walked down the church steps to the parking lot. "It's okay, really." She looked around. "Where's Ray?"

Steven pushed away from the truck door he had been leaning against. "I didn't see him, and I've been out here since church ended."

Elizabeth looked confused. "Did he tell you he'd be here today?"

"He was here, sitting in the back. He slipped in just after the opening prayer."

Steven climbed behind the wheel and started the engine. "Well, he must have slipped out again. There was no sign of him when I got out here."

162

"You mean I had both my boys in church with me this morning and I didn't know it? He should have come and sat with us. Steven, swing on by his trailer. Let's take him home for Sunday dinner. I didn't know he was staying in town or I would have called him myself."

The parking lot of the High Lonesome was empty and the windows were dark. "Check around back. He may have parked out by his trailer. Lainie and I'll wait for you here in the truck."

Steven disappeared behind the building, emerging a few seconds later to climb back in the truck. "Everything's locked up tight. I'd guess he went to his cabin after he closed up last night like he usually does on Saturday. Are you sure who you saw was Ray?"

"Yes, it was him." Lainie, huddled in the middle between Steven and Elizabeth and batting back tears, stared straight ahead. Clearly Ray had been so embarrassed for her that he couldn't even stay long enough to say hi.

Elizabeth chatted on, oblivious to Lainie's hurt silence, but Steven caught her eye in the rearview mirror and winked.

18

Fayette was standing on a chair draping silver garland over the kitchen door when Lainie walked in the door the next morning.

"Oh, good. Hand me a couple pushpins, would you?" She adjusted the swag, fastened the garland, and climbed off her chair, dusting her hands. "I like to get these decorations up right after Thanksgiving so we can enjoy them as long as possible. Don't you just love Christmas?"

Lainie bent to pick up an empty ornament box. "I don't know. It's all right. Just another excuse to party, I guess. Kind of like Cinco de Mayo with presents."

Fayette stood with hands on her hips, surveying her work. "Oh, honey, is that all Christmas has been to you? You are in for such a treat. You don't have the faintest idea of Christmas. Although all that music you've been working on should have given you a clue."

Lainie added her ornament boxes to the stack on the counter. "Could we not talk about Christmas music? It's not my favorite subject right now."

Fayette flapped a dismissive hand as the flash of headlights cut through the gray dawn outside and the morning's first customer pulled into the parking space by the door. "Oh, for pity's sake, so you were a little nervous. Who isn't their first time up? You'll be fine next time. Now take care of those folks for me while I run this stuff back to the storage room, would you?"

The morning passed, as Monday mornings always did, in a flurry of activity. Everyone who had been to church the previous day, maybe two thirds of the breakfasters, had a comment to make about Lainie's first solo.

The front door opened as Lainie walked past, and Lurlene came in. She grabbed Lainie in a hug. "I'm not staying, but I just wanted to run by and tell you how proud I am of you. I had company coming for lunch yesterday, so I couldn't stay till you were through talking to Juanita. She wasn't giving you a hard time, was she?"

Lainie shook her head.

"Well, good. But I want you to sing again next Sunday. Just the third verse of 'Silent Night,' which we're doing as the offertory. Think you can manage that?"

"No!" Lainie didn't hesitate, but Lurlene didn't seem to hear her.

"Good. I'll count on you then." She headed out the door, holding it open for Manny and Patsy Baca as they arrived with their family. "The best thing you can do is get right back on that horse."

Manny, with a twin on each arm, smiled his thanks. Patsy followed, holding Manuelito's carrier in both hands.

"Well, look who's here." Fayette stopped on her way to the kitchen to pat the chubby cheek of the little girl closest to her. "What are you all up to?"

"See Santa." Faith still held the remnants of a candy cane in her sticky fist.

Grace, whose thick black lashes were still wet, puckered up. "Bad man."

"No, honey. Santa isn't a bad man. We like Santa." Patsy sighed and looked up at Fayette as she set the carrier down on the seat of the largest booth and dug for a tissue to wipe Grace's nose. "A creepy guy from California stopped by the station last week and scared her. She's been leery of strange men since. Poor Santa didn't know what hit him."

"The guy had a lot of tattoos and some scars, but that doesn't make him creepy." Manny took the saltshaker away from Faith.

Patsy looked at him like he had sprouted antlers. "He touched our kids! He got right down in Lito's face and pretended to box with him. And he picked Grace up and asked her to be his girlfriend. That's beyond creepy in my book."

Manny rolled his eyes. "He said he was sorry for scaring Grace. He felt really bad."

"And I didn't like all those questions either." Patsy pulled out a baby wipe and scrubbed at Faith's sticky fingers.

"What kind of questions?" Lainie tried to keep her voice from shaking as she put the menus on the table.

"Nothing much, just small talk." Manny set the menu aside. "I'll have the special."

"He wanted to know how big Last Chance was, how long we'd lived here, if everyone was pretty much a native or if new people ever came to town. Why should he care?"

"He didn't. He made friendly conversation while he filled his tank, and then he drove on out of town. Happens all the time. You're just not usually there."

"I still say he was creepy." Patsy poured the milk Fayette brought into a sippy cup and handed it to Grace.

Grace held the cup in both hands and tipped her head back to drink it as Patsy pulled her onto her lap and cuddled her.

Lainie hoped no one noticed her hand trembling as she put the order on the rack. She walked through the kitchen and out the back door. The brisk air cooled her face as she sat on the top step. She took a deep breath. On the plus side, this happened last week and the creepy guy filled his tank and drove on out of town. He could be a thousand miles away by now. On the minus side, if the creepy guy *was* Nick, he had found her, even if he didn't know it yet. Maybe she could stay through Christmas, but then she was going to have to leave.

—⁂—

Lainie had her coat on and was ready to head home for the day when Steven came in.

"Hey! Glad I caught you before you left. I was driving by and thought this was about the time you got off. Want a ride?"

"I'd love one. It's been a long day. You've got perfect timing."

She waved at Fayette, who was answering the phone, and was headed out the door that Steven was holding open for her when Fayette called her.

"It's Ray." She held out the phone.

Lainie hesitated before she went back inside and took the receiver. "Yes?"

"Good! You're still there. Can you stop by? Maybe for another cup of my world-famous cocoa to warm you up for your walk home? I didn't get a chance to talk to you after church yesterday."

"I noticed." Funny. Yesterday she had been so hurt thinking Ray didn't care enough to stay. Now it just made it easier to leave. "But I need to get on home and Steven is here to drive me."

A long pause followed. "Are you mad?"

"Mad? Should I be?" Lainie could see Fayette and Carlos pretending they weren't listening. Steven had gone outside and was waiting in Elizabeth's truck.

"I don't know. You sure sound mad."

Lainie closed her eyes and gripped the phone. Maybe this would be a way to end it now. "You sure were in a big hurry yesterday.

You didn't even stay long enough to tell me how bad I was. What? Couldn't you face me?" Carlos slammed out the back door, came back in just long enough to grab his jacket, and slammed out again.

"What do you mean? You were great."

"Really? Did you even stay long enough to hear me?"

"Of course I heard you, even though the mic wasn't working all that well. You were really good."

"Right. Bye." Lainie hung up and stuck her head out the back door. Carlos was sitting on the back step hunched into his jacket. "All clear. You can come in now."

Steven reached across the cab and swung the passenger door open when Lainie walked out of the Dip 'n' Dine. He winced when she slammed the door but didn't offer a comment. He cleared his throat a block or so from home and broke the icy silence.

"So, looks like my brother really must have messed up this time." Lainie didn't say anything. Steven tried again.

"Look, I'm not trying to get in your business, but I know him pretty well, you know. Maybe I can help."

Lainie took a deep breath or two. Thinking about leaving had never been this hard. She shook her head. "I doubt it."

Elizabeth stuck her head out of the kitchen when the front door opened. "Good! I'm just about ready to put dinner on the table."

The kitchen was warm and fragrant with baking cornbread. Steam fogged the window. Elizabeth seated herself and clasped hands with Steven and Lainie. After she finished praying, Lainie held Elizabeth's hand for an extra moment. Elizabeth smiled at her and then looked closer.

"Lainie, honey, what's the matter? Are you okay?"

Lainie swallowed the lump that had risen in her throat. "I'm fine. Just thinking how much I've loved being here with you."

"Well, gracious, Lainie, I've loved having you here too." She smiled and picked up a bowl of mashed potatoes to pass. "Did Rita ever get ahold of you, Steven?"

"What now?"

"Well, you know she's been planning this parade since she heard you were coming home. And then when you came home on Thanksgiving, that just threw her into a tizzy, because the Christmas parade is a week from Saturday."

"Yeah, we talked about that when we met for breakfast."

"Well, she's got it all worked out now. She wants you to be the grand marshal of the Christmas parade. And between you and me, I think that's a perfect solution. You'll be riding in Manny Baca's convertible with the homecoming queen."

"Ever ride in a parade?" Steven grinned at Lainie. "Want to sit with me? We can tell Rita we don't need the homecoming queen."

"I think you'd better go with the program, Steven. Rita's been working on this for months, and anyway, I have no intention of riding in any parade. You're on your own in this one."

Steven shrugged. "Suit yourself, but riding in a parade with a genuine hero could raise your social standing around here."

Elizabeth's frown deepened. "Steven, I'm not sure I like this attitude of yours. Nobody has to lift one finger to welcome you home, you know. Everything that's being done is being done because people were worried about you and are thankful you made it home safely."

"Oh, come on, Gran, you know I was just kidding. It just seems like an awful lot of fuss, that's all. But I'll go through with it if it means that much to everybody. Homecoming queen and everything."

If his grandmother even noticed Steven's knock-your-socks-off smile, she gave no indication of it. "I just wish you could show a little gratitude, that's all."

Steven stopped talking altogether after that, and Elizabeth said very little. Lainie was relieved when the meal was finally over and Elizabeth left the kitchen for the living room and her television shows.

Lainie picked up an armload of dishes and carried them to the counter. Steven was already tossing dishes into the sink. "Whoa. Those things break, you know."

Steven didn't look up. "I know. But she really"—he glanced toward the living room and lowered his voice before continuing—"ticks me off sometimes. You'd think I was, like, twelve and needed to be reminded to mind my manners. I didn't ask for this parade. And if I was asked, I would have said 'no thanks.' I mean, who needs it? Who even needs this two-bit town, anyway?"

"Well, since you've got a business to run here, I'd say you do. And from a purely practical point of view, at least pretending this means something could build up a lot of goodwill."

"Right. You want to wash or dry?"

They finished the dishes saying little more than was needed to carry out their tasks. Steven worked with such concentration that Lainie could practically hear the wheels turning in his head. When she finally pulled the plug from the sink and he gave the dish towel a final snap and hung it to dry, the self-mocking grin had returned.

"I need to run over and see Ray. Want to come? Or are you still mad?"

"No, I'm not mad, but I guess I do need to talk to Ray. What about you?"

"Nah, I'm good. I just let Gran get to me, that's all. She just knows how to push my buttons."

"Really? I've never thought of Elizabeth as being much of a button pusher."

Steven leaned in, and Lainie felt his breath on her neck as he whispered in her ear. "She didn't raise you. Believe me, she's the queen of button pushers."

19

The bar was nearly empty when Steven and Lainie walked in. The only occupants were a couple of younger men huddled over their beers in one of the booths. When they saw Steven, one got up and approached him with a wide grin and an outstretched hand.

"Well, look what the wind blew in." He grabbed Steven's hand. "Heard you were home. Come join us. We'd be more'n honored if you'd let us buy you a beer, you and your pretty girl both."

"Thanks." Steven returned the smile. "I'd be pleased to join you. I don't know about the pretty girl, though. She's not my girl, sorry to say."

"Oh?" Both men looked at Lainie with renewed interest. "Offer still holds if you'd care to join us."

Lainie shook her head. "Thanks, but no." She climbed on a bar stool and nearly laughed at the apprehension in Ray's expression. "Relax. I'm not going to kill you."

"That's a relief. So just exactly what is it that I need to apologize for? Whatever it is, I'm sorry."

"Oh, I don't know. It's been a really bad couple of days. I messed up that solo so bad. Everyone was telling me I did just fine and it all sounded so phony. I guess I was counting on you to, I don't know, make me believe I was okay—even when I knew I wasn't.

171

Then when you couldn't even face me . . ." Her words dwindled into silence.

"It wasn't about facing you. It was about facing everyone else. I told you how weird I felt going to church after being in here until 2:00 in the morning. I'll be back one day. I'm really looking forward to it. But I just couldn't do the prodigal son routine. Not yet."

"So where'd you take off to so fast?

"I needed to get to my cabin. I'm working on a special piece right now, and all I could think about was that I'd missed half a day already."

Lainie's smile was sad. "You're really anxious to get back to your work, aren't you?"

"Yeah, I guess I am. I'd sort of pushed that part of my life to a place where I wouldn't have to think about it, but now that Steven's home, that's hard to do."

Lainie fell silent. She watched Steven, lost in animated conversation across the room, until she felt Ray's hand cover hers.

"Wish I knew what you were thinking."

"I don't know, Ray. Who knows what the new year holds? You might be leaving. I might be leaving too." There. She'd said it.

Ray picked up her hand and held it against his face. "I don't want to think about that now. You're right. We don't know what the new year will bring, so let's not waste the time we have now. Can't we keep taking things one day at a time? When the time comes, we'll know what to do."

Lainie looked away. She should tell him no. This was a recipe for heartbreak, and she needed to end things now.

"Well? What do you say?" Ray's smile was tender when she looked back, and his warm brown eyes caught her in their gaze and held her there.

Her voice came as barely a whisper. "One day at a time."

Steven sauntered up and broke the moment. "Remember Tito and Phil, Ray? I played football with them in high school." He turned to Lainie. "We were undefeated for eighty-four games straight. There were kids who entered high school as freshmen and who graduated four years later without ever seeing us lose a game. They even wrote about us in *Time* magazine. True, we were single-A, but so was everyone else we played. Man, it doesn't seem like it could be that long ago." He leaned against the bar and shook his head. "I remember one time when Tito, Phil, me, and someone else, maybe Manny, went to Juarez . . . How we kept from winding up in jail, I'll never know." He laughed. "Those were some good times."

Ray smiled. "You were something, all right. I don't know how you made it out of high school. If there was a party anywhere within thirty miles, you were in the middle of it."

"Well, somebody had to uphold the Braden reputation in these parts after Dad quit rodeoing." Steven clapped his brother on the shoulder. "You sure weren't doing it. I think you were born old."

Ray glanced away. "Maybe so. There just never seemed to be time to get into trouble. Too much to do."

"Ah, I'm just giving you a hard time." Steven looked at Lainie. "If you want to know the truth, I couldn't be prouder of my big brother. He's always known just what he wanted and gone after it with everything he had in him. And he's made a success of it too. Look at this place. How he keeps it going is more than I know."

"Well, bro, I can show you anytime you're ready."

"You got it." Steven slapped the bar. "Just let me know when you have some time."

Ray looked out the front window. An eighteen-wheeler was rumbling through town, but other than that, the streets were empty. "What about right now? It's a pretty quiet night. We could at least get started."

173

"Hey, why not?" Steven sounded enthusiastic. "Let's get going on this thing." He stopped as if he noticed Lainie for the first time. "Oh, but what about Lainie? I really should get her home first. We can't very well leave her sitting here doing nothing."

"It's okay, really. I'll just sit and listen to the music. It feels good to get off my feet."

"No way, I don't know what I was thinking. Ray, we'll just have to do this another time. I need to get Lainie home. She put in a full day."

Lainie felt a flare of anger. "Are you even listening to me? I don't need you looking out for me. You go on ahead with Ray. If I get all that tired, I'll just take the truck and you can walk home."

Steven looked from Lainie to Ray. Both just stared back. He shrugged and grinned. "Okay, then, let's do 'er. Just trying to be a good guy, but suit yourself."

"Well then," Ray said, "I guess the first thing we need to do is get you on the schedule. How many days a week do you want to start with?"

Ray led the way into his office while Lainie made herself comfortable in a booth. She slouched down, stretched her legs to rest her feet on the bench opposite, and cradled a mug of coffee in her hands. She shook her head as she gazed into the dark, steaming brew. How did she come to be sitting in a perfectly good bar drinking coffee? She must be hanging out with the wrong crowd—a crowd it was going to break her heart to leave. Through the open door to Ray's office she could see his brow furrow in concentration as he consulted his computer screen. Steven leaned both arms on the desk and stared into space. When he caught Lainie watching, he rolled his eyes and gave her a wink. Lainie looked away. It was becoming increasingly clear to her, if not yet to Ray, that any enthusiasm for Steven's taking over the bar was all on Ray's part. Steven was a runner. She knew the signs too well.

The breakfast crowd came in two bunches the morning of the Last Chance Christmas parade. The doors hadn't been unlocked ten minutes before the first carload of marching band members poured through the door. And by the time the early morning sun broke over the mesas east of town, every booth and table was full of paraders, parents, and sponsors. Lainie, Fayette, and Monica—one of Carlos's nieces brought in to help with the expected crowd—ran from table to table delivering plates of pancakes and platters of ham and eggs. The din grew louder as tables of diners fought to be heard over the next booth until the walls themselves seemed to throb. Finally, a shrill whistle split the noise and attention turned to the bandleader standing at the door.

"Okay, everyone, five minutes. Pay your tabs and be at the parade grounds in fifteen minutes, tops. Demerits for anyone who's late."

Junior rodeo riders and 4-H members took the cue as well, and within ten minutes the diner was empty.

"Well, that takes care of it till after the parade." Fayette handed busing bins to Monica and Lainie. "We have an hour, if we're lucky, before this place fills up again."

Lainie started piling dirty dishes into her bin. "Who's left? I'd have guessed everyone in town has already been in."

"Nope. Those were just the kids. Everyone else will be in after the parade before they head up to San Ramon to start their Christmas shopping."

Lainie grinned at Fayette. "Sounds like you've got this all worked out."

"Honey," Fayette said as she hoisted her bin and headed to the kitchen, "some things never change—the sun, the seasons, and the Last Chance Christmas parade."

Half an hour later, the dining room was spotless and Lainie poured herself a cup of coffee and slid into a booth by the window. The sun that poured through warmed her, even though outside the occasional passerby was bundled against a biting wind. Off in the distance, she could hear the muffled sounds of "Jingle Bells" being played by a marching band. She smiled and cradled her cup in her hands. The one thing she had always been able to count on in her life was that she couldn't count on anything. It felt good to be someplace, even for a while, where a Christmas parade was as constant as the sun and the seasons.

Sunday morning, as Lainie met with the choir in the adult Sunday school room before the service, she tried hard to focus on the music and not on the panic that was trying its best to swallow her whole. In a few minutes she was going to be standing in front of the church singing another solo. Everyone told her that she only had to sing her first solo once, and it was behind her. But the rapidly approaching second solo was even more terrifying than the first.

"Okay, people, listen up." Lurlene tapped the black lectern with a pencil. We've only got a couple minutes. I heard from the Christmas Eve Festival folks in San Ramon and we've got the 7:00 to 7:20 slot. So be there by 6:30 at the absolute latest, okay? We can work up some car pools if you want to. Any questions?"

When the choir filed into the sanctuary, Lainie was surprised to find the stampeding butterflies in her stomach had settled down a bit. Lurlene had closed the brief rehearsal with prayer and specifically asked for peace and confidence for Lainie. To Lainie's even greater surprise, Juanita had taken her hand and held it all during the prayer, giving it a warm squeeze and echoing Lurlene's "amen."

The church was full, and Lainie read warm encouragement in

every familiar face. Steven sat next to Elizabeth, and if his mocking grin tried to engage Lainie in a private joke, it was lost in the outright love emanating from Elizabeth's warm smile.

Just as the ushers began their procession to the front of the church to take the offering, the back door opened and Ray slipped in and sat in the back pew.

The offertory was simple: two verses of "Silent Night" sung by the choir, Lainie's solo on the third verse, and the congregation joining in on the fourth to fill the small sanctuary with the joyful celebration of the Savior's birth. Instead of being tied in knots over the seconds ticking toward her solo, Lainie found herself enveloped by the beauty of the simple words, and when Lurlene turned to her with a nod, Lainie opened her mouth and sang.

The notes were pure and sweet and filled every corner of the small wooden building, and as the third verse came to a close and Lurlene turned to raise the congregation to its feet, Lainie saw Elizabeth and a few others as well dabbing their eyes. In the very back, Ray stood with the others, and for a moment Lainie thought he might be going to stay. But he stepped to the door, gave her a wide smile, brought his index finger and thumb together in a sign of perfection, and silently slipped outside.

20

Ray came by just at dusk Christmas Eve to pick up Lainie and Elizabeth, and on the way to San Ramon, the orange and crimson sunset faded to purple and the first stars tentatively appeared in the growing twilight.

Elizabeth peered up through the windshield into the darkening sky. "This is the time I used to watch for when I was a little girl—the moment when it was really, truly, Christmas Eve."

"Seem weird not being at the ranch Christmas Eve?" Ray pulled off the highway at the San Ramon exit and joined the line of traffic snaking toward the town plaza.

"A little, maybe. But I've always wanted to see the San Ramon Plaza all lit up too, and with Lainie singing with the choir this year, well, here's my chance." She smiled at Lainie sitting between her and Ray.

"And here we are." Ray turned a corner that brought them onto the plaza.

Lainie stared at the soft glow that surrounded them. Every path, every curb, every rooftop was lined with thousands of softly glowing brown paper bags.

"I'll let you ladies out and go find a place to park. Meet you inside." Ray stopped the truck in front of a restaurant and came around to help Elizabeth climb down.

The plaza was already filled with families and couples strolling the paths between the luminarias, their hands stuffed in their pockets and their collars turned against the evening chill. A mariachi band was playing "Feliz Navidad" in the gazebo in the center of the plaza.

The warm, spicy aroma of chile drew them into the cheerful clamor of the busy restaurant, and Elizabeth waved as she followed the hostess across the red tiled floors to a table set before the kiva fireplace. "Oh, look. There's Juanita and Russ and the Montoyas. Looks like they had the same idea we did."

Lainie was rereading the menu when Ray pulled out his chair and joined them. She looked up with a confused expression. "Do you all even eat chile and stuff on Christmas Eve?"

"What do you mean, even on Christmas Eve? Especially on Christmas Eve is more like it. Why, what do you have on Christmas Eve in California?"

Lainie tried to remember. "I don't know. It depends, I guess. There was usually a party somewhere, so we had chips and some kind of platter from the grocery store."

Ray shook his head. "Trust me. This is better."

They were nearly finished with their meal when Juanita stopped by on the way out the door. Russ was still at their table counting his change.

"Merry Christmas, you all!" She finished tugging on her gloves and pulled her knit cap from her coat pocket. "What happened to Fayette? She get held up at home?"

"I never heard anything from Fayette. Was I supposed to? She's riding up to the ranch with us tomorrow morning, but we didn't talk about Christmas Eve."

"Russ and I asked her and Matthew to have dinner with us up here, but since we had to do some last-minute shopping in San

Ramon this afternoon, she said she'd meet us. We haven't seen her, so I thought maybe you knew if something had come up."

Ray rolled his eyes and pulled his cell phone out of his pocket. "Great invention, ladies. You ought to give it a try." Elizabeth and Juanita watched as he punched in the numbers. "Fayette? Hey, everything okay? Here's Juanita."

He handed the phone to Juanita, who muttered, "I hate these things," before she smiled into the room and raised her voice so that people sitting across the room turned to see what was going on. "Fayette? Are you okay? We're worried about you."

They all watched her shake her head and tsk, and when her brow furrowed, so did Elizabeth's. "Oh, honey, I'm sure he's just lost track of the time. I'm just sorry you had to miss the music. But listen, we'll be done singing in the plaza at 7:20. Russ and I will stop by here and pick up your Christmas Eve dinner and have it to you before it even cools off."

They could hear Fayette's tinny protest, but Juanita would not be dissuaded. "No, this is one night you are not going to cook. Now, what can we bring you? Mmm-hmm. And Matthew? Okay, see you around 8:00. Now you take care and stop worrying.

"Here, I don't know how to turn this thing off." She handed the phone back to Ray. "That boy! He'd better get himself turned around and right quick."

"So he's not home?" Elizabeth's face was a mask of concern.

"No, she hasn't seen him since three this afternoon when he promised he'd be home no later than five. You'd think on Christmas Eve, of all nights, he'd show a little consideration for his mama. After all she's been through . . ." Her voice trailed off and the table fell silent for a moment. Juanita shook her head and puffed a loud sigh. "Well, I'd better go get that order in so we can pick it up after we sing."

180

"Wait, Juanita. Can I ride back with you?" Elizabeth called after Juanita. "I don't want to rush Ray and Lainie."

Lainie dropped her hand to Elizabeth's shoulder. "I think you just want to go check on Fayette."

Elizabeth reached up and patted her hand. "Well, Christmas Eve is never easy on her, and she should not have to sit there alone wondering where her boy is."

At 7:00, when the handbell choir from San Ramon Methodist Church filed out of the gazebo in the plaza and the choir from the Church of Last Chance filed in, Lainie couldn't tell if her shivering was due to nerves or the cold. She could see Ray bend down to say something to two young men sprawled on a park bench in front of the gazebo, watched him clap one on the shoulder and shake the other's hand when they got up to make room for Elizabeth, and then her attention was drawn to Lurlene standing just down the steps with hands and eyebrows raised. The choir drew a collective breath, and the plaza was filled with the sounds of "Angels We Have Heard on High."

The concert was over almost before Lainie knew it began. Ray and Elizabeth stood at the foot of the stairs, and Ray swept her into a hug.

"That was amazing! Fantastic!"

Elizabeth blew her nose on the hankie she held clutched in her hand. "Lainie, honey, I don't think I've ever heard the third verse of 'Silent Night' sung so beautifully. You have a God-given gift in that voice, young lady. I hope you know that."

Lainie tried to think of something to say. She felt shaky, and exhilarated, and happier than she could remember having felt in a long time.

"You did real fine, Lainie. We're all proud of you." Juanita appeared at Lainie's side and gave her shoulders a squeeze. Her smile was actually warm and relaxed. "Are you ready to go, Elizabeth? Russ has gone to pick up Fayette's dinner, so we can go on and wait in the truck if you want."

"Here, let me see you to your truck, ladies." Ray offered his arm to his grandmother.

"No, that's not a bit necessary." Juanita grabbed Elizabeth's hand and tucked it in her own elbow. "The truck's right over there. You two go on and enjoy yourselves."

Ray jammed his hands in his pockets and watched the two ladies make their careful way through the glow of the luminaria-lined path to the pickup parked on the curb. He took a half step toward them as he watched Elizabeth struggle to hoist herself into the cab. But she settled herself before he could take more than a step, and he stopped and shook his head. "These ranch women . . . stay out of their way or get run down."

He turned to Lainie with a smile and held out his hand. "We've been ordered to have a good time. Shall we get started?"

Lainie found herself humming another Christmas song as they joined the others wandering the plaza. Her hand felt like it belonged in Ray's. Walking next to him, occasionally bumping shoulders, not saying much, filled her with a warmth that could stay the coldest night. Overhead the stars faded in the warm glow of thousands of candles tucked into their small brown bags. Who could imagine that such heart-stopping beauty could result from something so simple, so homely?

They stopped in the shadow of an old church still standing where it had been built with handmade adobe bricks two hundred years earlier. Ray dropped her hand and took her face in both his warm hands.

"Your face is cold."

Lainie looked up at him. "Really? It doesn't feel . . ."

But Ray wasn't listening. He bent his head and she closed her eyes as he gently drew her face to his. From the gazebo a choir sang, *Gloria!*

—⁓—

It was nearly midnight when Ray walked Lainie to Elizabeth's front door. The music was long over, the stores had all closed, and they had been two of the last to leave the plaza. Only as the luminarias began to burn out one by one could they admit that the evening had come to a close.

"Want to come in for some coffee or something?"

Ray shook his head. "Better not. Gran has ears that can pick up a gnat's sneeze. You wait. You won't be five steps in the house before you hear those fuzzy slippers of hers coming down the hall. She'd just send me home anyway. It's late."

"It's almost Christmas."

Ray looked at his watch. "Five more minutes." He put both arms around her waist and drew her to him. "Aren't you supposed to start Christmas Day off with a kiss?"

"I think that's New Year's Day." She smiled up at him.

"Let's start a new tradition." He brushed her lips with his.

From inside they could hear the phone ring and keep ringing.

"Who could that be? And why isn't Elizabeth answering it? She has a phone right by her bed." Lainie grabbed the door handle and ran in. Ray followed.

"Hello?"

"Oh, you're home. Good. I was starting to get worried." Elizabeth didn't sound at all perturbed.

"Where are you?"

"I'm here at Fayette's. Matthew's still not home, and I didn't want her to wait alone. I just wanted to make sure you got home all right and to tell you where I am."

"Shall I come over too?"

"Oh, no, honey, you go on to bed. I'm sure Matthew will be here soon and Fayette will drive me home."

"You're sure?"

"I'm sure. Goodnight, darlin'. I'll be home soon. Don't wait up."

Lainie hung up and explained the situation to Ray.

Ray scowled. "That jerk. I wish I knew where he was. I'd boot him all the way home."

"Oh, come on. He's sixteen. Doesn't making bad decisions come with the territory?"

"There's more to it than making a bad decision. Either he's the most clueless kid to ever walk on two legs or he's being deliberately cruel to his mom."

"Cruel? What are you talking about? He may be clueless, but he's not cruel and you know it."

Ray tried to smile, but his jaw muscles still looked tight. "Maybe you're right. I hope so, but if he even gave a thought to his mom, he'd know what she'd be going through." He stared at the floor a moment before looking at Lainie. "You know his dad was killed on Christmas Eve, right?"

"No! I knew he died, but no details."

"Yeah, it happened up by Flagstaff when Matthew was about five. Bud Hall was a long-distance trucker, and he stopped to help a stranded motorist. On his way back to his truck, another car skidded on the ice and hit him. He was supposed to be home by Christmas morning, and Fayette waited up for him, like she's waiting for Matthew right now."

Lainie's hand flew to her mouth. "Poor Fayette. No wonder she gets so worried."

"Well, now you know why I'd like to wring his neck sometimes." He jammed his hat on his head. "Call me when you hear something, will you?"

184

Lainie followed him to the front door, and when he turned, a gentle smile replaced his scowl. "It was an amazing Christmas Eve, Matthew and all." He brushed a strand of hair from her face. "I'll be by to pick you all up at about 9:30. Merry Christmas."

Lainie locked the door and walked slowly back to her room, leaving a small lamp in the living room on for Elizabeth when she came in. Steven had gone to the ranch earlier in the afternoon, and even Sam the cat was nowhere to be seen. After Lainie got ready for bed, she turned out the light and leaned her elbows on the windowsill. The sky over Last Chance was nearly white with stars. She tried to imagine what it would be like to be sitting on a hill watching sheep with a sky like that and then have everything split wide open with a huge star and angels and everything. No wonder the first words out of the angel's mouth were "Fear not." If she'd been there, she'd have passed out cold.

She turned back the homemade quilt and climbed into bed. Even if she'd be gone by the first of the year, tomorrow they'd have Christmas at the ranch—a big family Christmas like the ones in all the Christmas specials on television. She knew there'd be something under the tree for her. Elizabeth had all but thrown herself over a present she was wrapping when Lainie came home early one day last week, and Ray and even Fayette had acted smug and mysterious when the subject of Christmas Day came up. But even more exciting were the gifts she had for everyone else. She and Ray had gone Christmas shopping in San Ramon one Saturday afternoon on a rare day off, and her carefully chosen gifts were wrapped and tucked away in her closet to take to the ranch in the morning. She knew if she let herself think beyond tomorrow her heart would break, so she closed her eyes and let visions of a candlelit plaza lift her into quiet sleep.

21

Lainie gradually became aware of a shrill ringing. Slapping at the snooze button on the clock radio didn't make it stop. The time 2:32 blurred into focus. Why was it ringing at 2:32? The phone. It was the phone. Lainie opened her bedroom door and ran to the kitchen, dimly lit by the lamp she had left on in the living room for Elizabeth.

"Lainie? Matthew's been in an accident. They're taking him to San Ramon and I need you to come drive us to the hospital."

"An accident? Is he okay?" Lainie leaned against the counter, trying to wake up enough to understand what was going on.

"We don't know and we don't have time to talk. I can't drive at night and Fayette's not driving off in the state she's in if I can help it, but I'm only going to be able to keep her here for about five more minutes. Get over here as fast as you can."

"But wait . . ."

"Lainie! Now!" Elizabeth slammed the phone down, and Lainie stared at the receiver for only a second before she bolted down the hall to her bedroom. Wide awake now, she jammed her legs into her jeans and yanked a sweatshirt over her head. If Elizabeth, usually the voice of comforting calm, was yelling, it was time to move.

Fayette and Elizabeth were waiting in the drive of Fayette's mobile home, and Lainie barely brought the pickup to a stop before Fayette jumped in. Elizabeth climbed in after her.

"Go! Go!" Fayette pushed her hands against the dashboard as if she could propel the truck by sheer will. Lainie stepped on the gas, and the truck careened out onto the road.

"Lainie, take it easy." Elizabeth's voice had regained its calm. "It won't help Matthew one bit if we're in a wreck too. Fayette, we're going to get you there. Ben said that Matthew's on his way to the hospital right now. What we need to do now is pray."

Her gentle voice filled the cab of the truck as she prayed for Matthew, for the other boys who had been with him, for Fayette, for the doctors, even for Lainie and her driving. Gradually, Fayette's breathing slowed, if only by a little, and she loosened her death grip on the dashboard.

She leaned forward again as blue flashing lights appeared ahead on the dark two-lane highway and put her hand to her mouth with a low moan when they passed the mangled wreck being loaded onto a tow truck. Elizabeth continued her praying.

Fayette nearly knocked Elizabeth out of the cab trying to get out when Lainie pulled up at the emergency entrance of the hospital, but Elizabeth managed to get out of the way in time and followed Fayette through glass doors into the emergency room. When Lainie joined them, Fayette was demanding to see Matthew, and the nurses were telling her that she'd have to wait.

"They're already taking him into surgery, Mrs. Hall. The faster we can get him in there, the better his chances are. Just have a seat and the doctor will come talk to you just as soon as he knows something."

"Come over here and sit down, Fayette." Deputy Ben Apodaca, who had been waiting just inside, tried to lead her to a chair, but Fayette grabbed his arm.

"Ben, what happened? Is he going to be okay?"

The deputy took Fayette's elbow and steered her to a quiet corner of the nearly empty waiting room. He seated her, then sat in the chair next to hers and leaned close. Elizabeth and Lainie took chairs on her other side.

Ben took a deep breath. "I won't lie to you, Fayette. Matthew is in pretty bad shape. But I happened by the accident just after it happened, so we got him here just as fast as we could and he's in good hands."

"But what happened?" Fayette's voice rose to a wail.

"There was only one vehicle involved. From the tire marks, it looks like they may have been speeding and missed the curve."

"Who else was in the car?"

"There were three boys. Matthew was in the backseat."

"And the other boys? How are they?" Elizabeth asked.

Ben stood. He looked grim. "I can't talk about the other boys until I've talked to their parents. They're on their way, and I guess I should go out and wait for them. " He settled his hat on his head, touched Fayette's shoulder, and walked back out through the double doors to wait in the drive.

Silence fell in the waiting area. The room was bathed in harsh, greenish fluorescent light, making even the Christmas tree in the corner look sad.

Outside, a car screeched to a stop under the awning and a couple scrambled out. Ben stepped to meet them and led them into the emergency room through a side entrance. Fayette jumped to her feet.

"Why do they get to go in and not me?" She crossed to the nurses' station. "I want to see my son. Why won't you let me see him?"

The nurse came around the desk and put her arm around Fayette's shoulder. "Mrs. Hall, Matthew is in surgery right now. I assure you he is getting absolutely the best care he can get. Meanwhile, can I get you a cup of coffee?"

"No, I don't want any coffee. I want to see my son!" Fayette's voice broke, and she covered her face with her hands. Sobs shook her shoulders.

Elizabeth got up and put her arms around Fayette, rubbing her back for a few seconds before leading her back to her chair. "Come on, honey. We might as well get comfortable because I think we have a long night ahead of us. That coffee might do you some good. Lainie, would you get a couple cups for us, please?"

Lainie went to the cart parked by the door and drew three cups of pitch black brew. The powdered creamer she added lightened it somewhat, but not much. Fayette didn't seem to notice when Lainie handed her a cup. She set it down without looking at it. Elizabeth took one sip and screwed up her face. "Mercy!"

The third family showed up and was ushered into the emergency room right away. Fayette nearly came out of her chair again, but Elizabeth placed a hand on her arm.

"Fayette, they've told you Matthew's in surgery and they'll let you know the minute they know anything. Now you sit here with me and we'll pray for Matthew. That's the best and only thing we can do right now." To Lainie's surprise, Fayette did as she was told, using a soggy tissue to dab her eyes with one hand while Elizabeth held the other.

The eastern sky was beginning to lighten and they had still heard nothing when Elizabeth stood and stretched. "We need to call Brother Parker. I probably should have called him long ago. I just didn't think about it. And I'll bet Nancy Jo and Joe Jr. are up, so we should call them." She looked around. "I wonder if there's a pay phone somewhere."

Lainie jumped to her feet. She was more than ready to do something. "I'll go. I need to call Ray too."

Elizabeth pulled a tattered yellow address book, held shut with a rubber band, out of her purse and handed it to Lainie. "Thanks, honey. The phone numbers are in there. And tell Nancy Jo and Joe Jr. not to wait on us. Those children have been counting the minutes till Christmas morning."

The squeaking of Lainie's sneakers on the highly polished floors was the only sound in the early morning hospital corridor, though the smell of breakfast being brought on trays already wafted through the halls. She found the phone bank near the lobby. The folks at the ranch were already up, just as Elizabeth said. Lainie promised she'd stay in touch. Next she called Brother Parker, who said he'd get the prayer chain going and be right there. Then she took a deep breath and dialed Ray's number. He answered on the first ring.

"Well, you're up early." Lainie felt calmer just hearing the sound of his voice.

"Hey there. Merry Christmas! Yeah, I'm trying to get something finished before I come pick you and Gran up. What's the word with Matthew?"

Lainie began to tell him of their night at the hospital. She only got a few words spoken before he was interrupting her.

"Why didn't you call me before?"

"There wasn't time before we left, then we've been waiting for something to be able to tell people. I guess we didn't know what good it would do to wake everybody up."

"What good would it do? I could have been with you. I could have been there for Fayette and Gran. Well, I'm on my way now. Should be there within the hour."

Lainie hung up and leaned against the wall. Ray was on the way. Until he said he was coming, she'd had no idea how much she needed him to be there.

The waiting room was empty when she returned. Fayette's untouched cup of cold coffee sat on the floor under the chair where she had been sitting.

The nurse looked up. "The doctor came in while you were gone and they've gone into the chapel to talk. They should be back pretty soon."

She went back to her charts, and Lainie slid into her chair and stretched her legs out in front of her. Her head fell against the narrow chair back, and she let her eyes drift shut. How long had they been waiting? It seemed only a few minutes since they had passed the wreck on the deserted road, and at the same time, she felt she had been sitting in that chair for days.

"Did you get in touch with the folks?" Elizabeth touched her arm.

Lainie didn't think she had dozed off, but she didn't remember Fayette and Elizabeth coming back in, and yet they were sitting in the chairs next to her. She straightened up in her chair and shook her head to clear it.

"Yeah, Ray and Brother Parker are on their way. How's Matthew?"

Fayette ignored her question and got up and paced the room, stopping to gaze out the glass doors. Elizabeth shook her head. Her voice was so low that Lainie had to lean close to hear her. "Not good. They're going to fly him up to Albuquerque as soon as they get him stabilized."

Lainie looked at Fayette, standing and staring out the doors as the first rays of Christmas morning topped the hills and found their way across the polished floors of the waiting room. "So she still hasn't seen him?

Elizabeth shook her head. "Not yet."

Brother Parker was the first to get to the hospital. He drove one of the few sedans in Last Chance, and when Lainie saw it pull into the parking lot and the tall, lanky frame of the pastor slowly emerge and amble toward the doors, she felt a knot between her shoulders loosen. His lined face was a picture of warm concern, and he took Fayette's hand in both of his.

"How's our boy?"

Fayette opened her mouth to answer, but nothing came out. She shook her head as her face contorted in pain and sobs shook her frame. Brother Parker put his arm lightly across her shoulders, bent his head to gaze into her face, and waited. Finally, Fayette took a deep, shuddering breath and tried again, and again she collapsed in tears. Elizabeth got up to join them. Lainie could see the pastor nodding slightly as Elizabeth talked, but her voice was too low to hear everything she said.

They were still huddled by the door when Ray's pickup careened to a stop outside. He burst through the doors looking like a wild man, and Lainie couldn't help wonder how well-dressed, slow-moving Brother Parker had managed to beat him to the hospital.

He stopped just inside the door, and Elizabeth started over with the story of Matthew's accident. Lainie got up and joined them.

Ray turned to Fayette. "So are you going to Albuquerque with Matthew?"

She nodded. "There's a place near the hospital where parents can stay, and they're checking to see if they have a room for me. I don't know how I'm going to do it, though, with the diner here and Matthew up there."

Lainie took a deep breath and silently prayed that Nick, if it had been Nick, had kept right on going. There was no way she could leave Last Chance now. Fayette needed to be with Matthew. "Carlos and I can manage just fine. You go ahead and stay as long as you need to."

"Are you sure?" Fayette looked as if she were being torn to pieces. Lainie made her voice strong, even though her knees felt like string. "You bet. The only thing you need to think about right now is Matthew and getting him well."

Fayette brushed back tears. "All right then, I'll go home and pack when he leaves for Albuquerque and drive up this afternoon."

"I'll drive you." Ray put his arm around her shoulders and squeezed. "You've been up all night, and we don't want you falling asleep at the wheel. We'll get you all settled in your new digs, then I'll take the bus back."

"But what about your place? I know you're closed for Christmas, but will you be back in time to open tomorrow?"

"You know, that bar is Steven's problem. I've only been holding it for him. If he wants to open it tomorrow, he can open it."

At that moment, the doors to the waiting room pushed open and a doctor in scrubs and a jacket came through.

"Mrs. Hall? We're getting ready to take off. Do you want to come in for a minute before we leave?"

Fayette nodded without speaking and followed him through the doors.

While Elizabeth and Bother Parker continued talking in low tones, Ray squeezed Lainie's hand and led her a chair. He dropped down beside her. "How are you holding up?"

Lainie sniffled and swiped the heel of her hand against her cheek as tears began streaming down her face. "I don't know what's the matter with me."

Ray pulled her head to his shoulder, and the warm scent of his neck soothed her almost as much as the gentleness of his hand stroking her hair. "It's been a rough night. Are you going to be okay driving back to Last Chance?"

Lainie closed her eyes and nodded yes against his coat. When she felt Ray straighten and move to stand up, she opened her eyes and saw the doctor usher Fayette back into the waiting room, still talking.

"I want you to get some rest before you leave for Albuquerque, understand? You're in no condition to drive."

"I'm driving her." Ray crossed the room and put his arm around Fayette's shoulder. "She can sleep on the way."

"Have you been here all night too?"

"Nope. I just got here."

The doctor nodded distractedly and turned to leave. "All right, then. See you in Albuquerque."

The door swung closed behind him, and Elizabeth touched Fayette's arm. "How is he?"

Fayette shook her head and fought to control her voice. "He's all bandages and tubes. If they hadn't told me it was Matthew . . ." Her voice broke and she took a deep breath. "They put him in an induced coma for the trip."

"Let's pray for Matthew and the doctors. And his mama." Brother Parker's smile was warm as he reached for the hands of Fayette and Elizabeth. Ray and Lainie completed the circle while the pastor prayed. At the amen, everyone took a collective breath.

"Okay, let's get going." Ray took charge and ushered the group toward the door. "I'll take you home to pack, Fayette, then I'll go throw a couple things in a duffle bag and come back for you."

"Now, you let us know the minute you know anything, you hear?" Tears sparkled in Elizabeth's eyes as she drew Fayette into a hug. "He's our boy too, you know."

Fayette nodded. "I will. And if you have any questions whatsoever about the diner, Lainie, you have my cell phone number. I don't know if I can use it in the hospital, but I'll call you back." She spoke over her shoulder as Ray led her out the hospital doors.

"Fayette, the pastor who took over my church in Albuquerque is a fine man. I'll give him a call and tell him you're on the way. If I know that congregation, and I do, you'll be well taken care

194

of." Brother Parker opened the passenger door of Ray's truck so Fayette could get in.

"Fayette, wait a minute." Les Watson stood by his battered truck a few spaces away. His hands were shoved in his jeans pockets. "The boy . . . Is he gonna be okay?"

"Don't know, Les. I'd appreciate your prayers, though." She started to climb into the cab of Ray's truck.

"Wait. Wait just a minute. I got to say something." He took a few hesitant steps closer, and they could see tear tracks down his weathered cheeks. "Fayette, I got to tell you. It's my fault those boys got in that crash. I could have stopped it, and I didn't. I know there's no way on God's green earth you could ever see your way to forgive me, but I got to tell you I would give my own life to go back to yesterday and do things different."

Fayette froze in midstep. "Your fault? How?"

"I seen those boys standing outside the liquor store in San Ramon yesterday afternoon. They was around the corner so the proprietor couldn't see them, but they give this old boy some money and he went in and bought them their booze. I should have gone on up and put a stop to it, but I just thought boys got to sow their wild oats. I did the same when I was their age."

Fayette's voice was a horrified whisper. "Did you buy them alcohol?"

"Oh, no ma'am! I'd never do any such of a thing. No, this was some old boy I never seen before."

"But you watched him give my son alcohol?"

Les nodded. He didn't meet her eyes.

"And you didn't do anything, not even call me?"

Les looked up. Agony tore at his features. "Fayette, you couldn't think any worse of me than I do of myself. I could kill myself right this minute—"

Fayette held up her hand to stop his outpouring of grief. "Don't say any more. I can't listen to you. I can't . . ." She got in the cab and slammed the door.

Ray put his hand on Les's shoulder. "This isn't the best time, Les, but I know it took a lot for you to come this morning." He looked as if he had more to say, but he just squeezed Les's shoulder and got behind the wheel. Fayette stared straight ahead as they drove out of the parking lot.

Elizabeth looked at Les and shook her head. "Oh, Les, what have you done?" She pulled the passenger door of her own pickup open, and for the first time, the step up proved too much for her. Lainie helped her climb in, and she leaned back against the seat and closed her eyes.

Lainie had to turn her eyes from the raw grief and hopeless despair in Les's face, but as she looked in the rearview mirror, she saw Brother Parker lead him back into the hospital, whether to the cafeteria or the chapel, she could only guess.

22

Elizabeth didn't speak or open her eyes for most of the way back to Last Chance. Lainie, glancing at her, was startled at how frail and small, even old she looked. No matter that she was eighty-six, "old" and "Elizabeth" didn't belong in the same sentence. She looked back toward the road. They were passing the spot where the accident took place. Nothing remained to show that lives had been changed, maybe even ended, but tire tracks leaving the road and disappearing into an arroyo ten yards from the road. Other than that, it could have been any morning. The sky was a heartbreaking blue, the hills facing the rising sun almost imperceptibly changing from rose to lilac.

"You know who I keep thinking about? Evelyn."

Lainie glanced at Elizabeth again. "I thought you were asleep."

Elizabeth shook her head. "No, just thinking. That poor woman goes around like a whipped pup as it is, and now this."

Lainie didn't speak for a few moments, then chose her words carefully. "You really think this is all Les's fault?"

It was Elizabeth's turn to let the highway disappear beneath them for a while before she sighed and answered. "No, not really. Maybe he could have stopped the boys from drinking yesterday. He surely should have tried. But when it comes down to it, choices we make—and that goes for Matthew as well as Les—are ultimately our own. I know no one could have tried harder than Fayette to raise that boy right. But she'll be beating on herself, wondering what she did wrong, what she could have done differently."

They passed the WELCOME TO LAST CHANCE sign, and Lainie slowed down as the highway became the main road through Last Chance. The road was completely deserted, and a cold wind made the silver garland and giant red bell on the street's one stoplight dance just as the rising sun made it sparkle. It should have looked festive, but Lainie thought it only looked lonely. She turned onto Elizabeth's street. "Ray told me about Fayette's husband dying on Christmas Eve."

"Yes. That's why I wanted to stay with her last night until Matthew came home." Elizabeth's voice broke off and her mouth worked as she tried to control her tears. "Then when the phone rang . . . oh my, I hope I never have to see another human being look like she looked." She groped in her purse for a tissue and blew her nose.

"It's lucky you were there."

Elizabeth lifted her arm as if it weighed fifty pounds and reached for the door handle. "You know better than that, Lainie. Luck had nothing to do with it."

—◠◠◠—

The Dip 'n' Dine was dark and looked oddly forlorn when Lainie arrived the next morning. No matter how early she had ever turned up for work, Fayette was always there ahead of her with the lights on and the big neon doughnuts in the window dipping their way into the neon coffee cup. Light filtering through the darkened dining room from the kitchen indicated that Carlos was already hard at work. Lainie took a deep breath and let herself in, relocking the door behind her.

"Hear anything from Fayette about Matthew?" Carlos looked up from the biscuits he was cutting.

"Not since yesterday."

"When you do talk to her, tell her not to worry. I've spent the last five years wondering why she hangs around my restaurant so much."

Lainie smiled. "I'll tell her, Carlos."

By the time the first car pulled up, the diner was beginning to feel like itself. The lights were on, the coffee was nearly done, and the room was almost warm enough for the heater to shut off. Lainie glanced at the clock. It was still a half hour before opening. Fayette always let early arrivals in, but Lainie hesitated. She had a lot left on her to-do list, but maybe they'd be okay with a cup of coffee until she was ready to open. Fayette wouldn't consider it a real help if she started out by alienating the regulars.

Juanita and Lurlene tapped on the window and waved. Lainie unlocked the front door and let them in. "What are you two doing up so early? Going shopping in San Ramon?"

Juanita took off her coat and rubbed her hands to warm them. "Good heavens, no. I am shopped out until at least Easter, maybe even till the Fourth of July. We're here to help."

"Help?"

"Sure. Well, of course, when Brother Parker started that prayer chain for Matthew yesterday morning, we all got to praying right away, and then when he called later to say that Fayette was going to Albuquerque with Matthew for who knows how long and you were going to try to run this place all by yourself, why, we just decided to give you a hand. How is Matthew, by the way? Have you heard?"

"Ray called when they got in last night. Matthew made the trip okay, but no update on his condition."

"Well, everyone in town is praying for him, and we figure if Carlos can bring in some help for the kitchen and the church can staff the dining room, we ought to be able to keep this place humming.

199

Rita's bringing a big jar for the counter so people can donate tips and whatnot. We don't know what Matthew might need when he gets home, but there's bound to be something."

Lurlene chimed in. "There'll be two of us here every day till Fayette gets back. Rita's organizing the sign-up sheet, and that girl can organize. Juanita and I drew the first shift because I don't have any family here for Christmas, and Juanita is just looking for an excuse to get away from hers."

"Well, I wouldn't put it that way, exactly, but they have been here since last week, and I could use a little break."

Lainie looked from one expectant face to the other. "I don't know. Does Fayette know about this?"

"No, and as far as I'm concerned she doesn't need to know, at least not right away. She's got enough on her plate." Juanita held up her coat. "Now, where do I hang this?"

Lainie must have still looked doubtful, because Juanita huffed in exasperation. "You think a farmer's wife doesn't know anything about serving meals? Lainie, I guarantee you, no matter how many cups of coffee you've poured, eggs you've dished up, or tables you've scrubbed, I've got you beat. Big-time."

"And it's been a few years, but I did waitressing when I was in college, so make the most of what you've been given, Lainie. You're the boss. Just tell us what to do."

By midmorning, Lainie had to admit to herself that she was thankful for the help. The diner had never been busier, and except for a tendency to stop and visit with the customers, Juanita and Lurlene were doing a great job.

Rita bustled in about 11:00 lugging a five-gallon jar and waving a yellow legal pad. "You got a minute, Lainie? I want to go over this schedule with you."

Lainie looked around the room. The breakfast rush was segueing into the lunch rush without a break, but at the moment everyone was taken care of. "Yeah, I guess I've got a minute. Not much more than that, though."

"Good." Rita set the jar by the cash register and looked around the room for a free table. Finding none, she slapped the legal pad on the counter and leaned on her elbows. "Okay, we've got two shifts a day to start with, six days a week. We'll keep the same schedule from week to week, with those who can't commit to a regular shift acting as subs." She lowered her voice to a confidential whisper. "A few of these folks aren't exactly what you'd call naturals in the hospitality industry, but I paired them with the more capable people, so it should work out."

Lainie looked over the penciled list and nodded. She didn't know what to say. Juanita and Lurlene had assured her that she was the boss, but apparently the news hadn't been transmitted to Rita.

Rita tapped the pad with her pencil and took a deep breath. "I'm still not sure about this pair, especially since Evelyn said she was too broke up to help out." The final names on the list were Brother Parker and Les Watson. "But Brother Parker insisted both he and Les wanted to come. And he wanted the late shift on Friday too." She glanced out the window at the still darkened High Lonesome and shrugged. "Well, we can give him a week if Brother Parker says so, but to be honest, I have my doubts. I'll stop by each shift to make sure everybody turned up like they said they would. And if they didn't, just leave it to me."

"Adam and Eve on a raft and blowout patches," Lurlene yelled through the window as she went for the coffeepot.

Carlos looked up from the stove in impatience. "What are you talking about?"

"Poached eggs on toast and pancakes. Isn't that how you say it?"

"Just put the order on the rack. That's all you need to do."

Lurlene did as she was told. "Well, you don't have to get snippy about it. I was just trying to speed things up."

Rita picked up her legal pad and patted the jar next to the cash register. "I need to get a catchy sign on that just as soon as I think one up. I thought about 'Money for Matthew,' but I don't know, I think I can do better than that." She smiled up at Lainie and squeezed her arm. "Don't you worry. You'll have your hands full, but you can do it. And I'll be just down the street at the motel if you need me."

It was after dark when the phone finally rang. The people of Last Chance liked to eat breakfast and lunch out but dinner at home, so there were only a couple tables occupied. The two church volunteers perched on stools at the end of the counter taking a coffee break. In the kitchen, Carlos's nephews were scrubbing pots and Carlos was doing prep work for the next day. Until she went to answer the phone, Lainie had no idea how tired she was. As she pushed through the swinging door to the kitchen, she simultaneously was struck with the realization that a day just like this one awaited her tomorrow, and the next day, and the next till Fayette got home, and the knowledge that this was Fayette's life—and had been for years. She shook her head in awe of her friend and picked up the phone.

"Dip 'n' Dine."

"Lainie? How's it going?"

"Fayette! I was just thinking about you. Everything's great here. How's Matthew?"

Through the window, Lainie could see that every eye in the restaurant was on her, and in the kitchen all activity had stopped. She heard Fayette draw a deep breath.

"It's still early, but they've given me reason to hope. He was awake for a little while this afternoon and he knew me."

"Well, everyone here is pulling for him." She cleared her throat. "Um, praying for him." The word felt at once strange in her mouth and right somehow.

"I know that, and I can't tell you how much I depend on it."
There was a silent pause on the line. "And the other boys in the
car? Have you heard anything about them?"

It was Lainie's turn to hesitate. "Well, yes, we've heard. One, the
driver, is going to be okay. He got a few stitches on his forehead,
but other than that, not a scratch. But the other boy . . ." She took
a deep breath and pushed on. "Well, he didn't make it. They think
he was killed instantly."

Lainie heard Fayette's breath catch. "Oh, that poor family. And
they'd all been drinking? Matthew certainly had."

Lainie nodded before she realized Fayette couldn't see her. "Yeah,
especially the driver."

"Well, I need to get back to Matthew. I just wanted to make sure
everything is going okay at home. You're sure you can handle this?"

Lainie looked into the dining room. One of the second-shift
volunteers, a deacon, blew a straw wrapper across the room at one
of his friends sitting in a booth. It landed in the middle of the floor
and he got up to retrieve it. Maybe now would not the best time
to tell Fayette that her diner had been taken over by well-meaning
volunteers. "Sure, we're doing fine. Don't worry about a thing.
Just take good care of Matthew for us."

"Will do. Well, better go. Bye-bye."

"Bye." Lainie replaced the phone on its hook and gave everyone a
thumbs up. "He's still not out of the woods, but it's looking good."

A murmur of satisfaction rippled through the diner, and everyone
went back to what they were doing. Lainie picked up a clipboard
and began going over the next day's order. Where was Ray? Fayette
hadn't mentioned him, and Lainie hadn't had a chance to ask.

—⁓—

Ray came home early Friday afternoon. Lainie saw him drive in
across the road, take his duffle bag from the cab, and walk behind

the building toward his trailer. They had talked a few times on the phone, but Lainie was either too busy or too tired to do more than exchange a few words. She did know, and had been able to pass along to others, that Matthew was expected to recover fully, although it would take a while.

A few minutes later, Ray came out the front door of the tavern and crossed the road to the Dip 'n' Dine. Lainie just stopped and watched him come. When she looked around and saw everyone looking at her and grinning, she retreated to the kitchen where she could blame her warm cheeks on the hot stove.

"Hey stranger, welcome home. How's our boy doing?" Brother Parker had come in with Les just after 1:00 to work the afternoon shift, and his booming voice filled the diner.

"Pretty good, I guess, but it's going to be a long haul." Ray took off his hat and hung it on a hook by the door. "I stopped by the hospital on my way out of town this morning, and I got a smile out of him. It was good to see."

"How's Fayette holding up?"

"Like always. I don't know how she does it. Your old church, by the way, has been great. They've really taken those two under their wing. They sure think the world of you. Wanted to make sure we were treating you right down here."

"They're good people."

Lainie grabbed a tray of clean cups and pushed the door to the dining room open. Ray clapped Les on the shoulder and shook his hand. "How's it going with you?"

Les hadn't said much since he'd followed Brother Parker into the diner, and he didn't return Ray's warm smile. "I'm doing a lot better than that boy laid up in the hospital up there, and I'm sure as shootin' doing better than that other boy. You hear about that?"

Ray nodded. "Yeah, I heard."

"You know I'd give my right arm to do things different, don't you?"

Ray nodded again. "I know, Les."

"You think Fayette can ever forgive me?"

"She's got a good heart. Just give her some time."

"Well, I tell you one thing I done. I told the sheriff where them boys got that booze and I give a description of the old boy who bought it for 'em. So they was able to figure out who done it. They're talking about charging him with manslaughter. And I'll tell you something else. I'm done with booze. Not another drop, so help me."

Brother Parker came up behind him. "Take it a day at a time, Les. I think the order for table four is ready, you want to take that over?"

Brother Parker went to bus a table and Ray climbed on a stool at the counter. His eyes looked tired, but his slow smile was warm and spoke of all he couldn't say in the crowded and very attentive diner. Lainie tried to look detached and businesslike when she came to take his order.

"Welcome home. Glad you made it back okay. What can I get you?"

Ray slapped the menu shut. "The special, I guess. Can't go wrong with that." He grinned up at her. "So how are you holding up? Looks like everything is under control."

Lainie shrugged. "So far, so good. Honestly, though, I don't know what I would've done if the church hadn't stepped in to help out, and I sure don't know how Fayette has done what she's done all these years. I had no idea how much work goes into running this place."

"She's a remarkable woman, one of those folks who just does what needs doing, no excuses, no complaints."

He had swiveled his stool around and was watching Les serve tables when Lainie brought him his plate. "So how's Les working out? I have to say I was a little surprised to see him in here."

"You're not the only one. The word that he saw the boys get the liquor and didn't stop it got around really fast. A lot of people, Les included, think he was to blame for the accident. I wasn't sure his being here was a good idea, but he wanted to do something to help, even if he took a lot of grief over it. I don't know what would happen if Brother Parker weren't here to run interference. I've seen him step in more than once this afternoon when things started to heat up."

"Well, Les has a lot of flaws, but I've never known him to lie to himself or anyone else. He'll take his medicine like a man. And he's got a good ally in Brother Parker." He turned to his plate. "I guess I'd better eat. Steven left me a big mess to clean up before I open."

"Where's Steven?"

"He didn't say. I called to tell him I was on the way home, and when I got here, there was a note saying he had to take off for a few days and he'd see me early next week."

"You seem to be taking it all right."

Ray mopped a bit of red chile sauce off his plate with a folded tortilla and stuffed it in his mouth. "Oh, yeah, I was bugged when I saw it, but then I thought about how I was nearly done with that place. I can clean it up this time. Pretty soon it will be Steven's to clean or let rot, and it won't matter to me one way or the other."

He finished eating and stood to pay his tab. "If you're not too tired, come on by when you close up. I'll give you a cup of cocoa or something."

Ray took his hat from the hook by the front door and with a wave to Lainie that included the rest of the diners, crossed the road and entered the High Lonesome. All the diners returned to their meals, but Lainie and Les watched until the neon beer sign flickered to life in the window, and Lainie noticed Les's hands had picked up a slight tremor when he began piling dirty dishes in a plastic busing bin.

23

The church was full, even this first Sunday after Christmas, and the Christmas greenery, looking a little tired now, still looped down the walls and across the front of the church. The choir had the next two Sundays off, and Lainie followed Elizabeth to her spot on the third row on the left. A low buzz moved through the sanctuary in the moments before the service started, and when the room suddenly fell silent, Lainie looked up expecting to see Brother Parker about to open the service. Instead, everyone was looking toward the back. Lainie followed their gaze and saw Les, followed by a downcast Evelyn, slip into the back pew. Evelyn never lifted her head and huddled in the pew as far away from her husband as she could. Les looked uncomfortable, determined, and . . . clean. That was the best word Lainie could come up with to describe Les. His grey hair, still damp, slicked back from his forehead and tucked behind his ears, showed the marks of his comb. His suit, one of the few being worn that morning, was dark gray and somewhat shiny. Lainie hadn't seen many suits, but this one had such wide lapels and broad shoulders.

She felt a gentle nudge in her ribs and turned to look at Elizabeth, whose eyes were directed toward the front of the church. Lainie got the message.

When Brother Parker welcomed everyone, Lainie saw his smile

widen as his gaze swept the back of the church, but by the end of the service Les and Evelyn were gone. Rita, who was sitting just in front of them, had seen the whole thing.

"You know, I was absolutely in shock when Les came in with Evelyn. I don't think I've seen him so much as darken the door since his kids got baptized, and that must have been thirty years ago. I shouldn't say anything, I guess. If anyone needs to do some repenting, it's Les Watson. But when they got up when the altar call started, I just about fell out of my pew. I thought, 'If Les Watson goes forward this morning, I'm just going to drop my teeth.' But it was just Evelyn making a break for the door before the service was over, and Les following her out."

Juanita came up behind her. "Did you see what I saw? Was that Les Watson in that old suit? I don't know which was stronger, the smell of mothballs or that aftershave he had on."

Elizabeth pulled herself to her full five foot two and turned to face Juanita.

"Juanita, that is about the tackiest thing I have ever heard you say, and you ought to be ashamed of yourself. Right here in the Lord's house on the Lord's Day too."

Juanita fell back as if Elizabeth had slapped her. "Well, I'm sorry if I stepped on any toes, but I happen to think he's got some nerve coming in here this morning. Everyone in this church is torn up by that Christmas Eve car wreck. All of us have known Matthew since he was a baby, and some know the families of the other boys too. Les as good as caused that wreck, and if you won't say so, I'm not afraid to."

"The thing that caused that wreck was boys drinking and getting behind the wheel. How and where they got the liquor and whose fault it is, is for the sheriff to work out, not you." Elizabeth's voice never rose, but the tone sharpened considerably. "And if Les wants to get his life right, well, I can't think of a better place for him to start than right here."

Juanita's eyes blazed and she opened her mouth, but before she could say a word, her husband, Russ, came up.

"Good night, you two sound like a couple'a cats on a fence. What's going on?"

Juanita put her hands on her hips and turned to answer, but Elizabeth beat her to it. Both hands flew to her cheeks. "Oh my lands, I do, don't I? And after having the gall to take Juanita to task for the very same thing." She put her hand on Juanita's arm. "Juanita, I am so sorry for being so presumptuous. Would you forgive me?"

Juanita looked as if she had a lot more to say, but she shut her mouth and glared at Elizabeth before turning and walking out the front door. Russ shook his head and followed her down the steps and across the parking lot.

Left in the vestibule, Lainie turned to Elizabeth. "Why did you ask her to forgive you? She was the one acting like a jerk, not you."

Elizabeth tucked her Bible a little more securely under her arm, slung her purse over her shoulder, and led the way to her truck. "Because I was in the wrong, that's why. I was angry and judgmental, and instead of trying to set things right, I just jumped into the fight. I shouldn't have done that."

"But Juanita started it!"

Elizabeth smiled at her. "You sound like one of my great-grandkids. It doesn't matter who started it. I'm only responsible for what I say and do. And I needed to ask for forgiveness."

—⁂—

Ray stopped by Elizabeth's that evening and was still there eating ham sandwiches and coconut cake when Steven came in a little later.

"Well, look who blew back into town. Have a good time?"

If Ray's greeting sounded lukewarm, Steven didn't appear to notice. He tossed his duffel bag in the corner behind the door and filled the room, as he always did, with his personality.

"Hey, bro, glad you got back okay. How's Matthew?" Before Ray could respond, Steven leaned down and squeezed his grandmother's shoulders in a one-armed hug. "Hey, beautiful, you think I could score some sandwiches and cake too? I'm starving."

Elizabeth looked up from her recliner and adjusted the afghan she was crocheting. "I'm sorry, Steven, but as far as I'm concerned, that kitchen is closed. You can go help yourself if you want to."

Steven looked pointedly at Ray's plate. "I guess you have to rate around here to get any service." He dropped onto the arm of the sofa. "What's going on? Why's everybody mad at me?"

"I'm not mad, sweetheart, just tired. I haven't budged from this spot since this afternoon." Elizabeth crossed her ankles on the footrest and leaned the recliner back even further. "Lainie fixed a little something for Ray when he got here."

Steven turned his award-winning smile on Lainie. "If I asked you real nice, would you make me a sandwich too?"

"Dream on. Your arms don't look broken."

Steven's eyebrows rose. He slapped Ray on the shoulder as he headed toward the kitchen. "You've got to let me in on your secret, bro."

He came back a few minutes later holding a sandwich in one hand and a hunk of cake in the other. Elizabeth gave a squawk of indignation.

"For goodness' sake, Steven, get a plate and a fork!"

Lainie shook her head and handed Ray's empty plate to him. He smiled his thanks but didn't receive a smile in return.

"Okay, what'd I do this time?" Steven tossed his full plate aside.

"Where'd you go, Steven?" Ray's voice was low, but there was no mistaking the irritation in it.

"Didn't you get my note? I left it where I was sure you'd find it."

"I found it. And the mess you left me. I got the place open in time anyway, no thanks to you. Where were you? You forgot to mention that in your note—or when you'd be back for that matter."

Steven seemed to be trying for nonchalance. "Some buddies dropped in on their way to Juarez, so I thought I'd tag along. You were on your way home, so I didn't think there'd be any harm. Sorry I didn't have time to clean things up. It wasn't all that bad, was it?"

"Bad enough." Ray leaned forward and propped his elbows on his knees. "Steven, you can't run a business that way. It's hard work, and you do it whether you want to or not. You need to make up your mind right now about the bar. I'm about done holding it for you."

Steven was silent a moment. "Yeah, well . . ."

"What?"

"Truth, bro? I'm not sure I really want the bar."

Ray just looked at him, waiting, but Elizabeth jumped right in. "Don't sell it. Just close it down."

"No, that's not what I'm saying. I'm not ready to get rid of it yet. I'm just not quite ready to take it over and put in the hours Ray puts in. Maybe I can work my way into it, sort of get used to it."

Ray shook his head. "Nope. It's not working that way. I put my life on hold and kept the place open for you because Dad asked me to. If you don't want it, you can do what you want with it. But I'm through."

"You mean I've got to tell you right this minute what my plans are? I didn't say I was ready to walk away, I just said I wasn't sure yet. Can't you cut me a little slack?"

Ray got up and took the Grayson and Sons Funeral Home calendar off the wall. "How much time do you need? I mean to decide what you want and get completely up to speed. I want a date I know I can walk away."

"Three months? That ought to do it." For the first time, Steven looked like he was taking things seriously.

Ray stared at him. "You're kidding, right? That's not till the end of March."

"I know it's a lot to ask, but it's been a long time. I'd just feel better knowing you were in it with me for a while."

Ray sighed as he pulled a pen from his pocket. He flipped through the pages and circled a date with a heavy black line. "Okay, but only if you put the work in. The minute you start slacking off, I'm out of here. Got that?"

Steven's grin was back and he extended his hand. "Fair enough. And thanks, bro. I really appreciate all you've done, and I mean that."

Ray clasped his brother's hand. "For Dad." He stood and held his hand out to Lainie. "Walk me to my truck?" He touched Elizabeth's shoulder. "'Night, Gran. You take care."

Ray closed the front door behind them and took Lainie's hand. "Three months is a joke and way more than he needs, but at least it's a solid date, and then that place is behind me. I can't believe I've been here all this time and he doesn't even know if he wants it."

"What did your mom think about your dad opening a bar? Was she as set against it as your grandma was?"

Ray stepped off the porch and walked with Lainie down the sidewalk. "She was just glad to be back in Last Chance to stay. It wasn't too long after we got here that she got sick. After that, no one said much about the bar. Granddad and Gran were too busy taking care of her and riding herd on Steven and me to take on Dad and the bar too."

"Your grandparents took care of your mom? Why not your dad?"

Ray reached the truck and leaned against the door. He shrugged. "That's just the way they were. Where their family was involved, they just took charge. And to tell the truth, Dad was okay with that. He didn't deal with Mom's illness very well at all. I don't think he could stand to see her getting sicker and weaker and not be able to do anything about it. So he took care of the bar, and they took care of us."

Lainie grinned. "And she's still at it."

"Well, she tries." Ray pulled Lainie close and nestled his face in her hair. "Mmmm. You smell good. You know that?"

Lainie leaned against him. "And you smell like oil paints. What were you working on?"

"Something for you."

Lainie leaned back and looked at him. "Really? What is it?"

He grinned down at her. "You'll just have to wait and see. It was supposed to be a Christmas present, but things got crazy after Steven came home, so I didn't get to my cabin to paint as often as I thought I would."

"Can't I even have a hint?"

"Nope." Ray dropped a kiss on her forehead and nose.

"Will I be able to take it with me? Most of the paintings I've seen of yours are awfully big, and I'm guessing we're talking about a painting."

"What about 'wait and see' don't you get? When it's done, I'll bring it to you. And just where are you planning on going, anyway? I thought you had a diner to run."

"Well, yeah, I'm not going anywhere at least till Fayette gets back, but you know I'm not here forever."

"Aren't you?" Ray's voice was a murmur in her hair.

Lainie pushed away and looked in his face. "No, I'm not. And from what I just heard, you aren't either. Let's get real. Whether or not Steven wants the bar, you're out of here by the end of March. And your grandma treats me like family, but who are we kidding? I'm not. I'll stay till Fayette gets back, but when summer rolls around again, I'll be gone."

Ray was silent as he searched her face. "Really? Where will you go? Still headed to El Paso?"

Lainie shook her head. "No, not there. I'm not sure where I'll go. Someplace no one would ever think to look for me."

"Is someone looking for you, Lainie?" Rays voice was gentle and Lainie longed to lose herself in it, but she shook the feeling off.

"I don't know. I hope not."

"Would you tell me about it?"

Lainie shook her head. "There's nothing to tell. And I hope it stays that way."

Ray's gaze held hers for so long that she finally looked away. He sounded sad when he spoke. "I wish things didn't have to change."

Lainie turned her collar up to ward off a chill wind that gusted down the street, rattling the bare branches of the cottonwood trees. "But they always do, don't they?"

24

Cold spring winds filled the air with dust and tore at the green-tipped branches of the old cottonwood trees before anyone heard anything definite about Fayette's plans. She wasn't coming back to Last Chance, not to stay anyway.

"I just don't believe it. What does she know about this so-called history teacher, anyway? She's known him how long? Three months? And she's going to chuck everything she's got right here in Last Chance? Friends? A thriving business? A church family that stepped in and ran it for her? I think worry must have driven her completely out of her mind, that's what I think."

The breakfast crowd had thinned, and Lurlene and Juanita were perched on stools at the counter having a cup of coffee. Despite three months of regular shifts, the volunteers still acted like they were serving guests in their own homes, but Lainie knew she never could have kept the diner open without them.

"Well, I for one am glad she's found a little happiness. If anyone deserves it, it's Fayette." Lurlene added another dollop of cream to her coffee and gave it a stir.

"But who is he? Does anyone know him?" Juanita was not about to let some stranger waltz off with one of her friends without a good deal more scrutiny.

"Brother Parker does." Lainie hoisted a tray of dirty dishes from

215

a booth by the window and walked past them on her way to the kitchen. "He said Ken—that's his name, by the way—is a deacon in that church Brother Parker pastored in Albuquerque, and that he's a fine man. His wife died about fifteen years ago, and he raised his two kids by himself. They're both married now."

"He has married kids? How old is he, anyway? He sounds like some old coot looking for a sweet young thing to do his cooking for him, if you know what I mean."

"For Pete's sake, Juanita, what is wrong with you?" Lurlene stared at her friend. "You don't have to have one foot in the grave to have married kids, and Fayette isn't a child. She's what? Past forty for sure."

Juanita pursed her lips and stared out the window. She had clearly said all she intended to say on the subject, at least for the moment.

"So do you have any idea what she's planning on doing with the Dip 'n' Dine?" Lurlene swiveled around on her stool so she could better talk to Lainie, who had returned from the kitchen and was washing down tables.

Lainie shrugged. "Sell it, I guess. She can't very well run it from Albuquerque."

"Well, who in the world would buy it? I can't think of anyone around here in the market for a restaurant, can you, Juanita?"

Juanita still wasn't talking. Unmistakably miffed that Lurlene had summarily dismissed her concerns for Fayette's happiness, she slid off her stool, brushed the donut crumbs off her slacks, and disappeared into the kitchen.

"Good grief, Juanita, I didn't mean for you to get in a huff. I'm sorry." Lurlene waited a moment, but the only sound in the kitchen was Carlos banging on pots and talking to his nephew. She turned back to Lainie. "Well, I don't know then. I'd hate to see this place

close down. We'd have to go all the way to San Ramon every time
we didn't feel like cooking. What about Ray? What's he going to
do when he hands over the High Lonesome to Steven? Isn't that
supposed to happen in the next couple weeks?"

Not only Juanita, who reappeared at the kitchen door, but also
the couple in the last booth lingering over their coffee stopped to
see how Lainie would answer Lurlene. Things even got quiet in
the kitchen.

Lainie raised one hand and shook her head. "I'm not even going
there. That's what the plan was, but I haven't heard anything about
it for a while, and if Steven and Ray are discussing it, it's not when
I'm around, thank goodness."

"Really? Is there some sort of problem?" Juanita apparently
decided to break her silence and plopped herself back on the counter stool.

"Steven still wants that place, doesn't he?" Lurlene asked. "I can
remember him talking about growing up to be his dad's partner
from the time he was a little guy. Steven just idolized that man.
Cutest thing in the world to see him, not even as high as his daddy's
belt buckle and dressed just like him—hat to boots—marching
along behind him like a little Bantam rooster."

Lurlene and Juanita fell into reflective silence and slowly stirred
their coffee.

Juanita slammed down her spoon and jumped off her stool.
"That's Fayette! I'd know that car anywhere."

Lainie looked up as the sun-faded red Dodge pulled off the
highway and into the parking lot of the Dip 'n' Dine. Just seeing
the familiar face smiling through the windshield as Fayette parked
her car eased the tightness Lainie hadn't even realized she was carrying between her shoulders.

Juanita headed for the door with Lurlene close behind. By the time Fayette climbed out, they were waiting by the car door, vying to see who could give her the first hug. Lainie couldn't hear the words they said, but the squeals that came through the plate glass window left no doubt of their excitement that Fayette had come home. She watched Juanita grab Fayette's left hand to examine the ring and Lurlene grab the hand from Juanita. They were still exclaiming over the ring when they ushered Fayette through the door and into the diner.

Fayette gently pulled her hand from Lurlene's grasp and opened her arms as Lainie crossed the room to meet her. She meet Lainie halfway and enveloped her in a tight embrace.

"You can never know what you have done for me." Lainie felt Fayette's tears on her cheek as her friend whispered in her ear. "I can't even begin to think what I would have done if you hadn't been here for me. Matthew was hurt so bad, and if I had not been able to be with him, I would have died."

Lainie brushed her own hand across her eyes when Fayette released her and stepped back. "I had help, you know." She gestured toward Juanita and Lurlene, who still stood beaming by the door. "The whole church pitched in. They've been here every day."

Fayette turned her damp face and open arms to the ladies at the door and hugged both of them in one embrace. "I know. And I love each and every one of you for it. If I had all the treasure in all the world, it wouldn't make the tiniest dent in the debt I owe. Thank you. Just thank you."

Juanita pulled a packet of tissues from her pants pocket, took one, and passed the packet to Lurlene. "Well, you're welcome, I'm sure. We're just glad we can help. Now, what brings you back home, and why didn't you tell us you were coming?"

Fayette took a tissue from the packet Lurlene proffered and wiped her nose. Her smile was a bit watery, but it was happy. In fact, Lainie had never seen Fayette look so relaxed, red nose and all. "It seemed like a good time. Matthew is doing well with his physical therapy. He's got lots of company, thanks to the youth group at church. And there are some things I need to take care of here in Last Chance. I wanted to see how you all are doing, for one thing."

Carlos had come from the kitchen and gestured around the room with a grin. "Hey, we're doing great. Business is good. These ladies keep things going smooth all the time. Maybe we even do better without you."

Fayette laughed and gave him a huge hug too. "Well, don't make me feel too welcome, Carlos. I'd hate to feel needed or anything."

He shifted awkwardly and patted her back. "You hungry? I got a big pot of posole in there."

"You know, I haven't had lunch. And it's a perfect day for posole. That wind out there is cold."

"Well then, missy, you sit right here and we'll serve you." Lurlene pointed to a booth. "Now, what do you want to drink?"

Fayette laughed. "I don't think I know how to be a customer. In all the years I've owned this place, I don't think I've ever been the one served."

"Well, it's high time you were." Juanita brought the diet soda Fayette ordered and slid in the booth across from her. "Now, tell us all about your fiancé. Why didn't you bring him with you?"

Color actually flushed across Fayette's cheeks, and her shy smile made her look like a girl again. "His name is Ken Maxwell, and he's a middle school teacher. That's why he didn't come this time. He's teaching."

"Yes, we know that much. But what's he like?" Lurlene scooted in next to Juanita. "Is he tall? Good looking? Do you have a picture?"

"No, he's not too tall. He's a little taller than me, maybe. I think he's nice looking, but more than that, he's a good man. He's kind. And he and Matthew get along so well."

"Have you set a date? You're not getting married in Albuquerque, are you?"

Fayette smiled her thanks when Lainie set the bowl of posole in front of her and returned her attention to her inquisitors. "That's one of the reasons I came down. I want to talk to Brother Parker because we do want to get married here."

Lurlene and Juanita exchanged triumphant glances.

"It wasn't that easy a decision," Fayette continued. "Everyone in that church just adores Ken and they've been so good to Matthew and me, but when it came down to it, I just couldn't see getting married anyplace but the Church of Last Chance."

"So when?"

"June, maybe. Ken gets out of school at the end of May."

"But that's just three or four months. We'll have to get crackin'." Juanita grabbed a paper napkin and took a pencil from her apron pocket. "Now, do you have any idea what day in June you want to get married? It'll be a Saturday, of course, so that'll narrow it down some."

"And the music," Lurlene chimed in. "Who's going to sing? You know, I went to a wedding once where the whole choir sang the 'Hallelujah Chorus,' and it was just lovely."

Fayette put down her spoon and threw up both hands with a laugh. "Wait! I haven't even talked to Brother Parker yet. And as lovely as that wedding must have been, Lurlene, I've been single too long to have the choir bust into the 'Hallelujah Chorus' when I head down the aisle. I don't think even I could keep a straight face."

Lurlene's brow furrowed. "I think it was the recessional, but I see what you mean."

"Okay, ladies, coffee break's over now." Lainie came up to the table and put her hand on Lurlene's shoulder. Lurlene, then Juanita scooted out of the booth, and Lainie picked up Fayette's empty glass and set another diet soda in front of her. "I just called Elizabeth. She said you were to come to dinner. No argument."

Fayette smiled. "I learned better than to argue with Elizabeth a long time ago, and I'm not about to start now, especially over something like a dinner invitation."

"How long are you going to be in town?"

"I'm thinking maybe a week, depending on how Matthew does. I want to go over everything here at the diner, just to see what's going on. And I need to see to my house. It's been empty for a while, and I need to see what I need to do to get it ready to sell."

Lainie shook her head. "I can't believe you're leaving Last Chance for good."

"I can't either, now. When I'm in Albuquerque, it just seems natural, like that's where home is, but driving back into town this afternoon, it's like I became someone I used to be. The Last Chance Fayette, I guess."

"If you're going to be around for a week, you should know that Les works here on Friday afternoons with Brother Parker. Are you going to be okay with that?"

Fayette nodded. "I think so. I've had some time to think, and Ken and I have talked about it. I know that no one is responsible for Matthew's actions but Matthew. But when I look my at my son in such pain and struggling so hard to walk and I think that maybe, just maybe, he could have been spared all that if only Les had said a word, something inside of me just gets so hard and angry."

"Well, I can either tell him not to come in Friday, or you can use that day to work on your house. If you're not ready to see Les, there's no reason why you need to. But you should also know he's been coming to church."

Fayette looked skeptical. "Really? Well, good for him. I'm glad. But as for work, can we just play it by ear?"

Lainie smiled. "Sure. You finish your lunch and I'll go tell Elizabeth to count on you for dinner."

———∞———

Lainie pulled Elizabeth's pickup into its usual spot in the church parking lot and checked her watch. She knew she'd get a look from Lurlene for getting to the choir room late, but Elizabeth had insisted that Sunday lunch would be the perfect time for Fayette to talk to Brother Parker about the wedding plans, so this morning there was chicken to fry and cobbler to make.

A crowd had gathered on the church steps, and she could see Fayette's blonde topknot in the middle. Lainie couldn't help remembering Brother Parker's sermons on the lost lamb, and the lost son, and all the rejoicing that went on when they were found again. Fayette hadn't exactly been lost. Everyone knew where she'd been, but she was home again, and if the fatted calf hadn't been killed, a fatted chicken was waiting at home under a foil tent.

Les's battered old truck wasn't there, though. Maybe Evelyn had talked him into staying home this morning. Since the accident, Les had never missed a shift at the diner and was, in fact, one of the hardest workers. Evelyn, on the other hand, wore shame like a clammy blanket and rarely ventured from home. "Poor Evelyn and the heavy burden she was called to bear" was often the subject of conversation when the church ladies got together, Lainie always wondered when Elizabeth, who had the kindest of hearts, never seemed to sympathize but always briskly changed the subject.

She was right about the look Lurlene gave her when she shrugged into her robe and slipped into line just as the choir began filing into the choir loft. Juanita, just in front of her, turned her head and whispered, "Where were you?" Lurlene said, "Shhh!" and then they were in the sanctuary, and the service began.

Elizabeth had claimed Fayette, and the two sat side by side in the third row. Steven was nowhere in sight. No surprise there. More and more, he evaded Elizabeth's "everyone under my roof Saturday night goes to church Sunday" edict by not coming home Saturday night.

The small congregation shuffled to its feet as the pianist played the introduction to the first hymn. The voices filling the church covered the sound of the door in the back opening, and since everyone had their noses in the hymnbooks, almost no one but the choir knew that Les Watson had slipped in and was sitting alone in what was becoming his regular spot in the back row.

Brother Parker gave Fayette a special welcome and gave her a minute to give an update on Matthew. Fayette blew a kiss to the choir as she mounted the few steps to the podium, and her smile as she turned to face the congregation was relaxed and filled with joy. Lainie couldn't see her face as Fayette told of Matthew's amazing progress and gave her thanks to the church for making it possible to stay in Albuquerque with him, so she didn't know if Fayette's expression changed when her eyes landed on Les, but if she was at all disturbed at finding him there, her voice gave no clue.

The rest of the service went by in the usual order. Evelyn never did turn up, and Lainie half expected Les to slip out before the altar call, but he stood to his feet with the rest of the congregation and joined in the first verse of "Just as I Am." By the second verse, he was no longer singing but shifting restlessly from foot to foot, and Lainie expected him to bolt for the door at any moment. Sure enough, when Brother Parker instructed the congregation to close their eyes and pray while the choir sang the third verse, he put his hymnal down and stepped out into the aisle. But instead of heading out the door, he walked down the aisle to the front of the church. Brother Parker took his right hand and placed his left arm across Les's shoulders while they whispered their conversation.

When Brother Parker finally nodded to Lurlene as a signal to end the altar call, most of the congregation had peeked and knew that Les was at the front of the church. You could have heard a bulletin float to the floor.

Brother Parker stood with his hand on Les's shoulder. His eyes swept the congregation for a long moment before he spoke.

"Les Watson has come this morning to make a public profession of his faith in Jesus Christ. This moment has not come quickly or easily, but I've talked with Les at great length and prayed with him, and I believe in the sincerity of his confession. Will you join me in welcoming Les into the kingdom of God?"

Lainie watched Fayette as the congregation erupted in applause. She clapped politely with the others, but her face was expressionless. Les, however, was clearly ill at ease. He shook his head and grabbed Brother Parker by the shoulder to mutter something in his ear. Brother Parker raised his hand to quiet the congregation. "Les has something he'd like to say."

The church fell silent again and Les cleared his throat.

"I appreciate it. I really do. I don't deserve your kindness, but I appreciate it all the same." He glanced at Brother Parker, who gave him an encouraging nod. "Brother Parker can tell you that I was planning to do this this morning even before . . ." He glanced at Fayette. "Even before Fayette came home. And to tell the truth, I thought maybe I should put it off for another day. You know, I didn't want to cause more hurt than I already done. But Brother Parker told me that once you take the step to follow Jesus, well, the best thing is to tell folks as quick as you can, so here I am."

He broke off for a long moment. When he spoke his voice was

224

shaking with the effort to control tears. "I'm so sorry. I've messed up so many lives. Fayette's, that boy in the hospital up in Albuquerque, and who knows how many I don't even know about. Evelyn, for sure she didn't deserve everything I've put her through. I wanted her to be here this morning so I could apologize in public, just like I've disgraced her in public all these years, but she has a bad headache."

He pulled a handkerchief from his pocket and blew his nose. "Anyway, I know Jesus forgives me, but I need to ask your forgiveness too. I want you to know I haven't touched a drop since Christmas Eve. I can't promise I'll never slip up again, but with your prayers and God's help, I'm taking it a day at a time." He stopped talking and looked out at the stunned faces. "Thank you."

He tried to walk away, but Brother Parker took his arm. "Stay up here, Les. Your brothers and sisters want to welcome you to the family."

Les turned to face the congregation. For a long moment no one moved. Les looked at Brother Parker and shifted his feet again. Lainie caught movement from the third row as Fayette pushed past Elizabeth. Elizabeth was right behind her, but Fayette was the first one to reach Les. She put both arms around him, and as the Church of Last Chance lined up down the center aisle to welcome him to the family, Lainie heard her murmur, "I forgive you with all my heart. Can you forgive me for taking so long to do it?"

25

"Mmmm, smells good in here!" Fayette smiled at Lainie and gave Elizabeth a squeeze, and Lainie noticed again how happy she looked. "Hope I'm not late. I waited around so I could talk to Les a little bit after everyone left."

Elizabeth shook her head. "No, you're the first one here. Brother Parker and Ray should be here in a few minutes, and I'm not sure about Steven. He's sort of his own man these days." She pulled the pan of fried chicken out of the oven where it had been warming and turned up the heat for the biscuits. "How did things go with Les, or do you mind saying?"

Fayette dropped in a kitchen chair and propped her elbows on the table. "Good, I guess. I had no idea what he'd been putting himself through since Matthew's accident. Of course, I knew he blamed himself, and part of me was glad, I'm ashamed to admit. I blamed him too, at first. But I've had people around me to help me see things different, and he's just been going through the torments of you-know-where."

Elizabeth nodded. "It hasn't been easy for him. But Brother Parker's been right beside him every step of the way."

"Do I hear my name? I hope that means you're calling me to dinner." Brother Parker came in, followed by Ray. "I met this young man on the front walk. Hope you don't mind if I brought him along."

Elizabeth held up her cheek for Ray's kiss. "Hello, honey. Thought we might see you in church this morning."

Ray caught Lainie's glance and rolled his eyes. "Yes, I hoped I'd make it, but I had some work I had to finish before I could come over this afternoon."

Elizabeth's voice was low but clear as she ushered everyone to the dining table. "Six days shall a man work, but on the seventh . . . Now, Pastor, you sit there at the head of the table. Fayette, you sit here."

She went on assigning seats, and Ray bumped Lainie's shoulder with his own. The message was clear: "Help me out here!" Lainie gave him her most innocent smile and took the seat Elizabeth indicated.

Steven didn't come in until after dinner. He spoke to Elizabeth, Brother Parker, and Fayette, who were still seated at the dining room table discussing wedding plans, and came through to the kitchen where Ray and Lainie were doing dishes.

"Anything left over?" He stuck his head in the refrigerator and came up with a chicken wing. "Wings and backs. And all the cobbler's gone. Thanks."

"Sorry, bro." Ray picked up a wet glass off the drain board and polished it with his dish towel. "If I had only known, I never would have taken the last drumstick. We haven't seen much of you around here lately."

Steven took a long drink of the glass of milk he poured for himself and wiped his mouth with the back of his hand. "Is that supposed to be a dig?"

Ray shrugged. "All I'm saying is whether you're up to speed or not, I'm out of here in ten days. If you want to make a go of the place, I'd suggest you show up."

Lainie handed Ray a dripping plate. "What are the chances that Steven could take over this Friday? Fayette's given me the day off. Maybe we could do something."

Ray's face lit up. "That sounds great. I don't remember when I've taken a whole day off in the middle of the week." He looked at Steven. "What do you think? Ready to try another solo run at the bar on Friday?"

Steven tore the last remnants of meat off the chicken bone with his teeth and threw the bone in the trash. "You should have thought of that before you hogged all the chicken."

Ray bristled and opened his mouth to speak, but Lainie beat him to it. "Come on, don't be a jerk. You've been telling me I need to get to Juarez for the day. This is my chance."

"Wait a minute. Who said anything about Juarez? No way we're going to Juarez." Ray turned from the cupboard still holding the plate he was going to put there.

"Oh?" Lainie leaned against the counter and folded her arms. "Really. So where are we going?"

"I don't know. There are lots of places we could go. It might be fun to pack a picnic and go out to the ranch and ride up into the hills. We could go up to Silver City and see some galleries. But Juarez is off the table. Don't you read the papers? It's a war zone."

"Oh, come on. Don't be such an old lady, Ray." Steven perched on the kitchen table and plopped his feet on the seat of a chair, glancing into the dining room to check if Elizabeth could see him. "You know that's all media hype. Bogeymen sell newspapers."

Ray looked angrier than Lainie had ever seen him. "Some of those bogeymen were arrested between here and the border Tuesday, and a bunch more last month. This is serious. I know most of those poor fellas are just looking for a way to support their families, but there are some bad dudes out there." He looked at Lainie. "Drop the idea. Pick someplace else, because we're not going to Juarez."

Lainie stared at him. No one told her what she could do. "Excuse me? Maybe you don't want to go, but what makes you think you can order me around?"

Ray tried to backpedal. "Okay, I put that wrong. I should have said it's just a really bad idea right now. Pick someplace else for us to go, and we'll hit Juarez when things calm down. I'm just trying to take care of my girl."

His smile was pleading but ineffective. Lainie's voice was cold. "I'm a big girl, Ray. I can take care of myself just fine without your help. And I think I want to go to Juarez Friday. Are you going to take me? Because if you won't, I'll bet Steven will."

"Sure, I'll take you." Steven had been following the conversation like a spectator at a tennis match. He grinned. "This whole thing is blown way out of proportion. You can stay out of trouble if you know what you're doing."

Lainie looked at Ray, willing him to change his mind. The angry set of his jaw was easy to ignore. The hurt in his eyes, not so much, but she was too mad to stop there. She turned a brittle smile on Steven. "All right then, what time do we leave?"

—⚏—

It hadn't taken long after Ray left Sunday for doubt to start nibbling at her righteous indignation. She didn't even like Steven all that much, and now here she was spending the only day off she'd had in months going to Juarez with him in a car he'd borrowed from Manny, while Ray . . . Well, what about Ray? Had she messed things up forever with Ray?

Steven turned up the radio. "This is a great song." In another moment he was singing along and slapping the steering wheel in time with the music.

Lainie couldn't help laughing at his falsetto. "You've got a really rotten voice, you know that?" Steven glared at her in mock umbrage but didn't miss a note. "No, I mean it. You're really bad."

Steven continued to sing as if she hadn't spoken, and the childlike exuberance of his voice coupled with the sunshine spilling down the rocky hillsides lifted her spirits. She even tried to harmonize with his ever-changing key.

They reached the outskirts of El Paso in late morning. Lainie's breath came faster as they drove past the sprawling suburbs toward a skyline that loomed from the desert floor. She had never realized until now how much she missed the city. When they joined the line of cars to cross the bridge into Juarez, she was jazzed and ready to go.

"It doesn't look like a war zone." Lainie craned her neck and looked all around them.

Steven laughed. "Nope, I told you it was all hype."

"Why are all those people walking across the bridge?"

"More weenies. They're scared something might happen to their cars, or they're afraid someone might pull a scam and they'll wind up in jail." He snorted in derision.

"That stuff never happens?"

"Not if you know your way around." Steven grinned at her and eased onto the street. "And I know my way around."

The day they spent in Juarez was everything Steven had promised. He parked the car, paid a kid to watch it for them, and took Lainie's hand as he led her from shop to shop through streets filled with tourists. It seemed odd to have vendors calling after them and even following them down the street, but Steven spoke easily in Spanish and mostly waved them off. The first time someone asked if they wanted to get married and offered to help, he looked at Lainie in thoughtful consideration.

"What do you think? That would really shake them up back home. Want to go for it?"

Lainie's mouth flopped open and shut before she gasped, "No!"

Steven laughed and squeezed her hand. "Chicken."

When the sun disappeared behind the buildings and the shadows filled the streets, Lainie glanced at her watch. "Don't you think we should be heading home? We have quite a drive ahead of us."

"After dinner." He steered her into a cantina where the music had already begun to pour out onto the streets. "This is one of the best places in town. You can't come to Juarez and just pass it by."

Lainie reluctantly allowed herself to be led inside. With the setting sun, her desire to be away from home had evaporated. The day had been fun, but it was over and time to go home.

Steven didn't hide his annoyance when Lainie insisted they head for the car as soon as they finished their dinner. Clearly he had planned to continue their tour of Juarez's nightlife, but this time Lainie was adamant.

"You told everyone we'd be home by bedtime, and that means Elizabeth will be waiting up. I don't want her to worry."

"Gran always worries. She's as much of an old woman as Ray." Steven put down his empty glass and signaled the waiter for another. Lainie stood up.

"I'm not even going to try to answer that, but we're done here." The waiter arrived with the fresh drink, and Lainie picked it up off the table and put it back on his tray. "No. The check, please."

Confused, the waiter hesitated and looked from Lainie to Steven. Steven glowered and reached for his wallet. His irritated expression quickly changed to one of alarm as he jumped to his feet and began searching all his pockets.

"It's gone. My wallet's gone. I can't believe it. It's got to be somewhere." He slapped all his pockets in turn.

The waiter's expression changed from confused solicitation to hard suspicion. He wrote out the ticket, placed it on the table, and stood watching Steven do the missing wallet dance.

Finally convinced that his wallet wasn't hiding from him, Steven dropped his hands to his side and stated the obvious. "Someone took my wallet."

The waiter cleared his throat. "Señor . . ."

Lainie opened her purse. "I'll take care of this. We need to get on the road."

The car was waiting where they had left it and from a quick examination appeared to be in good shape. Lainie held out her hand.

"I'd better drive. Hand me the keys."

Steven dropped them in her hand. "That's right. I lost my driver's license with my wallet."

Lainie opened the driver's side and got in. "Yeah, right. I'm worried about your driver's license. All the tequila shots don't mean a thing."

The line of cars snaked slowly toward the border, and the butterflies in Lainie's stomach started doing the Macarena. Something about having an officer stick his flashlight in your car and ask questions did things to your breathing—like stop it altogether.

The border crossing proceeded without a hitch. Lainie glanced at the instrument panel and merged onto the freeway.

"I hope we have enough gas to get us home. Paying your bar bill cleaned me out."

"Yeah, well, I'll pay you back for that. I'd pay you for a tank of gas too, if you want to put one on your credit card."

"I don't have any credit cards. We have two dollars in my wallet and whatever change you have in your pockets to get us home, so pray nothing else goes wrong."

They came around a curve on the freeway to find traffic stopped and a sea of flashing red lights ahead. Lainie hit the brakes, praying the borrowed car had good ones, and brought the vehicle safely to a stop. She barely had enough time to breathe a sigh of relief, however, before the squealing of brakes suggested that the car behind them was not similarly equipped and the grinding thunk that threw them against their seat belts confirmed it.

"Are you all right?"

She turned her head. Her neck still worked. "I'm okay. You?"

"Yeah, I think so. Let's hope the car came out okay too."

The seat belt clasp still worked, and the door latch. Lainie slid out the barely opened door and stood by the car. The freeway resembled a parking lot as far as she could see both ahead and behind. The two cars appeared welded together in an accordion of mangled metal. Despair slid around her shoulders and pooled in her stomach. This car wasn't going anywhere. She took a deep breath. *Okay, I know I'm not going to spend the rest of my life standing here in traffic staring at a wrecked car. This will all get worked out somehow.* She clenched her jaw and squeezed her eyes shut to force back tears. *I just wish I had the slightest clue how.*

"Whoa. Lucky you were driving, huh?" Steven huffed into his cupped palm to check his breath and eyed the police officer making her way toward them. "This could have been bad."

A half hour later, as they watched the tow truck hoist the car off the pavement, the officer handed them forms to sign. "Do you know anyone who could come get you?"

Steven, who had tried to keep his distance and had opened his mouth as little as possible, shook his head no. Lainie started to agree with him but stopped in midsentence.

"Wait, I do know someone." She dug in her purse for her address book and flipped through the pages. "Hand me your phone and pray she's home."

Steven handed it over. "I forgot to charge it before we left home, so it's nearly dead. Where's your phone, anyway?"

"Don't have one." She jabbed at the keypad and stared at the pavement until a grin crossed her face and she gave Steven a jubilant thumbs-up. "Lindsay? It's Lainie. You'll never guess where I am."

26

She'll be here in ten minutes." Lainie handed the phone back to Steven. "You call home and tell them what's going on while I finish up here. I'm supposed to open the Dip 'n' Dine for Fayette tomorrow."

Lindsay drove up as the tow truck eased its way back into traffic.

"I can't believe it! Where have you been? We all thought you were dead or something. Nick was so worried when you just disappeared."

Lainie ignored Steven's raised eyebrows and his silently mouthed "Nick?" and climbed into the passenger seat beside Lindsay. "It's a long story, and I just want to get off this stupid freeway. Can we go now?"

"Sure. Whatever you say." Lindsay's smile faded and she checked her rearview mirror.

Steven leaned forward from the backseat and thrust his hand between the seats. "I'm Steven. And I'll be the one to thank you for coming to rescue us. Lainie's still a little shaken up from the accident. She'll come around in a little bit, maybe even introduce us."

Lainie leaned her head against the headrest and closed her eyes. She didn't have to see Steven's dimple or his slow, lady-killer smile. She could hear them in his voice. She sighed. "Did you call home?"

"Yeah, left a message."

"Who with?"

"Fayette. Isn't she the one you were worried about?"

"Yes, and your grandmother, and Ray. All of them will be looking for us pretty soon."

"Fayette will pass the word along. I really wasn't all that anxious to talk to either Gran or Ray. Besides, my phone died as I was leaving the message at Fayette's. Totally out of battery charge."

Lainie twisted so she could see into the backseat. "You did leave a message, though? They know where we are and that we might need someone to come get us?"

"Yeah, yeah, we're good." He dropped the impatience from his tone and slipped the syrup back in. "So tell me, Lindsay, how do you two know each other?"

Lainie's stomach clenched and she stopped breathing. What had she been thinking, calling Lindsay, anyway? She'd spent the better part of a year pretending that part of her life had never existed, and now she had just invited it back in.

She shot an anxious glance at Lindsay, silently imploring her to keep it short, but Lindsay seemed totally mesmerized by the purring voice at her shoulder. "Oh, we've been friends forever, since we were kids back in LA. I came out here about three years ago, and Lainie was on her way to stay with me when she fell off the face of the earth last summer." She lightly shoved Lainie's arm. "What happened to you anyway? You call to say you're stuck in some crummy wide spot in the road and then nothing. I never even knew the name of the place where you were stuck, or even what state you were in."

Steven leaned back and laughed. "That would be Last Chance, New Mexico. And is that any way to talk about the place that opened its arms and took you in out of the cold, Lainie?"

"Well, I was worried sick." Lindsay picked up where she left off. "I wanted to call the police, but Nick said you were probably just still mad because of that fight you had and that you'd turn up when you were ready, so I didn't."

"Nick said what?" Lainie swallowed to try to moisten her mouth. "When did you talk to Nick?"

"Maybe a couple of months ago. He's not in California anymore. I forget where he is. I'm not even sure he told me."

"What did you tell him?" Lainie fought the terror that threatened to choke her.

"The truth. That I hadn't heard a word from you."

"And if he calls back, that's the story you're sticking to, right?"

"If you say so. But I wish you'd just talk to him."

"Who is this Nick anyway? Lainie seems to have forgotten to mention him." Steven leaned forward again and rested his arm on the back of Lainie's seat.

"Oops! Did I open my big mouth when I should have kept it shut?" Lindsay's eyes sparkled at Steven in the rearview mirror and she glanced at Lainie. "Nick is Lainie's boyfriend, at least he thinks so, but if you guys . . .?" Her voice trailed to a question mark.

"Nope, Lainie and I are just friends, aren't we, Lainie?" He dropped his hand to Lainie's shoulder. She shrugged it off in silence and looked out the side window. "Well, it's sort of an on-again, off-again friendship, I guess, and right now it seems to be off. But this thing with Nick—pretty serious, was it?"

Lainie glared over her shoulder at Steven, but Lindsay, intent on navigating traffic, didn't catch the look. "Yeah, it was serious. How long were you two together, Lainie? Five years? I couldn't believe it when you called to say you were leaving and coming to El Paso. I figured you'd tell me why when you got here, but you never showed up."

"Can we change the subject, please? My personal life really isn't anyone's business but mine." She turned around to glare again at Steven. He wasn't even trying to suppress his grin. "You really are enjoying this, aren't you?"

Steven laughed. "What can I say? I've been wondering about the mystery woman since I got home. Does Ray know about Nick, by the way?"

Lainie turned back around and stared out the windshield. Nick was supposed to go from the hospital to jail. What had happened? Where was he? And why, why, why had she ever called Lindsay?

Lindsay turned off the thoroughfare and Lainie watched a row of small, flat-roofed houses huddled in dusty yards behind barred windows slide past. The car stopped at the corner in front of a pair of two-story boxes facing each other across a small gravel strip.

"Here we are." Lindsay shut off the ignition and fitted a steel bar to her steering wheel to lock it. "I'm upstairs on the end in that building there."

Steven prowled the apartment, peeking into the single bedroom before he flopped down on the couch, spreading his arms along the back.

"You guys hungry?" Lindsay opened her cupboard and scanned the few contents. "I've got some chips and some Mallomars, but that's about it. I didn't think to ask while we were out, but there's a drive-through on the next block that should still be open."

"Why don't we go out? It's early yet." Steven glanced at his watch and grinned. "Sort of."

Lainie glared at him, but Lindsay jumped at the idea. "Sure! Let me change real quick." She closed her bedroom door behind her, then stuck her head out again. "You like to dance? There's a couple of great clubs I know about."

"Sounds great." Steven looked at Lainie, who hadn't budged from the faded armchair she had sunk into. "You up for this?"

"Nope. I've had enough fun for one day, thanks. Besides, I'm broke, remember? And so are you, unless you found your wallet."

Steven flashed his grin and gave her a wink. "Don't worry, I'll think of something."

Lindsay emerged from her room wearing a short skirt, high heels, and a clinging top that revealed more than it covered. She struck a pose. "Ready?"

Steven practically leered. "For what?" He opened the door with a flourish, and as she passed through, he glanced over his shoulder at Lainie and raised an eyebrow. "Don't wait up."

Lainie blessed the quiet that enveloped her with the closing of the door. Not even the sound of the television next door intruded on her solitude. For the time being, until Steven and Lindsay returned or until they heard from someone in Last Chance, no one wanted anything, not even a comment from her.

Not until she heard the sound of Lindsay's car starting up at the curb and driving away did she remember that Steven couldn't have left Lindsay's address or even her phone number in his message. And Steven's phone had died. So much for not having to talk to anyone. She spotted a beige phone with a curled and twisted cord hanging on the kitchen wall and hauled herself out of her chair. It had no dial tone, not even when she clicked the button a few times. She pushed aside feelings of anxiety that threatened to turn to panic. Everything was all right. Fayette would tell Elizabeth where they were and that they were okay. No one was likely to come for them until tomorrow anyway, and by then Lindsay would be home with her cell phone. She grabbed a throw pillow, plumped it with a few punches, and curled up on the sofa. It couldn't have been just that morning that Steven had picked her up at Elizabeth's. It seemed like days.

Gray light was filtering through the bent slats of the blinds when a fumbling at the door woke Lainie. She had only seconds to figure out where she was before Lindsay and Steven stumbled in, giggling and shushing each other. The only thing that seemed funnier to them than Steven tripping on the doorsill was the sight of Lainie sitting up on the sofa and glaring at them. Lindsay collapsed against Steven, but even though he held her around the waist, neither of them looked too steady.

"Oops, did we wake you? Shhh. Go back to sleep. We'll be quiet." Lindsay made her way to the kitchen and swung open the cupboard doors again. "I'm starving. Anyone want a Mallomar?"

For reasons that escaped Lainie, Steven found that hysterically funny. He fell into the armchair squeaking with laughter and wiping his eyes.

Lindsay, holding a Mallomar in each hand, headed for the bedroom. "I'm going to bed now, Steven. You can sleep there." She gestured toward the sofa where Lainie sat. "Oh, wait, you can't sleep there. Lainie's there and she looks really, really mad."

Lainie stood up. "The sofa's yours. I think you could both use a couple hours of sleep. But before you go, Lindsay, would you leave me your phone? I'd like to call home when it gets a little later."

Lindsay's eyes widened and she patted her skirt, although the most casual observer could see there was nothing in there but Lindsay. "Oops, I left it somewhere. Probably Pedro's."

Lainie began to feel cut off and panicky again. "Where does Pedro live?"

"Pedro's not a person." Lindsay leaned against her doorjamb, giggling. "He's a bar. And he's closed. But don't worry. I've left my phone there before. I'll just go back and get it when they open. G'night." She waved a Mallomar in Lainie's direction.

Steven had already crawled to the couch and was lying face down in the throw pillow. Muffled snoring told Lainie that air

239

was actually reaching his face, but she yanked the pillow to turn his head. "It would serve you right if you smothered, you jerk."

When noon came without either Lindsay or Steven waking up, Lainie couldn't wait any longer. She opened the front door and stepped into the quiet neighborhood. There weren't many more signs of life at midday than there had been the night before. The harsh sunlight showed faded, peeling paint on the window frames and illuminated the battered cars crouching in the shadows of carports.

Lainie set off down the street. She traveled three empty blocks and never saw another soul. She didn't have any better luck when she did find a main thoroughfare. She spotted a phone booth outside a convenience store but found only a single wire protruding from the back wall when she got there. She went inside and tried to borrow the store phone, but the proprietor didn't even look up from the magazine he had spread open on the counter. He just pointed to a sign taped to the front of the cash register that read "No restroom, no phone."

Defeated, Lainie retraced her steps back to Lindsay's. The car was no longer parked at the curb, and a note on a scrap of yellow paper was taped to the locked door. "We've gone to get my phone. Back soon. Sorry about locking you out. Where are you, anyway?"

When Lindsay's car rattled to a stop at the curb a few minutes later, Lainie didn't bother getting up off the top step where she waited. Lindsay climbed out of the car waving her phone over her head. "It was at Pedro's, just like I said."

Steven slid from the passenger side with a pair of very high heels hooked over two fingers. "Yeah, and that's not all she left." He held them up and shook his head.

"I have no idea how I got home without my shoes." Lindsay brushed her shoulder against Steven as she passed him. "Why didn't you tell me I was barefoot?"

"Oh, man, I don't think I could have told you my name last night. How'd we get home, anyway?" Steven followed Lindsay up the stairs, lightly bumping into her when she stopped suddenly halfway up.

"What's wrong? You look mad."

Lainie slowly got to her feet. "I've been walking all over town looking for a phone. Thanks for waiting for me, by the way."

"What is your problem?" Lindsay pushed past Lainie and un-locked the door. "We were only gone, like, ten minutes. And we didn't know where you were. I'm the one who bothered to leave a note. You didn't."

Lainie held out her hand. "May I borrow your phone, please? I really need to call home."

"Steven already did on the way back here. He got it all settled." She disappeared into her bedroom. "I've got to get ready for work. And I feel like—" The closing door cut off the rest of her sentence. She opened it again and stuck her head out. "I don't know what they did to you out in Lost Gulch or wherever, but I don't care for it. You're not the Lainie I used to know, that's for sure."

Lainie turned to Steven, who had found the remote and was settling into the armchair. "So what's going on? Everything okay?"

Steven didn't look up from his channel surfing. "Yeah, Manny's bringing the tow truck when he closes up the garage. He said he'd be here about eight."

"What about the diner? Did it get opened okay? Did you call your grandmother to make sure she wasn't worried?"

Steven turned to Lainie with an irritated sigh. "Look, I said everything was okay, didn't I? Manny said he'd try to close up early, so let's just relax, all right?" He turned back to his remote.

Lainie curled up in a corner of the couch and gazed out the window. Had she changed as much as Lindsay said she had? It was hard to tell. She could hardly remember herself before she landed in Last Chance. Only passing moments, like seeing Lindsay head out for a night of partying in her short skirt or hearing that Nick was still out there, stirred the sleeping memories of her abandoned past. And they left her feeling sick inside.

"Well, I'm off." Lindsay breezed out of her room and headed for the door. "If you leave before I get home, just make sure the door is locked and pulled tight shut." She bent over the sofa and offered an awkward hug somewhere in the vicinity of Lainie's head. "I'm so glad I got to see you, Lainie, and I'm sorry I was such a witch. I'm just not feeling my best right now. Do you have a phone number where I can reach you? I don't want to lose track of you again."

When Lainie hesitated, Lindsay rushed on. "Just write it on that pad on the counter. I've got to go. If I'm late again, I'm dead." She blew a kiss at Steven. "Loved meeting you, Steve. And don't forget, you promised the next night out is on you, so call me." The door slammed behind her, and her quick steps faded down the concrete stairs.

Steven went back to his TV watching without saying a word to Lainie. Usually she had to beg him for five minutes silence, but those cartoons certainly had his attention. Something was up, but it was clear there was no way he was going to talk about it.

"I can't just sit here and listen to that television. I'm going outside." Lainie jumped to her feet and grabbed her jacket.

"Don't get lost." Steven switched the station without looking at her.

A cool wind blew a fast-food bag down the street, and Lainie pulled her jacket around her. She dropped to the step where she had waited for Steven and Lindsay and leaned against the railing, watching Saturday afternoon unfold around her. Even though she had never seen the neighborhood before last night, there was a hopeless familiarity in the barred windows and dusty streets. Down the block a group of boys, not much older than Matthew from the looks of them, leaned against a parked car, laughing and calling out to some girls, who turned around in fury and yelled something Lainie couldn't hear. She didn't have to. She knew what the boys said; she knew what the girls answered; she knew what the car cruising slowly down the street was looking for. This had been her world. And it would be her world today if that red warning light hadn't shown up on her dash last summer. "Lucky break, I guess."

A half smile crossed her face as Elizabeth's indignant voice popped into her mind. "Luck had nothing to do with it, young lady, and you know it."

Maybe not luck, then. Maybe Elizabeth was right and God was in control, even when you didn't even know who he was. Tears stung her eyes.

"God, did you really see me last summer? Was it you and not my dumb car that got me to Last Chance? I want to go back there, God. I want to go home. I mess things up so bad when I try to make my own plans. Will you take over for me? I like your plans so much better."

She closed her eyes as a warm peace filled her until she wanted to burst out singing. "And, God? I'm going to bring Ray to church with me. It's time he came home too."

—※—

Manny arrived in his tow truck just past 7:30. Lainie saw him pull up, and she and Steven met him on the walk as he ambled toward the stairs. Never had Lainie seen him without a joke or a smile, but he was almost grim as he turned on his heel and headed back to the driver's side of his truck.

"Come on, let's go get my car. I need to get back. The girls are sick and Patsy was not happy I was taking off after work instead of coming home to help her."

"Sorry about the car, dude." Steven opened the side door and slid in after Lainie. "The guy that hit us has insurance, though. I've got all his info."

"Yeah, we'll see." He started his engine. "Now, where's my car at?"

"Is everything okay at home?" Lainie moved her knee so Manny could shift gears. "No one was worried, were they?"

Manny looked at her, exchanged a glance with Steven, then returned his attention to the road in front of them. "Ask him."

"I told you everything was fine, didn't I?" Steven dropped the arm he had stretched across the back of the seat to give her shoulder a squeeze. "Now stop worrying, okay?"

Lainie waited in the truck while they hooked the wrecked car to the tow and then settled between Manny and Steven for the ride through the darkness to Last Chance. Neither man was inclined to talk—certainly a change from the norm for both of them, but Lainie relished the silence. She'd stop by the garage Monday to try to make amends with Manny for the wrecked car, and as for Steven, well, it would be a while before she had anything more to say to him.

The headlights flashed on one of Rita's roadside signs. "Make Last Chance Your Last Stop—10 Miles." Lainie smiled into the darkness. She couldn't get there fast enough. She had a few fences to mend with Ray, and hopefully Elizabeth wasn't too put out with her, but she was going home.

27

The porch light was on and the glow of a lamp shone through the curtains of Elizabeth's front window when Manny dropped them off at the curb. Lainie took a deep breath before starting up the walk.

"Looks like she's waiting up. I hope Fayette called her before she started wondering where we were." Lainie glanced back at Steven, who was standing with his hand on the gate.

"She's probably just watching some old rerun of one of her cop shows." Steven closed the gate, leaving himself on the outside. "You know, I feel kinda bad about leaving Ray with the bar when I said we'd be back. Why don't you make up with Gran, and I'll talk to Ray. I should have had Manny drop me there."

"Are you kidding me?" Lainie stared at him. "You get back here. You're not leaving me to face her alone."

But Steven had already started walking down the darkened road. He raised a hand over his head in farewell without looking back.

"Coward!" If Steven heard her, he gave no sign. She sighed and walked up onto the porch and opened the door.

Elizabeth sat upright in her recliner, her slippered feet flat on the floor. The ever-present television was dark and silent, but what really caught Lainie's attention were Elizabeth's red and swollen eyes.

"Elizabeth? What's wrong?" Lainie dropped onto the sofa and reached for Elizabeth's hand.

Elizabeth moved her hand out of Lainie's reach as tears welled up and spilled over her plump cheeks. "Would you mind telling me just where you've been? And why you left me sitting here not knowing if you were even alive?"

"What do you mean? We called just as soon as we could to tell you what was going on. Fayette gave you the message, didn't she?"

"We didn't get any message. We had no idea what had happened to you until Manny called to say he'd heard from you early this afternoon." Elizabeth groped for a tissue and her voice broke. "Do you have any idea how frightened I've been? You know the kinds of things that have been going on down there. Ben made some calls and said as far as he could tell you hadn't been killed, but that was all anyone knew."

Lainie shook her head to try to clear it. None of this was making any sense. "But Steven told me he left a message on Fayette's answering machine. Didn't she get it?"

Elizabeth blew her nose. "Fayette's back in Albuquerque. She got a call right after you left that Matthew had taken a fall in physical therapy, so she had to leave."

"Oh, Elizabeth, I'm so sorry." Lainie put her hand on Elizabeth's arm. "Steven did call Fayette just as soon as we could. His phone only had enough charge for one call, but we did try."

Elizabeth blew her nose. "I can appreciate that Fayette would be glad to know you were okay, but did you ever think that maybe I would like to hear from you? Couldn't you have found a phone somewhere and called me? Or Ray? He was about to head over to Juarez to look for you himself when you all called Manny today."

"I did try." Lainie's voice trailed away. Her mind played over her long search for a phone, but the story still sounded implausible, even to her. "Really, I did try."

Elizabeth glanced sideways at Lainie and blew her nose again.

After a moment of uncomfortable silence, Lainie tried again. "What happened at the Dip 'n' Dine this morning?"

"When no one came to open up, Carlos called here to see if you'd overslept or something. So we real quick called Juanita and Lurlene. They managed."

The sick feeling in the pit of Lainie's stomach grew until it completely swallowed her. "I'm so sorry. I just don't know what I could have done differently." Tears that had been clogging her throat spilled down her face. "I did everything I could."

Elizabeth took her hand and looked into her eyes. "You could have listened to people who care about you and not gone in the first place."

Lainie didn't try to defend herself. The one thing that had put her in that car with Steven was Ray telling her she couldn't go, and she knew it.

When the phone rang, she started to get up to answer it, but Elizabeth waved her back. "I'll get that. I'm sure it's someone calling to see if you're back yet. The phone's been ringing off the hook all day."

Lainie reached for a tissue from the box on Elizabeth's end table. She leaned back against the sofa and closed her eyes. It didn't help to realize Elizabeth was talking to Ray.

"Yes, she got in a little while ago . . . No, she's okay. She's had a rough time of it, though." Compassion crept back into Elizabeth's voice. She could be as stern as she felt she needed to be when she talked to you, but she invariably took your side when someone else landed on you. Lainie could only imagine what Ray must be saying to put Elizabeth on her side again. "You know, I was so relieved to see her walk in the door that I didn't think to ask." She put her hand over the receiver. "Where's Steven? He came back with you, didn't he?"

Lainie sat up. "He left me at the gate and went to set things straight with Ray. Isn't he there?"

Elizabeth went back to her conversation. "She said he was on his way to see you. If he's coming he should be there shortly." Her voice sounded sad. "I can't say it would surprise me if he didn't turn up, though. Facing the music has never been one of his strong suits. I had hoped he'd grown up some these last few years."

Lainie took a deep breath and stood up. She needed to face a little music of her own. "Can I talk to him?" She held out her hand for the phone.

"Hon? Lainie wants to talk to you." Elizabeth started to take the phone away from her ear then pulled it back. "Are you sure? She's right here . . . Okay, I'll tell her. Take care, honey. Looks like everyone's home safe and sound."

Elizabeth hung up the phone and turned to Lainie, whose out-stretched hand slowly drifted to her side. "Ray said he'd be over in the morning before church to talk to you. Now, I think we need to get some sleep. It's been a long two days for both of us."

Lainie nodded, tears welling up again. "Elizabeth, I'm so very sorry about all this. I wish I could go back and do everything differently."

"I know you do, honey. But even if there's no going back, there's always tomorrow. Things will look better in the morning." Elizabeth's smile was weary, but she reached up and patted Lainie's cheek. "Now go on to bed."

Dawn was just softening the early morning sky when Lainie heard Elizabeth get up and pad down the hall to the kitchen. If she had slept at all, it had been fitfully, and she lay quietly listening to the sounds of coffee being made and pans clanking on the stove.

Why hadn't Ray wanted to talk to her last night? She needed to hear his voice. Even if he was furious, as he had every right to be, they couldn't start working things out until she could tell him she knew how wrong she'd been. She got up and put her robe on and joined Elizabeth in the kitchen.

Elizabeth turned from the stove with a warm smile. There was no sign of the hurt and anger that had marred her face the night before. "Good morning, sweet thing. The coffee is just ready. How did you sleep?"

Lainie dropped in a chair at the kitchen table and shook her head. "I didn't. I feel like such a loser."

"You put that out of your head right now. You are no such thing." Elizabeth poured two cups of coffee and sat across the table from Lainie. She cradled her cup between her hands and looked into Lainie's eyes. "But I need to ask you something, so don't you tell me it's none of my business. You didn't do anything you shouldn't have, did you?"

When the significance of what Elizabeth was saying sank in, Lainie's eyes flew open and she sat back in her chair. "No! Steven? You've got to be kidding. Eew, no!"

The swallow of coffee Lainie took felt curdled and sour, and she gritted her teeth to keep it from coming up again. "Really? Is that what everyone thinks?"

"I don't know what most people think, but there are bound to be those who do. So you need to be able to hold your head up and look those folks squarely in the eye."

Lainie stood up. "I'm sorry, Elizabeth. I'm just not ready for this. I can't walk into church this morning thinking that everyone is sitting there wondering if I spent the night with Steven. That just makes me want to throw up."

"You know, I think you're right." Elizabeth leaned back in her chair to look up at Lainie. "It might be better if you stayed home this morning. If anyone has anything to say, they can just say it to me and I'll be happy to tell them that you are home safe and sound, resting."

"I'm going to go shower." Lainie headed out of the kitchen. "Do you think Ray is up? I'll call him and tell him he doesn't need to get here so early."

———

The house was quiet when Lainie went into the kitchen to make a fresh pot of coffee and wait for Ray. No sound came from Elizabeth's sewing room, but since the door was now closed, Steven had doubtlessly come home when he thought the coast was clear. She had so much to tell Ray. He had to hear her out, to believe she wasn't the same person who stormed off with Steven. She was relatively sure Steven wouldn't interrupt them, even if he did wake up. If he had gone who-knows-where last night rather than face either Elizabeth or Ray, he was not likely to appear this morning.

"You big chicken," she muttered at the closed door.

When she saw Ray pull up, it felt not like butterflies but like frogs jumping around in Lainie's stomach. She watched him tuck a flat, square package wrapped in brown paper under his arm and head up the walk. He was hunched into his sheepskin jacket against the wind. If only she could read his expression she would have an idea of what she was about to face, but his head was ducked to keep his battered Stetson from blowing off. She took a deep breath, pasted what she hoped was a winsome smile on her face, and went to open the door.

She had spent the night preparing her explanation, but all her words deserted her when Ray raised his head and she saw the pain on his face.

"Come on in." Lainie held the screen door open for him. "I made a fresh pot of coffee, and Elizabeth baked a coffee cake for breakfast. Have you eaten?"

Ray set his package on the sofa and shook his head. "I can't stay long." He glanced down the hall. "Did Steven ever turn up?"

"I think so. His door is closed, so my guess is that he's still asleep."

The smallest trace of a smile lifted one side of Ray's mouth. "Wow, Gran went to church and let both of you stay home? She must be getting soft. Hang on, I'll be right back."

Lainie watched him knock once on Steven's door and disappear inside. She sank onto the arm of the sofa and stared at the closed door. No sound came from the room. She almost would have preferred angry shouting. At least then she'd know what was going on.

Finally, the door opened again and Ray emerged. He couldn't have been in Steven's room for more than about five minutes, but Lainie felt she hadn't drawn a deep breath in hours. She found herself on her feet again when he stopped in front of her. Before he could say anything, she put her fingers against his lips.

"Wait. Let me say it first. I was a total idiot to go to Juarez with Steven. I know it. I guess I knew it before we even got out of town. But Ray, I've always been that way. The quickest way to get me to do something is to tell me I can't do it." She smiled up at him, hoping to coax a smile in return. But Ray just looked sad.

"Yeah, well, I was wrong. But going to Juarez, and with Steven, was such a bad idea on so many levels. And you weren't hearing me, so maybe I got a little heavy-handed."

Lainie searched for a rebuttal and came up empty. Ray waited a second, then continued talking. "Then when you didn't come home when you said you would, and didn't even call . . ."

"But we tried to call. Didn't Manny or Elizabeth or anyone tell you that? Steven left a message on Fayette's phone. We didn't know she wasn't in town."

Ray shrugged. "I waited up for you, you know. I thought maybe if I left the lights on in the bar you might stop by and let me know you were home safe."

Lainie looked away. She was afraid if she tried to speak the lump in her throat would choke her.

"When the hours went by and you didn't come, every news story that has come out of Juarez in the last year played through my mind like a piece of video." Ray's laugh was short and bitter. "I actually found myself hoping that you and Steven had just checked into a motel somewhere."

Lainie grabbed both his hands. "Oh, Ray, how could you think that? Steven? Don't you know how I feel?" Ray just looked at her, and Lainie took a deep breath. For once, her first thought wasn't her own protection. Too much was at stake. "I never even wanted to go to Juarez with Steven. Don't you know that? I just did it because you told me not to, and I know that was stupid. Can you forgive me? All I thought about the whole time we were gone was how much I wanted to be here with you. And on our way home, every milepost we passed made me even more eager to get here and tell you so. For the first time in my life, I actually felt like I was going home." She searched his face looking for a sign of forgiveness, but the pain there was etched even deeper.

"Lainie, come here." He led her to the sofa, and they sat facing each other. "I need to tell you that I'm leaving Last Chance."

"Leaving? Where?"

"I'm going to Santa Fe. You know I had planned to leave when Steven took over the bar. My life's been on hold long enough. I'm done. I just told him he can run the bar, close it up, or burn it down. I don't care. I'm out of here."

"When?" Lainie's voice came as a whisper.

"Now. Today. I cleaned out the trailer yesterday, and now I'm going to pack up the paintings I've finished and get the rest of my stuff from the cabin. Then I'll hit the road."

Lainie tried to will her heart to turn back into ice, but it was too late. Tears spilled over her lashes. "I said I was sorry. You know nothing happened. I told you I wished I had never gone."

Ray gripped her hands. "But you did go, Lainie. And you went just to spite me. I can't do this anymore. I can't hang around here waiting for Steven to get his life together and you to figure out what you want."

"I do know what I want. I've been trying to tell you." Lainie couldn't be sure Ray heard her whisper. He had reached for the package he had brought in, and his back was to her.

"Here. This is for you. I brought it down last Sunday and was looking for the right time to give it to you." His laugh was short and bitter. "I guess now's as good a time as any."

Lainie pushed the tears off her cheek with the heel of her hand and tore the brown paper away from the canvas. It was the view from Ray's cabin across the valley to the distant hills on the horizon. In the middle distance a dust devil reached from the valley floor to the heavens. A hawk floated on spread wings at the top of the column, while far below another climbed to meet it.

"Remember?" Ray's voice had softened. "You said that hawk was you, soaring high and free, away from everyone."

Lainie nodded and ran her finger over the lower hawk. "You said that one was you, coming to get me."

Ray sighed before he stood up and put his hat back on. "Well, you flew too high for me, girl. I couldn't get there."

She followed him to the door and he turned and pulled her close, pressing his lips against her forehead for a long moment.

"Take care of yourself, you hear?" His voice sounded husky, and he cleared his throat. "And tell Gran I'm sorry I missed her. I'll call her tonight when I get in, and I'll see her when I come back for Fayette's wedding."

He didn't look back, and Lainie watched him get in his truck and drive away. She picked up her painting again and sat on the sofa studying it. The hawk that once looked so wild and free now just looked alone.

28

The second Saturday in June, Lainie worked her last shift at the Dip 'n' Dine, handed her keys to Chris Reed, the new owner, and stepped out into the warmth of the fading afternoon. All day, customers and former volunteers had been stopping by to say good-bye, wish her well, and have a piece of the cake Chris had brought in to commemorate her last day. Nearly everyone asked her why she had to go, and even Chris had said there was a job for her at the Dip 'n' Dine as long as she wanted one. But her time in Last Chance was coming to a close. It was time for her to go.

Across the road, weeds were beginning to push through the gravel parking lot of the High Lonesome. With its boarded windows and padlocked doors, it looked just plain lonesome now.

She lifted her hair to let the breeze cool her neck and headed to Elizabeth's, and to the ongoing discussion as to why Lainie should stay in Last Chance.

"I'm sorry, but you have not been able to give me one reason that makes any sense at all." Elizabeth sat back from the breakfast table Sunday morning and folded her arms.

Lainie sighed and tried again. "How about the fact that Nick managed to walk out of the hospital six months ago and no one knows where he is? But he knows where Lindsay is, and she knows where I am. I said I'd stay till the new owner of the Dip 'n' Dine was up to speed and Fayette got married, but I've been pushing my luck."

"How you can still be talking about luck is more than I can understand."

"Okay, bad choice of words. Luck had nothing to do with it, and I know it." She smiled at Elizabeth as she carried her dishes to the sink. "But, please, it's time for me to go, and I think you know it."

Elizabeth's blue eyes sparkled with unshed tears as they searched Lainie's face. "Okay, darlin', I understand. But you'd better call me every night until you get wherever it is you're going."

"I will."

"And you'd better come back and visit me often."

"Promise."

"All right, then." Elizabeth pushed herself to her feet. "We'd better get going if we're going to get to church on time.

The choir was just filing into the choir loft as Elizabeth led the way down the aisle to the third pew on the left. Her spot on the aisle was empty and waiting, as if no one would dare sit in what had been Elizabeth's spot for more than half a century. She stepped back to allow Lainie to slide in before her, then stepped in and reached for a hymnbook.

Lurlene turned from the choir to lead the congregation in the first hymn, and Lainie let the sound wash over her. She could hear Russ Sheppard's deep bass and Juanita's slightly sharp soprano. She smiled, even as tears threatened to choke off her own song. Everything about Juanita had seemed sharp and even terrifying when Lainie first met her. When did she first begin to see past

Juanita's bristly exterior to the tender heart she guarded so fiercely? Probably it was sometime during the months Juanita, as well as the rest of the church, showed up at the Dip 'n' Dine so faithfully and worked so hard.

Her heart swelled as she looked around the room at the faces she had come to love. Les and Evelyn Watson had moved from the back corner to a spot by the window near the piano. Rita, with her ever-present sheaf of papers she needed to see somebody about as soon as the service was over, caught Lainie's eye and mouthed something Lainie couldn't follow while making incomprehensible hand gestures. Lainie smiled and nodded. She'd find out soon enough what Rita was talking about.

As the hymn drew to a close, Lainie spotted Chris Reed sitting across the aisle toward the center of the pew. Lainie was confident he'd find in Last Chance the same loving acceptance she had.

A rustle and shuffle filled the sun-washed room as everyone settled into their places and Brother Parker moved to stand behind the pulpit. His booming "This is the day that the Lord has made!" filled the well-scrubbed sanctuary. And just as it did every Sunday, the congregation answered, "We will rejoice and be glad in it."

He opened the Bible, and Lainie settled in to listen. Focusing on his message gave her something to think about besides leaving. But the sound of his deep voice, rich in Western drawl, only served to remind her that this was her last Sunday among them. She determined again that she would not cry, but how did leaving get so hard?

─────

Elizabeth peered into Lainie's red and swollen face. "Are you sure you don't want me to drive? If you don't mind my saying so, you're a mess. Can you even see?"

Lainie slid behind the wheel of her almost-new Toyota and sniffled. "I'm okay now. And I was doing okay in there until the final hymn."

"Caring about folks is nothing to be ashamed of, especially when they care about you like we all do. I'd have thought you'd know that by now."

"Caring is one thing, falling apart completely is another." Lainie tried to smile at Rita, who was waving good-bye from her car. "Oh, shoot. I was supposed to see Rita after the service."

"She's coming over after lunch this afternoon. I talked to her while you were in the bathroom."

Lainie pressed cool fingers against her puffy eyes. They felt dry and grainy. "I hope I didn't knock her down trying to get out of there when the service was over. What did she want?"

"Well, she wanted to talk about the wedding shower on Thursday, but I told her since it's going to be a big barbecue at the ranch, she didn't need to trouble herself anymore about that. We're certainly capable of throwing a party. But there's still the rehearsal dinner, the wedding itself, the reception, and whatnot. I'm sure every last detail is organized to a fare-thee-well. But you know Rita."

Lainie pulled into the long driveway behind Elizabeth's truck. Elizabeth gathered her Bible and purse and opened the door. "Why don't we just make some sandwiches for lunch and see if we can sneak in a nap before Rita gets here this afternoon. I think I'm going to need more strength than I have right now to go over those wedding plans again."

A low rumble of thunder in the distant hills woke Lainie from the Sunday nap she had learned to enjoy. Her hand dropped to Sam the cat, snuggled in the curve of her hip. He rolled onto his back, stretching his front paws over his head, and turned on the purr. As she lay absently scratching Sam's ear and chin and trying to decide whether to go back to sleep, she became aware of voices from the living room. Rita. Elizabeth must have decided to let her sleep and taken on the meeting by herself. With a smile of contented gratitude, Lainie turned over and closed her eyes. A few seconds later she opened them again. Sleep was not going to happen. She sighed and swung her feet over the side of the bed. Might as well get this over with.

Lainie winced at the sight of herself in the mirror across the room. Her eyes were still slightly swollen and her hair hung lank to her shoulders. The little makeup she usually wore had been completely cried off at church and not repaired. To top it off, she had obviously slept on her arm, because a red crease ran from ear to jawline. She shrugged and caught her hair back with a rubber band. "Deal with it, Rita. If you come visiting during naptime, you take what you get."

She smiled to herself as she walked up the hall toward the living room. Elizabeth was talking and had yet to take a breath. No matter what she said about the chattiness of others, Elizabeth could give anyone in town a run for their money. Her voice rose in a question and paused for an answer just as Lainie reached the end of the hall. She froze as a familiar voice murmured a response. Too late, she took a step back into the shadowy hall. Ray, sitting on the piano bench across the room and slowly twirling his hat between his knees, raised his head and met her gaze.

Whatever he was saying died in his throat. His hat hung loose on his fingers, and he attempted a smile. "Hey, Lainie, how's it going?"

"Oh, it's you." Lainie eased into the room and lowered herself onto the nearest surface, the arm of the sofa. "I thought you were Rita."

"Rita? Nope."

"Isn't this a nice surprise? He just got here a minute ago."

Elizabeth beamed at her. "I was just on the way to the kitchen to get us some iced tea."

"I'll go." Lainie jumped to her feet, but Elizabeth waved her back and headed toward the kitchen.

"No, no. You stay put. I'll do it. I think there are some cookies left too."

"Can't I help?" Lainie heard the desperation in her own voice and could have kicked herself, but with a final dismissive wave, Elizabeth had disappeared into the kitchen. There was nothing left for Lainie to do but turn to Ray and say, "So, how are you? It's been a while."

Ray shrugged and began twirling his hat again. "Fine, I guess. You?"

"Fine."

In the kitchen Elizabeth clinked glasses and opened the refrigerator door.

"You came early. No one else is coming till Wednesday."

"Yeah, well, I need to spend some time cleaning out the cabin. I left behind a bunch of stuff that I need."

Silence filled the room again, and Ray dropped his eyes to the hat slowly twirling between his knees.

"Here we are!" Elizabeth came back in the room carrying a tray with three ice and amber–filled glasses. "And we had just enough cookies for each of us to have one."

Lainie took a proffered glass and stood up. "I think I'll just take mine back in my room with me, if that's okay. I need to start getting it ready for Fayette when she comes Wednesday."

"Oh, you can put it off a little while." Elizabeth pulled her tray back as Ray reached for a glass and turned to frown at Lainie.

"No, you guys need some time to catch up, and I really need to start sorting through all my stuff." Her smile felt painted on when she turned to Ray. "See you at the barbecue Thursday, I guess."

He nodded again, without smiling, and Lainie turned and willed herself to stroll back down the hall to her room, taking a sip of her tea as she went, and gently closed her door behind her. Once inside her room, however, her careful control deserted her. A splash of tea marred her dresser and the glass rattled when she set it down

"You are such an idiot!" the puffy-eyed girl with the tied-back hair hissed at her from the mirror. "Why are you acting like a teenager? Ray was history when he walked out months ago." Lainie stared back at the face in the mirror until it softened a bit. "It's been a rough day, but the worst is over."

Lainie was surprised at how quickly she was able to pack up everything and how few containers it took to hold it. Her new suitcase and a few cardboard boxes held her life. For a while, as she had allowed roots to begin sinking into the sandy soil of Last Chance, it had been hard to tell where she left off and Last Chance began, but now the boundaries were clear. They consisted of a few pasteboard enclosures and the click of a suitcase lock.

She turned away from the dresser and looked around the room that had been home to her for nearly a year. In a few days Fayette would be staying there, then after the wedding it would revert to Elizabeth's guest room. Lainie picked up a cardboard box to carry to the sewing room. "Thanks for giving me the guts to go, Ray. This could have been hard."

———

Saturday morning, the door to the sewing room cracked open and Fayette peeked in. When she saw Lainie awake, she came in and sat cross-legged at the foot of the daybed.

"This is the day! Can you believe it? I'm really getting married." Wild, springy blonde hair framed Fayette's scrubbed and freckled face, and her happy grin made her look like a little girl. "The kindest, gentlest, strongest, most wonderful man in the world is in this very town, over at the Last Chance Motel with my son and half the city of Albuquerque, and in just a few hours, he's going to marry me!"

Lainie flipped the hem of Fayette's flannel pajamas. "Has he ever seen you looking like this?"

"I should say not!" Fayette sat up straight and pushed her hair from her face. "There's no way he'd ever see me first thing in the morning until after we're married. You know that!"

Lainie pulled her robe out from under Fayette's leg and put it on. "Smart move."

Fayette's face fell into another grin, and she grabbed Lainie in a hug that nearly knocked her off her feet. "Go ahead, try to throw cold water on my day. It's not going to work" She planted a big, noisy kiss on Lainie's cheek. "Because I know you're just as happy as I am. And you might as well go ahead and smile, because trying not to is about to kill you."

The smile Lainie had been trying to suppress burst through, and Lainie returned Fayette's hug. "Of course, I'm happy for you. I couldn't be happier. Ken is one lucky man, and I hope he knows it."

Fayette slipped her arm around Lainie's waist as they headed to the kitchen. "You know, he does think he's lucky, at least that's what he tells me. Can you believe it?" A soft smile played around her lips. "I never thought I'd find what I had with Bud again. I mean, I knew everyone in town and all the good ones were married. Come to think of it, even the downright peculiar ones were married. Ray and old Mr. Calhoun were the only single men in town."

Lainie was silent, and Fayette gave her waist a squeeze. "Well, that was real sensitive, wasn't it? I'm so sorry. I guess I have bride brain."

Even Lainie could hear how false her cheer sounded when she

turned a bright smile on Fayette. "And why shouldn't you have bride brain? You're entitled."

Fayette faced Lainie, placing both hands on her friend's shoulders. "Seriously, how are you? You could have blown me over when he stopped in to see Matthew on his way to Santa Fe. Of course, he wouldn't tell me anything, but whatever it was that broke you two up, I'm sure it was his fault."

Lainie shook her head. "No, it was pretty much all me. He could have listened, and maybe I could have explained, but I think he was done with my explanations."

Fayette muttered under her breath. "Well, he always was a jerk."

Lainie smiled. "You are such a friend. He's not a jerk and you know it. He put up with more this last year than anyone could be expected to—from Steven, and from me too, I guess. He just got done."

Fayette slipped her arm around Lainie's waist again. "Well, I think you're being way too easy on him. Remember, I've known him all his life. Have you seen him since he's been back?"

Lainie nodded. "Yeah, he came by to see Elizabeth when he got here last Sunday, and of course I saw him at the barbecue at the ranch Thursday, but not to talk."

"Well, all I can say is you two need to get together and work this out."

"Yeah, right. That'll happen."

When they entered the kitchen, Elizabeth turned from the stove and sang "Here Comes the Bride." Fayette grabbed a dish mop and held it in front of her like a bouquet, handing Lainie a spatula as she half-stepped across the kitchen floor. "Come on, maid of honor, let's have a wedding."

Lainie took the dish mop and pulled out a chair at the kitchen table just as the phone rang. "As maid of honor, my first duty of the day is to tell you to eat your breakfast and then go start getting ready. You've got a lot of work to do."

"Get the phone, would you, Lainie?" Elizabeth didn't even turn around. "I'm up to my elbows in pancake batter."

"If that's Ken, tell him I can't talk to him before the wedding. No, let me talk to him." Fayette pushed away from the table. "No, tell him I love him, but I'll see him at the church."

Lainie waved her back into her chair and picked up the beige receiver of the kitchen wall phone.

"Lainie? Is that you?"

"Yeah, this is Lainie. Who is this?"

"It's Lindsay. Listen, I need to talk to you."

Lainie stretched the curled cord around the corner into the living room and dropped her voice. "Lindsay? How did you get this number?"

"Oh, Steven gave it to me when you were here. I was supposed to call him, but it got buried in my purse somewhere. I just found it last week."

"Steven's not here anymore, if that's why you're calling."

"No, there's something else. I've been going back and forth and back and forth. Sometimes I think I should call you, but then I promised not to. I just didn't know what I should do."

"Lindsay, what are you talking about?"

There was a long pause, and then Lindsay blurted, "Nick called again."

Lainie felt her knees slowly give way, and she found herself sitting on the floor, back against the wall, knees under her chin.

"Before you say anything," Lindsay continued, "you need to know that he still loves you. He's never given up trying to find you."

She waited briefly for Lainie to say something before plunging on. "He told me that girl you saw him with wasn't anyone, just a girl he knew, and if you had only waited, he could have explained everything."

Lainie found her voice. "What did you tell him?"

"Well, at first I didn't tell him anything. You've been my friend a long time and if you ran out on Nick, I'd say you probably had a reason. But all he could talk about was how much he loved you, and how long he'd been searching for you, and how much he wanted you to forgive him."

"What did you tell him?"

"Lainie, he even cried. I didn't even know Nick knew how to cry."

"Lindsay, what did you tell him?"

"I told him you had been living in Last Chance. Are you mad?"

29

Dear Elizabeth,

 Yes, I've gone. I hope you forgive me not saying good-bye, but I found out this morning that Nick knows where I am. That means he'll be here soon, and for your sake as well mine I have to go. I'm so sorry. Tell Ben Apodaca that Nick is not quite six feet tall, real muscular, and has a tattoo of a panther on the left side of his neck—so he can be watching for him. I hope I can come back someday, but with Nick out there, I don't know if I can. Meanwhile, I want you to know how much living with you in Last Chance has meant to me. No one has ever loved me like you do.

> *I love you,*
> *Lainie*

Lainie finished her note and looked around the sewing room for a place to leave it where Elizabeth would be sure to find it. All the belongings she had accumulated during her stay in Last Chance and everything she had brought with her were packed and ready to go. All she needed to do was find a moment to slip away from the reception, swing by the house to grab her stuff, and she'd be gone before they missed her.

She put the note on top of the sewing machine cabinet, trying not to think about what Elizabeth would think of her when she found it. On impulse, she dug around in one of the boxes until she pulled out her Mickey Mouse snow globe and set it on top of the note. Elizabeth knew how much she cherished the memento. Maybe she would understand how hard it was for Lainie to go.

"Lainie, honey, are you about ready? We need to get the bride to the church." Elizabeth tapped at her door.

"Coming." Lainie took a last look at her image in the full-length mirror on the wall next to the sewing machine. The pale yellow dress Elizabeth had made for her floated around her like summer itself and made her eyes look even bluer. Squaring her shoulders and pasting what she hoped was a festive smile on her face, she left the sewing room, firmly closing the door behind her.

"My, don't you look a picture." Elizabeth, in her cornflower blue dress with a matching lace jacket, took both Lainie's hands and leaned back to admire her. "That is just your color. Let's go find our bride and see if she needs any help."

Lainie swept her into a long, tight hug that Elizabeth first accepted, then struggled slightly against. "Mercy, honey! Is everything all right?"

"Everything's great. I just get all gooey at weddings, that's all."

Elizabeth nodded, already distracted, and headed down the hall to Lainie's old room where Fayette was getting ready. "Mmm-hmm. Go get the flowers for Fayette's hair out of the refrigerator, will you? We need to be at the church in twenty minutes if we're going to get her out of sight before the guests start arriving."

—◊◊◊—

"How's it going in here?" Rita popped into the crying room off the vestibule where Lainie, Elizabeth, and Matthew waited with Fayette. "Good news, Fayette. The groom turned up."

Fayette's early exuberance had long since faded into hand-twisting nervousness, and she answered Rita's teasing with a weak smile that Rita didn't even notice.

"Well, it's standing room only in there now, so come on with me, Elizabeth. Time to get you seated, then I'll be back for the rest of you." She popped out again, leaving nervous silence in her wake.

"Tell me I'm doing the right thing." Fayette spoke to no one in particular.

"Mom, you are so doing the right thing. Ken's awesome."

Fayette's eyes filled with tears. "Are you sure you're okay with this, Matthew? For so long it's been just you and me. Are you ready to let someone else into our life?"

Matthew leaned out of reach as Fayette tried to cup his face with her hand. "Oh yeah, way ready. It's okay. Really."

Fayette laughed and dabbed her eyes with the lace handkerchief Elizabeth had tucked into her sleeve for something borrowed. "Well then, let's go get married."

Rita popped back into the crying room. "Time to go! Lainie, you first. Don't forget to walk slowly. Fayette and Matthew, you wait till I give you the signal."

They got to their feet and moved to the door of the crying room. Fayette slipped her hand into the crook of her son's left arm, and as Lainie stepped out of the room to begin her slow walk down the aisle, she noticed him cover his mother's right hand with his own.

"I do not believe it. Tell me my husband is not fixing to play horseshoes. Not at a wedding!"

Lainie, sitting with Juanita, Elizabeth, and Patsy Baca under the elm trees in back of the church, looked up to see Russ, with a couple horseshoes hanging from each hand, amble from the church toward the horseshoe pit where three other men waited for him with their jackets removed and sleeves rolled up.

"There goes Rita after him. I almost feel sorry for those boys." Elizabeth lifted another bite from the plate she balanced on her lap.

They watched as Rita marched up to Russ and stood with her hands on her hips. She was too far away for them to hear what she said, but she didn't look happy. Russ stopped, bent his head and placed his hand on her shoulder, then straightened, gave her shoulder a friendly pat, and turned and pitched his horseshoe. The clang of his ringer echoed across the grassy field where wedding guests gathered in groups of clustered lawn chairs eating lunch. Rita watched them ignore her for a few more minutes before she turned and stomped across the field toward Juanita.

"Don't waste your breath, Rita." Juanita held up a hand before Rita could speak. "If I told that man to leave a burning building, he'd stay inside just to show me I can't tell him what to do. They're not doing any harm. Just leave them be."

"But horseshoes at a wedding? I worked so hard to make every-thing just perfect." Rita sounded about to cry.

"Perfect's not family, Rita. And this is family. Just look." Eliza-beth gestured at the gathering on the shady field. Sounds of con-versation punctuated with laughter floated on the warm air. "Look at those kids chasing each other. Do you want to tell them that you're not supposed to do that at weddings? Anyway, you've done a magnificent job. It's too bad we don't get more weddings here in Last Chance. You could just close down the motel and do this full-time. I think you'd probably be the only wedding-planning mayor in the state."

"Go get a plate, Rita. Come join us." Juanita patted an empty lawn chair next to her. "It looks like the fellow who bought the Dip 'n' Dine is doing just fine with the catering."

"Well, they're going to cut the cake in a bit. I need to see about that."

"I don't think they'll be cutting the cake for a while yet. Look."

They looked where Juanita directed to see Fayette and Ken standing hand in hand at the horseshoe pit. While they watched, Ken took off his jacket, handed it to Fayette, and accepted the horseshoe Les Watson handed him.

"Good night, nurse! I don't know why I even try." Rita dropped her clipboard onto the empty lawn chair and stormed off toward the buffet.

Lainie tried to look at her watch without anyone noticing. There were still hours left of the reception. A dance floor and stage had been set up at one end of the field for the band that would arrive later, and the Japanese lanterns strung from the trees would be lit when it got dark. She should probably wait till after the cake-cutting, but after that, no one would look for her for hours.

"Oh no, somebody hide me. Here comes Manny with the kids. And they don't look happy." Patsy Baca put her plate on the ground beside her and waited for Manny to reach the group. The baby, in a pack on Manny's back, slumped against his shoulder, and a cranky, whiny little girl hung from each hand.

"Hey, everybody, anyone want some kids? Give you a good price. Pay you, even."

Patsy sighed and moved to get up. "I guess we should get them home. They are way past ready for a nap."

"I think Lito's already out, right?" Manny turned so they could see his pack.

"Yeah, he's sound asleep." Patsy stood and hoisted Grace to her hip. "I guess I'll go find Fayette and Ken to say good-bye. I'll be so glad when my life isn't completely determined by feedings and nap times."

"If all they need is a nap, why don't I take them inside and put them to bed in the nursery?" Lainie glanced at her watch again and stood up.

"Oh, no. I couldn't let you do that. They're such pills right now."

"It's no problem at all. We're old pals, aren't we, girls?" Lainie held out her hands to the whiny little girl on Patsy's hip, and to everyone's surprise, Grace leaned into Lainie's arms.

"See? I've got the gift." She held out her other hand to Faith. "Want to come with me?" But Faith turned her face away and hid behind her father's leg.

Manny laughed and swept the little girl onto his arm. "Why don't I come with you to get them settled? No need to wake Lito if we can help it."

With a satisfied smile, Patsy sank back into her lawn chair and picked up her plate, calling after them, "Make sure the girls go potty before they go to bed. I'll be in to see how you're doing in a little bit, and if Lito wakes up, come get me. He'll be hungry. Oh, and stop by the buffet and bring me another glass of tea when you get back, will you, Manny?"

The nursery was cool, and the light filtering through the nursery rhyme print of the drawn curtains softly illuminated the cribs lining the wall.

"It's nice in here. I could stay and take a nap myself. Here, help me with the pack, will you?" Manny turned his back, and Lainie supported the sleeping baby boy while he shrugged out of the straps.

"Look at that. The kid can sleep through anything, just like his old man." He gently placed his baby in a crib and stroked the little boy's thick, black hair.

Manuelito's face scrunched into an almost cry before he found his thumb and settled back into slumber, never opening his eyes.

"Come on, chicas. Mama says you need to go potty, and what

Mama says, goes." He disappeared into the hall with a curly haired toddler on each hand.

Lainie pulled three light blankets from the cupboard and had just finished tucking one around Manuelito when Manny returned with the girls.

"You sure you're going to be okay?" He edged toward the door.

"We'll be fine. Go on."

"Okay, then. Think I'll go show those guys how the game of horseshoes is played."

"Don't forget Patsy's tea."

Lainie grinned as Manny gave her a backwards wave over his shoulder, then turned her attention to the girls, who had found the toy chest.

"Are you picking out something to take to bed with you?"

Neither girl looked up.

"It's nap time now, but you can take one toy to bed with you."

"This." To Lainie's surprise, Grace handed her a plastic truck and scrambled to her feet. Maybe she was a natural with kids, after all.

"That's a great truck. How about you, Faith? What do you choose?"

Faith, busily trying to fit a triangle in the round space of a shape sorter, ignored her.

"Okay, girls. It's nap time." She scooped up Grace, gave her a kiss on her neck that made her giggle, and popped her and the truck in a crib.

"Come on, Faith. Nap time." Lainie bent down and took Faith's hand. She could almost see the wheels turning in Faith's mind as she considered her options. For whatever reason, she decided the nap would be okay and allowed Lainie to put her and the shape sorter in the crib across the room from her brother and sister.

Lainie slipped a CD of lullabies into the player, kicked off her shoes, and settled herself in a rocker to consider her own options. The girls were quiet. Grace was lying down looking at her truck, and even though Faith was still sitting up, her eyes were droopy. It shouldn't be long till they were asleep. Maybe when Patsy came in to check on them and feed Lito, Lainie could slip away. That would be the best time. The afternoon would be easing into evening, and if anyone thought of her at all, they would assume she was busy elsewhere.

"Nighty-night pants." Lainie looked up to see Faith standing in her crib frowning at her. "Nighty-night pants." This time a little louder.

Lainie went over and laid Faith back down. "Yes, it's nighty-night time. Go to sleep now. Here's your shape sorter."

"Nighty-night pants." Faith tugged at her ruffled panties and started to cry. "Want nighty-night pants."

"Oh! Do you wear diapers when you go to bed?"

"No! I no baby! Want nighty-night pants."

"Okay, now I have to figure out what nighty-night pants are." Lainie opened the cupboard and examined the contents. There were blankets, wipes, and diapers of every size, but nothing that could be called pants.

She turned back to Faith. "I'm just going to go check the toddler room and see if they have anything there. I'll be right back. Don't worry."

Faith, her message finally understood, returned to her shape-sorter.

The toddler room had a lot more stuff than the baby room did. Cupboards lined the wall, and Lainie hurriedly looked through them. She found a package that looked like it could hold diapers and from it pulled a pair of pants—thick, absorbent, disposable, and covered with pink and blue teddy bears. These could only be nighty-night pants. Pulling two pair from the package, she held them up and shook her head. "Who knew? Not me."

"No! Baby!" A panicked scream from one of the girls tore through the nursery. Lainie dropped the package she was holding and bolted for the baby room. Just as she reached the nursery, however, she pulled up short and ducked around the corner. Someone sat in the rocker holding little Lito, who was just beginning to howl his protest.

"Hey, buddy. These females and all their squalling getting to you too? We guys got to stick together, right?"

Lainie knew the voice. She didn't need to see him to know who sat rocking Manuelito Baca. He was facing away from the door, but she had already seen the prowling panther tattooed on his neck.

She pressed her back against the wall and stared at her bare feet. She didn't think he knew she was there yet, but he had to be counting on her coming to check on the crying children. How long would he wait before he came looking for her?

The door parents used to bring their children in on Sunday mornings opened onto the parking lot, and through its window she could see her car in its spot under the elms. When she bought it, Manny had given her a magnetic box to stick under the front fender to hide the spare key, and she could practically hear it calling her. What if she slipped out, drove to the closest phone, called the sheriff, and then kept right on going? How long would it take for him to get here? Or she could slip out, run around the building, alert everyone, and then leave during the commotion. She could scream and hope they could hear her. Or what if she just ran? Nick always had a soft spot for little things like dogs and kids. She was almost positive he'd never hurt them. She gave a last look at her car sitting in the parking lot, took a deep breath, and stepped around the corner into the nursery.

"Hello, Nick. Want to hand me the baby? He seems to hate you."

Nick turned and looked up at her with no surprise and went on rocking Lito. His nose had a bump in the bridge that she didn't remember, and it seemed off-center in a face marred with puckered purplish scars. He smiled a mirthless smile. "Still handsome as ever, right?" Lainie saw his hands tighten around Lito, who was working himself into a rage. "We're doing fine here, aren't we, buddy? It's these crazy women that really mess you up. No wonder you're crying."

"Give me the baby, Nick."

Nick ignored her. "So what do you think, buddy? How about you and me getting out of here?"

"Nick, get serious." Lainie hoisted the still screaming Grace from her crib and cuddled her as she crossed the room to slip her arm around Faith. She tried to make her voice sound stronger than she felt. "There are two hundred and fifty people out there. You're not taking that baby anywhere."

Nick just rocked and looked at her. His eyes hadn't changed. They were as cold and dead as those of any coyote lying by the side of the road. When he spoke his voice had become as dead as his eyes.

"So what'd you do with my stuff, Lainie? Sell it to buy that pretty dress? Maybe that car out there?"

"How do you know about my car?"

He laughed. "I've been watching you a while. You know, I always thought you were different. I wanted to take care of you, to give you the things you never had. And the minute you get the chance, you turn thief and run. You're just like the rest of them." He held a hiccuping Lito up to gaze into his eyes. "Learn it early, son. Never trust a woman."

Lainie shook her head. "I didn't steal from you. I didn't even know it was there till I got here."

"Yeah? Then why'd you take off so fast and try to cover your tracks like that?"

"Because you were becoming someone I didn't know, and I wanted to get away from you."

Nick narrowed his eyes and worked his jaw. "So, if you're too good for me, you still have the stuff, right?"

"No, I gave it to the sheriff."

"You what? You just waltzed in and handed it over? Just like that?" Nick's laugh was more of a bark.

"Pretty much."

"And he just said, 'Thank you very much,' and let you walk out?"

"Not entirely. I told him everything I knew about where it came from."

"Naming names, of course."

"Of course."

"Well, that answers a lot." Nick stood up. "Okay, I think we're done here. Grab the girls. We're leaving."

Lainie offered a quick and silent prayer for courage and took a deep breath. "No."

"No? I'd rethink that if I were you, Lainie. You owe me big-time, and you're going to pay. You can count on it. But these guys don't owe me anything. You can make it easy on them or hard. It's up to you."

"Why drag the kids into it, Nick? They're just babies. Leave them alone." Lainie put Grace in the crib with Faith and gave each one a quick hug. Slipping on her shoes, she picked up her purse. "I'll go with you if you leave the kids here."

Nick hesitated only a second before putting Lito in the crib next to the twins. "Okay then. Let's go."

With a last glance at her small charges staring wide-eyed from their cribs and with what she hoped was a reassuring smile, Lainie left the room. Nick put his hand in the small of her back and pushed her through the door and into the parking lot. As they reached her car, Lainie could hear the voices of first Grace, then Faith, and finally Manuelito raised in despairing wails.

30

Nick shoved her toward her car. "Hurry up. Those kids will have the whole town up here in a minute."

Lainie slid behind the wheel and rummaged in her purse for her keys. Nick grabbed her purse from her hands and dumped the contents into his lap. Snatching the keys from the pile, he threw them at Lainie, sweeping the rest of the stuff onto the floor.

"Go! You don't want to give me time to go back in there and grab a kid or two."

The engine jumped to life, and Lainie headed toward the entrance onto the highway.

"Turn left."

Lainie's mind started whirling. The highway passed right by the county sheriff substation. What if she pulled off the highway and drove right to the door? What would Nick do?

"Turn right."

"What? Where?"

"That dirt road ahead. Turn right."

Fear tightened its grip on Lainie's stomach. She had never been on this particular road, but she knew these dirt tracks. They were little more than trails, barely wide enough for one pickup, meandering across the desert and into the mountains, useful for a purpose unknown to any but the one who made them.

They bounced along for about half a mile before Nick spoke again. "That big bunch of bushes over there, head for that."

Giving the wheel a sharp left turn and trying to pick her way between the rocks and cactus, Lainie drove toward the mesquite clump he indicated.

"Okay, stop here. Get out."

Lainie turned off the engine and sat behind the wheel. Nick grabbed the keys from the ignition and got out of the car. Drawing back his arm, he threw the keys far into the desert. Then he walked around the car, opened her door, and yanked Lainie from the driver's seat with such force that she stumbled to her knees.

"I said, get out." He stood over her for a moment before grabbing her arm and jerking her to her feet. Her high heel turned on the gravelly desert floor, and she grabbed his sleeve for balance. For a long moment he looked at her hand on his arm, but when he turned to look in her face, she lifted her chin in defiance, and his eyes turned to stone again.

She didn't see the blow coming and briefly wondered why she was on her hands and knees in the gravel again with her head filled with ringing pain.

"I loved you!" Nick was standing over her screaming. "I had plans for us. Everything I ever did, I did for you. I wanted to give you everything."

Pulling herself to her knees, Lainie watched drops of blood fall from her face and stain the yellow dress. She looked up at Nick.

"You didn't do anything for me. I told you over and over I didn't want any part of that life. Whatever you did, it was to make you feel like somebody."

"Is that what you think? That last stash, the one you stole. That was going to be the beginning of something big for us. When I got home and found you and the stash gone, I couldn't believe it.

I thought someone had taken both of you. I was out of my mind. It wasn't till I called your friend in El Paso that I found out you'd been planning on running out on me for weeks. That was bad enough, but you took my stash. Didn't you know what they'd do to me? Or was that part of your plan?"

"Nick, you've got to believe me. I didn't know it was in the backpack. I promise you I would have left it behind if I'd found it."

"Yeah, right. Well, one way or the other, when you ran out on me, it went with you. And you can see what came of it." He turned his head so she could see his face from every angle.

"I'm sorry." Lainie's voice dropped to a whisper. "I never meant for that to happen. Please believe me."

"Well, it doesn't matter now. Come here." He yanked her to her feet and shoved her toward the clump of mesquite.

"Wait. I don't want to—" Lainie tried to pull back, but his grip on her arm was strong.

"Get in." Nick opened the passenger side of the car hidden in the thicket and shoved her inside. "We're taking my car from here."

He shoved the car into Reverse to pull out of the thicket and then gunned it back the way they came. Lainie clutched the door with one hand and held the other against the ceiling as they bounced over ruts and fishtailed through sand. Her eyes wouldn't close, but she silently prayed anyway. "Lord, even if no one else knows where I am, you do. Please, please, please . . ."

A loud curse broke the silence, and Nick slammed on the brakes and threw the car into Reverse again. Just ahead, a sheriff's car turned off the highway and barreled down the dirt road toward them. Another followed right behind, and a pickup that looked a lot like Ray's brought up the rear. Lainie grabbed the door and opened it when the wheels of Nick's car spun in the gravel as he reversed directions, but before she could jump out, the tires gained traction and the forward lurch slammed the door shut.

If Nick noticed, he didn't say anything. He just threw it into Drive and headed back toward the mountains. Lainie looked in the side mirror to see if the sheriff might be gaining, but if they were still back there, they were lost in the huge dust cloud trailing Nick's car.

Nick must have noticed the same thing. Jerking the wheel hard to the left, he took the car off the road and headed into the desert in a wide circle, creating a cloud of dust that enveloped as well as followed them.

"Nick, this is crazy!" Lainie was still hanging on for dear life. "Even if you do get back to the road, you know they've got radios. You'll have every law officer in this part of the state on your tail. Just pull over."

"Shut up." Nick leaned forward, trying to see his way through the dust. "This is all your fault anyway. And you're in it as much as I am."

"What are you talking about?"

But Nick didn't answer. He never saw the arroyo until they sailed over the edge. The instant the nose of the car hit the opposite bank, Lainie's head hit the side window and everything went black.

———

Lainie first became aware of voices, lots of voices, far off.

"I think she's coming around." Ray's voice. Where was Ray?

She opened her eyes. Her shoulder ached where the seat belt had grabbed her, and a big parachute-like thing was all over her lap. She turned her head to find Ray kneeling in the sand next to her open door.

"How're you doing?" His voice and his smile were gentle. Lainie closed her eyes again. When she opened them, he was still there. She tried to smile too.

"I'm fine." Sleepy, maybe, but fine.

The fear came first, and then memory fought its way through the fog.

"The babies—Nick." Her hand scrabbled at her seat belt until Ray covered it with his own.

"The kids are fine. I called Manny. Nick's not going anywhere. He's sitting in the backseat of the patrol car right now. And you need to stay still until the ambulance gets here."

Warm peace, the first she'd felt in months, coursed through Lainie. She closed her eyes and leaned against the headrest. "Good. But don't worry about me. I'm fine, really." Had she spoken aloud? She wasn't sure.

"Great, but you still need to stay put."

Lainie opened her eyes. Ray was still there. "How did you find me so fast? No one knew . . ."

He grinned. "You left a trail of dust a half mile long. It wasn't hard at all to know where you turned off."

"But how'd you know it was me?"

"I saw your note."

Lainie just looked at him.

"Gran forgot her comfortable shoes and asked if I'd run home and pick them up for her." He looked sheepish. "I'd heard you were planning to leave after the wedding, and I wondered if you were still going, so I checked to see if your stuff was still there. Is that weird?"

"Sort of." She was so tired, and her head throbbed.

"Well, I saw your snow globe sitting on the sewing machine, and then the note under it. I took it with me because I wanted to talk to you about it, but just before I got back to church, I saw your car pull out. You were driving, but there was a passenger."

"Nick."

"I was afraid of that, so I called the sheriff. Then I followed you."

Lainie thought she smiled as she reached for his hand.

"The hardest thing I've ever done was to wait on the highway at the turnoff for the sheriff. But he promised me that if he got there and found me on that road between him and you all, he'd run me in too."

Lainie's eyes drifted closed. The siren of the approaching ambulance whined to a stop. She felt Ray's hand brush the hair from her face and his lips gently touch her own.

"They're here for you now." His voice was low in her ear. "I'm going to follow you to the hospital. And then, when you're ready, I'll bring you home."

Epilogue

Two weddings within three months, and coming as they did in summer when the Last Chance Motel was at its busiest, would have been more than the average wedding planner/mayor/ motel owner could have handled, but Rita pulled it off. And no one was surprised.

She ducked into the crying room off the vestibule where Lainie waited with Fayette. "Standing room only, and I've closed the church doors. We're ready to get this show on the road."

Lainie glanced again in the full-length mirror Rita had placed in the room and let her hands drift over the soft ivory chiffon of her wedding dress. Her image, misty through the veil that brushed her shoulders in the front and trailed behind her, seemed to belong to someone else.

"You look beautiful." Fayette caught her hand and squeezed it. "And no one ever deserved happiness more."

Lainie took a deep breath. "Deserve it? I don't know about that, but I'm so happy it scares me. Is it even real?"

"It's real." Fayette squeezed her hand again and looked over her shoulder with a smile as Rita bustled her out the door.

Alone in the crying room, Lainie heard the piano music swell and the murmur of the wedding guests hush as Rita threw open the doors from the vestibule and Fayette began her slow progression.

"Now!" Rita's loud whisper and frantic wave brought Lainie to the head of the aisle. She paused and looked over the church. She was vaguely aware of the fragrance of late summer flowers and the sea of smiling faces as the guests shuffled to their feet.

Steven, handsome as ever, stood grinning next to Ray as Fayette reached the front of the church and turned to take her place on the other side of Brother Parker. The choir beamed at Lainie from the loft. From the moment Lurlene heard of the impending wedding, she had been planning the music, and it seemed right somehow that the choir would sing her down the aisle.

But it was Ray who caught her gaze and held it. He smiled his slow smile, and as he started up the aisle to meet her, Lurlene nodded to the pianist and the church was filled with the triumphant opening chords of the "Hallelujah Chorus."

Cathleen Armstrong lives in the San Francisco Bay Area with her husband and their corgi, but her roots remain deep in New Mexico where she grew up and where much of her family still lives. She and Ed raised three children, and when they were grown, she returned to college, earned a BA in English, and began to write.

Meet

CATHLEEN ARMSTRONG

online at

www.cathleenarmstrong.com

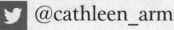 AuthorCathleenArmstrong

@cathleen_arm

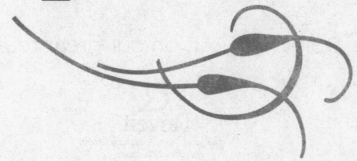